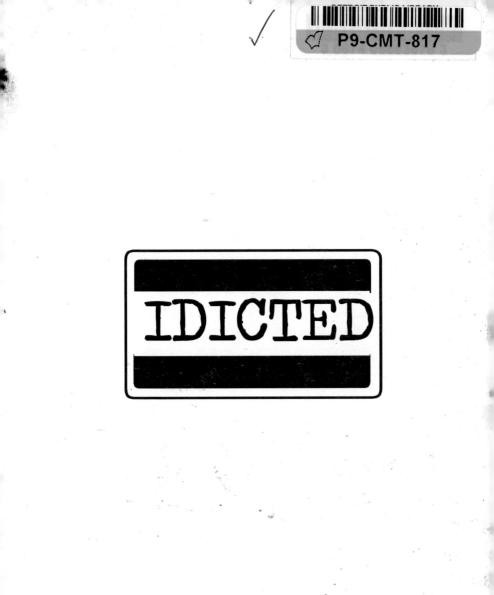

KEISHA MONIQUE

Life Changing Books
Published by Life Changing Books
P.O. Box 423
Brandywine, MD 20613

Library of Congress Cataloging-in-Publication Data;

www.lifechangingbooks.net

13 Digit: 9781943174195

DEDICATION

First of all giving thanks to God and my Savior Jesus Christ, this book is dedicated to my grandfather Mr. Henry-Lee Simon. (7/2/28 - 1/15/2005)

Grandpa, as I write this dedication to you, my eyes are clouded with tears of joy and sorrow. Words could never express how much I miss you...love you and thank you. No matter what I was doing or going through you were always there for me. Nothing or no one could change or alter the love you gave me. You taught me the true definition of unconditional love. You taught me that if I wanted something, to get up off my behind and go get it. You taught me to never let anyone define who I was... Never to let anyone or anything stand in my way. You taught me how to pray and let God carry me when I couldn't carry myself. You taught me to never give up and never quit... All our family vacations, trips back and forth to New Jersey, fishing expeditions where I would run from the worms and the fish..lol. All the times you held me while I cried, wiped away numerous tears telling me it was gonna be O.K.... to trust God. I remember your voice, your smile and most of all your laugh. I wish you were here to see me now; I made it grandpa. The drugs..the jails..the abuse... None of that broke me. You taught me to stand tall and have pride in who I am... My heart will always carry you with me. I know that you are smiling down on me from Heaven. Give my mom and my daughter a kiss for me. I thank you for everything; it is because of you that I am the woman I am today. Your great great grandson has your name - Melvin Henry-Lee Garrick III. He also has your hair..Lol. I'll make sure that he knows all about you. Rest in peace Grandpa, I'll see you on the other side.

I love you always!
Keisha

ACKNOWLEDGEMENTS

To my children Ashley and Melvin Garrick, Isaiah Shakur Sims and Darryl Duckett, I love you all. Thanks for riding with me. Especially Ashley Garrick you ALWAYS believed in me. Zay you are most definitely Momma's boy. Melvin I'm proud of how you have grown and matured. You're an awesome dad to M.J. Darryl even though I put you up for adoption; you came back to me with nothing but love and respect. Thank you.

My grandson MJ. I love you kid! You brighten my life. Kae'Leigh Sumpter - Grandma loves you lil' lady. Martin McKnight... Thanks for everything. . Sokoya Finch you are my role model, mentor and spiritual light. Thank you for enlightening me on who I am; my personality type and that I have the spirit of the Hawk lol. That has changed me more than you know. La'Faye Henry at FCI Tallahassee. You started the change in me. You saved me from myself. Officer Richardson at FCI Tallahassee. Thanks for all the notebook paper you gave me to write on. LaKeisha Butler thanks for the pen that got me started. Shannon Rhames, Jieisha Addison and Nichole Shelley…thanks for helping me type. We have plenty more work to do.

K'WAN (the author) thank you so much for all of your help, feedback and support. Wendy Florenco…a special thanks to you for helping me submit the manuscript. Krystal Jackson, thanks for my grandson. Jeanette Lofton thanks for giving me life. Calvin Henry Simon – Rest In Peace, I love you dad. Tonya and Yvette - The best big sisters I could ask for. Pandora Moye the matriarch of the family, you make 92 look good. I love you Aunt Pan. Quanisha, Tocarra, Brittany and Chad-my nieces and nephew.

Uncle Reggie, Michelle, Bianca, Sabrina, Shannell, Shirley, Jackie, Chevette, Ms. Hermina, Shaniqua, Geronimo, Durty Red,

Wesley Pough…thanks for your support and to all my friends and associates I love you all. Rosa Frazier…we will forever be Pinky and the Brain. Rest In Peace.

Life Changing Books, thanks for believing in me. Virginia Greene, thanks for all your help and direction.

ADDITIONAL THANKS:

PHOTO CREDITS
Hair- Tammy Lyles @ Hands of Style
Photography- Ernest Pelzer
EDITING-
Tracy Carter at Sister Girl Editing – your developmental editing and CPR on the manuscript really brought this book to life. Thank you so much.
Joy Hammond Nelson - copy editing. Thanks

Prologue

As I pulled up in front of Rosewood Middle School, I leaned over and kissed my son before he jumped out of the car and ran toward his class.

I wonder where I want to work from today, - I thought while driving around town. I needed to go online and do some more credit card applications and make a run to pick up the cards that should've been delivered today.

I pulled into the parking lot of Richland County Public Library and parked where I could keep an eye on my car. I found my favorite spot available in the library and sat down out of sight of the nosey library employees. I opened my briefcase and pulled out the list of names and social security numbers I'd be using.

After logging on to the Chase Visa Card website, I applied for ten different cards and got an instant approval on seven of them. I smiled knowing that each card will have at least a five thousand dollar credit limit. That wasn't bad for thirty minutes of work. I continued on and completed applications for Capital One, Citibank, Discover, and WaMu. When I finished, I had fifteen instant approvals and would probably get ten more when the rest processed.

I hopped back into my car and drove to the various houses that I used to have the cards delivered. I always looked for homes that had working families so that no one would be at home when it was time to retrieve the cards from their mailboxes.

I have three people on my team, my sister, Michelle, and my two best friends, Dream and Charla.

Life was pretty sweet. I was driving a brand new Cadillac DTS, my closet was packed full of designer clothes, and my son had everything he could ever wish for. I shopped so much that I'm known by face in all of the malls and boutiques.

This hustle is much better than selling drugs. I don't have to worry about getting robbed or having my door kicked in by narcotic agents. I bring home enough money to buy anything I want; you name it, I have it. It's the lifestyle I was destined to live, and I can't see it getting anything but better in the near future.

Or so I thought…

Chapter 1
Guess Who's Knocking

What the hell is wrong with this crazy ass dog? I wondered while I watched my pit bull, Diva, run from one room to the next barking and growling. Before I could even get the chance to tell Shy to hold on while I put the phone down, I was startled by loud knocking on my front door.

BAM, BAM, BAM. It sounded as if my door was going to cave in.

"Who the hell is knocking on my door like they the damn police?" I whispered to Shy.

He got all excited and yelled so loud into my ear that I damn near dropped the receiver on the floor.

"Rocky, who is that? Is that the police?" Shy asked.

BAM, BAM, BAM. The knocking started again as I walked towards the window to peek out to see who it could be. I wished my damn dog would shut the hell up so I could hear. *Oh, shit! It's the police at the door.*

After I peeped through a crack in my Venetian blinds, I saw a deputy sheriff walk around the side of my house. I crept silently back into my bedroom, trying not to make a sound.

"Shy, oh, shit. It really is the police outside my house," I whispered into the phone as I sat at the foot of the bed, too scared to move.

"Ra'Quelle, don't open the door!" Shy screamed as if to tell me something I didn't already know.

"Hold on, Shy, I'm about to see what they doing."

I decided to go back to the door to see if I could hear anything. I placed the phone down on the bed and tried to get up without making too much noise. Diva's loud barking provided enough of a distraction that the police couldn't possibly hear me walking across the squeaky hardwood floors. What I heard next though sent me into a paranoid state.

"Agent Wells, do you see or hear any movement inside the house?" someone asked.

"Negative, sir. Only a dog barking and our intel shows that she has a female pit bull."

Intel? Agent? What the hell? How do they know what kind of dog I have? My heart was pounding in my chest so hard that I was sure that they could hear it. I crept back into the bedroom to get my phone.

"Shy, oh my God! They said 'agent,' and they know what kind of dog I have. What kind of police is that?"

"The Feds have agents, and NARC officers are also called agents. Since you don't sell drugs, it's probably the Feds," he schooled. "Do you have anything in there that could get you caught?"

"What do you think genius?" I snapped.

"Well, you better get rid of it, just in case they kick your door in," he said, apparently ignoring my sarcasm.

"Oh Lord, do you think they'll do that?"

"They might, depending on what they want. Get that shit out the house, just to be safe."

"Okay, hold on, I'm going to put you on speaker phone while I try to get rid of all this stuff. Just don't talk too loud," I told Shy and placed the phone down on the bed.

Diva followed every move I made. I was growing more annoyed with her and wished that she would just sit down somewhere. I guessed she could sense my fear.

"Diva, sit. Sit, girl."

Man oh man; what kind of foolishness have I gotten myself into now? I didn't know what kind of police were at my door. I know I didn't violate my probation. *Hell, I just saw my probation officer last week*, I thought while I moved around the house like a crack head looking for the next hit.

4

I didn't sell dope, so it couldn't be the NARCS. *Now where did I put the rest of those Social Security numbers?* I found them just as quick as the thought left my mind.

How am I going to get rid of these checks and credit cards if I can't go outside? Man, I'm tripping. The police really had me shook up, got me running around this house talking to myself.

Lord, please don't let these people kick my door in. Please don't let me go to jail today. Who's going to get Isaiah off the school bus if I go to jail?

"Ra'Quelle, Ra'Quelle, can you hear me? Are you alright?" I heard Shy yell through the speaker on the phone.

"Boy, why are you screaming my name like that? I told you I had you on speaker phone so I could try and handle this shit," I reminded him, hoping he'd shut up.

"Oh, my bad, ma. I just didn't hear you saying anything, so I got worried. Are they still out there?"

"I don't know and I'm damn sure not going to see."

BEEP.

"Damn, now who's calling me?"

The caller ID read 'PRIVATE.' My first thought was that it was most likely the police. "Shy, let me call you back, I have to hang this phone up 'cause I think the police are calling me from outside, and they're gonna wonder why they don't hear the phone ringing inside the house. I'll call right back, okay?" I told him before hanging up the phone.

See, these people out here were playing games, but they had the right one because I refused to get caught up like that. That phone could ring until an AT&T operator answered it, I didn't care. I walked back to the door to see if I can hear something – anything – that would give me some kind of idea of what is going on.

"Agent Wells, how good is the intel we have on this phone number?" someone asked.

"Sir, the phone is listed under Ra'Quelle Summers. It has this address listed and the line is open. I can hear a phone ringing inside of the residence, but no one has answered."

"Affirmative, just keep trying it."

Yeah, okay, Agent Wells, or whoever the hell you are. You

keep on trying to get me to answer that phone, and I'm gonna keep on trying to destroy this evidence.

Think, Rocky, think. I racked my brain trying to figure out what to do with all of the evidence? I couldn't put it in the trashcan nor could I flush it, there was nowhere to hide it. Maybe I could get someone to come to the back door and get it. Let me call Peanut and ask him.

After dialing the number, I anxiously waited for him to answer. *Please be home; please be home.*

"Hello?" He answered thank God.

"Peanut, this is Rocky. What's up, what are you doing right now?"

"Girl, I'm sitting here looking at all those federal agents you have all around your house. That's what I'm doing. Shit, a better question is *what* are you doing, or what have you been doing, better yet? And why the hell are you calling my phone? I can't be talking to you, un-un, no, you hot." He laughs into the phone.

"Boy, quit playing so damn much. I need you to help me."

"If you think I'm playing, that's on you. I hope you don't think those marshals are playing on your front porch."

"Peanut, did you say marshals?"

"Yep! Marshals, feds, federallys, whatever the hell you want to call them," he said.

Holding the phone tightly in my hand, the tears began to fall. With all of the desperation that I had and feeling completely alone in that moment, I had to ask my friend for a solid. The uncertainty of his reaction ate away at me, but I had no choice but to ask.

"Hey Peanut, do you think I can make it out the back door and get over to your house?" I ask him being hopeful.

"Naw, big sis, don't even set yourself up like that. Your house is surrounded and they have your driveway blocked. Damn girl, who you killed?"

"I don't know, but I'm thinking I'm going to find out soon." I took a deep breath before continuing. "Alright peanut, good looking out. I appreciate you. If I go down, you have to get Zay off the school bus for me and get him to his daddy," I in-

6

structed with fear in my voice.

"No doubt, no doubt, I got you. Just lay low and keep quiet. They might just leave," he tried to reassure me. "They're really not doing anything but standing around and talking."

"Alright, bye Peanut." *Leave, my ass, those people aren't going anywhere. They're probably out there drinking coffee and smoking cigarettes and shit.*

"Come away from that door, Diva, and sit down some-where," I told my dog through clenched teeth.

Oh, snap, I know what I can do to get rid of all that stuff. I'll burn it. Yeah, why didn't I think about that earlier? Yep, y'all stay right on out there. Uh-huh, I got it now. Let me get all this shit together, these credit cards, receipts, and other peoples' mail. Mm-hmm, I'm going to burn all this shit right now. I had to talk to my-self in order to organize my thoughts because at that moment, the fear of the unknown consumed me.

I gathered all of the possible evidence that could be used against me and prepped it to be burned until I realized I had better take the battery out of the smoke detector. There are enough people out there now; I don't need the fire department to come too. By that point, it was a 'by any means necessary' moment and I had to do what was necessary to keep myself home with my baby.

Now where did I put that lighter fluid? I thought to myself.

The bathroom seemed like the best place to set this shit on fire because they wouldn't be able to see the flames through the window. I put the papers in a pot from the kitchen, soaked it in lighter fluid and lit it up. The fire was bigger than I thought it would be and black smoke filled the room.

I had prayed that the fire would hurry up and burn because the smoke was about to kill me. I could hardly breathe. I began to think that maybe I used too much lighter fluid. I wasn't trying to burn my damn house down. I threw some water on it and let the fire go out, but this caused even more smoke to fill the bathroom.

WOOF, WOOF, WOOF. Diva was barking, trying to alert me of the smoke.

"Shut up, Diva, I see the fire. Hell, I started it. It will be okay, ma-ma. Shh, be quiet. Good girl," I said trying to console my dog.

The damn phone rang again and I wondered who the hell it was. "Oh, that's Peanut," I said when I saw his name on the caller ID.

"Hey, Peanut, what's up?"

"Rocky, those people just left, so if you were trying to dip, you better go ahead and dip now while you can," he tells me while laughing into the phone.

"Are you sure they're gone? Did you check out back?" I questioned him, hoping they were really gone.

"Yeah, ma, they're gone. I watched them leave and I'm standing on my porch right now."

"Okay, good looking out. Do you have anything over there to drink? My nerves are shot."

"Yeah, I got about a half a bottle of Grey Goose left over here. You can get that."

"Okay, thanks. I'll be over there in a second. Let me take Diva out to pee."

"Okay, I'll see you when you get here."

Damn. I'm glad they are gone. *Thank you, Jesus.* I wonder what they wanted.

"Diva! Come here, Diva!" I called out for my dog. I knew that damn dog better not have pissed in my house or I was going to beat her ass.

"Come on, ma-ma, let's go potty," I say after seeing Diva come around the corner. While she's handling her business, I had better take that damn burnt ass pot outside too.

This smoke is smelling up the house. Damn, this shit stink, I say to myself as I placed the pot outside and waited for Diva to relieve herself.

"Look at you, ma-ma. You're such a pretty girl, yes, you are. She's my pretty baby, yes, she is. Did she go pee-pee? Is she a good dog? Yes, she is," I praised Diva for using the bathroom where she was supposed to. *I love this dog beyond life*, I thought while smiling to myself.

"Come on, let's go in the house," I said as I opened the back door and motioned for her to enter first. I left Diva in the house and went out the front door. It was a pretty day out; the sky's clear and the weather was warm, but I couldn't even enjoy it. I was out there looking behind me like a damn drug fiend. Those people had me shook.

I glanced down at my clothes and laughed at myself; standing outside in some low-ride capris, a wife beater, and my Debo slippers. It's all good though, I'll throw something on later.

Damn, Peanut needs to clean up his yard, look at all that shit out there. He had blunt guts, cigarette packs, and beer cans all in the front yard. Now he was one lame ass dude, for real. I knocked loudly on the front door.

"Who is it?" he yelled.

"Open up this damn door, boy. You know who it is! You knew I was on my way over. Damn!" I yelled as I waited for that fool to open the door.

"Aye, Peanut, on some real nigga shit, you need to clean up your damn yard. Real talk, that should be some kind of health code violation or something." I laughed.

"Ha-ha hell, Rocky, you laughing, and making jokes about my damn yard, but you know what I don't have in my yard? The feds, that's what. Now get your drink. As a matter of fact, take it all 'cause you're going to need it. Hurry up and take your hot, FBI, CIA, U.S. Marshal dodging ass back to your own house. We don't do the police thing over here. I'm trying to smoke my breakfast and you blowing my high. I got folks all on the side of my damn house trying to see into your house. Ain't that some shit? You better go home while you can, Hot Girl, and I'll get at you later." He stood there looking at me as if he truly wanted me to leave his raggedy ass house. I knew this nigga was not trying to play me.

"Okay, Peanut, you got that one off. You just make sure that you remember that. Laugh now; cry later. I want you to make it your business to remember how hot I am when Christmas time rolls around and you need me to get presents for all those sixty-three kids you over here laying a claim to. Remember how hot I am then, nigga! And don't come over to my house later after you smoked all that shit and your ass got the munchies, okay?" I reminded him giving much attitude.

9

"Girl, go ahead with that bullshit, you know you're my boo. I'm just fucking with you, Rock. You gonna always be my boo, no matter what, even if your ass is on fire." He laughed.

I rolled my eyes. "Whatever, dude." I slammed his door shut as I left.

Chapter 2
Trouble

When I got back to my house and I went straight to the kitchen because I really needed to fix myself a drink to calm my nerves. I almost forgot that I needed to call Shy back too.

Aww yeah, this Grey Goose is right on time. Where is my lighter? I need a cigarette. When I found it, I lit my Newport and inhaled deeply.

BAM, BAM, BAM!

"Open up this door, Ms. Summers, we know you're in there. We just saw you on the front porch." I heard someone say from outside the house. "Open up the door right now, or we will knock it down."

"Grrr, Grrr!" Diva growled viciously at the door.

"Shut up, Diva." Damn, I wished this dog would go sit down somewhere.

Shit! I'm going to have to open the door, I thought to myself as I slammed back what was left in my glass. I quickly poured myself another one while I looked for the damn ashtray?

The police were out there threatening to kick my door in and take my black ass to jail. I didn't want to go to jail. I looked down at my hands shaking so badly; I could hardly pour the liquor. *Hell, I'll drink it out of the bottle. This isn't the time to be worrying about being all cute. Damn. I'm going to jail. Let me call Shy back.*

"Shy, the police are back," I said when he answered the phone. "They know I'm in the house. I'm going down like the damn Titanic. Will you bail me out of jail please?"

"Rocky, just don't answer the door. They can't just run up

11

in your house," he said, trying to sound confident. I loved him, but sometimes I forgot how crazy he is.

"Shy, it's the damn Feds; they can do anything they want."
BAM, BAM, BAM... "Last chance, Ms. Summers. Open up the door right now!" I heard the voice yell for a second time

"Agent Wells, step aside, sir. I'm going to use force to open this door. She seems to think this is some kind of joke." Hearing that forced me into action because I did not want my door kicked in.

"Okay, okay. I'm coming, I'm coming!" I yelled as I tried to hot box my Newport.

"Who is it?" I ask, standing at the door drinking out of the bottle.

"You know damn well who it is, so open up the door now!"
Okay, Rocky, take a deep breath. Calm down. Here we go.

When I opened the door, they almost knocked me down rushing into my house. They came to a quick stop when they were face-to-face with a 90 pound, bow legged, huge headed, red-nosed pit bull. All movement stopped, everything seemed to be going in slow motion. Diva had taken her attack stance. Her head lowered, her teeth were bared, and her hind legs were crouched, bracing herself to spring forward.

I noticed the first two agents who entered the house just stood there. Peanut was right; they were the U.S. Marshals. A tall, lanky white dude with sandy blonde hair, a black U.S. Marshals t-shirt, tight form fitting Walmart jeans, and a blue windbreaker with yellow U.S. Marshals letters accompanied the infamous cowboy boots the feds are known to wear.

The one I came to know as Agent Wells is slightly to my right with a crew neck t-shirt and khaki Levi Dockers with a suicide crease in them. He didn't wear the classic blue U.S. Marshal windbreaker; however, his U.S. Marshal's badge swung proudly around his neck on a silver beaded chain. My eyes instantly locked onto his like a heat-seeking missile, trying to get a read on this guy.

Before I could devote my attention into trying to peep his game, my internal survival instincts sounded my mental alarm. I glanced slightly to my right and noticed another not so tall, overly stocky man who was coming from behind. My first thought was that he was about to draw down on me.

In one swift, smooth motion, this mysterious man had a dead lock with a red beam right smack in the center of Diva's forehead. As I watched him use his right thumb to slide the safety off the Ruger 9 mm pistol, I grabbed Diva by her thick collar and tried to maneuver myself into a position between her and this man, who seemed intent on laying Diva to rest.

My heart was beating triple time in my chest. I had dropped the Grey Goose bottle while reaching for Diva and the sound of the shattering glass put everyone on the edge. In the blink of an eye, all three of the agents had their weapons drawn. And for some reason, Agent Wells was the only one who had his weapon trained on me.

Okay, that's how it is, I thought to myself. I could see at that moment that he was the one I have to be leery of.

"Don't shoot my dog! Please do not shoot my dog!" I screamed while begging with my eyes.

Without looking away for even a second, Agent Wells instructed me to remove the dog from the room immediately. I attempted to coax Diva out of the living room and into the bedroom, but she was not having any of it.

She attempted to jump over the coffee table to get to the agents, but I caught her in a chokehold and tried to calm her down. She sensed my fear and like the rider that she truly was, her eyes had shown me that it's fight until the death in her mind. She would lay down her life for me without any hesitation before she'd let these strange beings lay their hands on me.

My mind was going seven different ways all at once. I knew for a fact that Diva was a thoroughbred; I raised her to be one. If I turned her collar loose, I had no doubt she would take out as many of these officers as she possibly could.

My car keys were right beside me on the table. I could see the multicolored yellow, orange, and green Coogi key chain from where I stood. I remembered that there's at least a half of a tank of gas in the Cadillac sitting out back. If I kicked off my slippers, I knew I could get to my car before they'd catch me. I'm much closer to the back door than I am to them anyway.

Naw, I refused to even try that because as soon as they hit my dog with some hot lead, going out the back door was no longer optional.

The bond I had with Diva was stronger than that. I would never leave her to fight my battles while I ran away like a coward. I bottle-fed her as a puppy, and I used to carry her around in my Michael Kors bag. She used to be so cute with her paws hanging over the side of the bag while she looked around. I loved her and I was just as true to her as she was to me. As crazy as it may sound, I'd lay down my life for her in a New York minute.

Since I had enough sense to know that there was no win for me in a shootout with the police in the middle of my living room, I gave Diva the one word that calms her down instantly. My brother promised me that having a safety valve for my dog might save her life one day.

A safety valve is a word or a set of words that brings a dog out of its attack mode immediately. It basically tells the dog that although she can sense danger and she could read my fear, she must fall back and trust her master to handle whatever is going on. *Stand down, soldier, Mama's got this.*

Diva's safety word is "Checkmate," as in game over, like a game of chess that has just been won when one opponent out maneuvers the other and removes the head nigga in charge – the king – from the board. True to her respect and trust for her master, Diva instantly stood down and allowed me to lead her into the other room.

I locked her in the room and returned to the living room where I knew the games were about to begin. Before they started to question me, I asked if I could get a broom to sweep up the glass from the liquor bottle I dropped. As I entered the kitchen, I looked around and took in the spoils of my riches.

I noticed the hand carved gray marble counters, the solid oak cabinets with the brass handles and hinges. I wondered if I'd ever cook again on the stainless steel Kenmore glass top range.

Damn, this really could be the end for me. I had a good run and I obtained a lot of material things, but it doesn't look good for the home team right now.

My sister had been bugging me to give her this gorgeous black Maytag front loading washer and dryer. But if things go wrong, she just might be getting it quicker than she thinks.

I grabbed the broom and dustpan from behind the sub-zero fridge and wondered why the hell I paid six stacks for a damn re-frigerator. After sweeping up the glass and tossing it into the trash, I went back into the living room. I'm looking at them and they're looking at me. I hope someone breaks the silence soon because I ain't saying shit.

A caramel sister with a long ponytail and honey brown eyes wearing a Richland County Sheriff's Department uniform stepped forward and ended the silent standoff.

"Ms. Summers, I'm Officer Smith with the sheriff's depart-ment. You do know why we are here, don't you?" she questioned, looking as if she expected an answer.

Now what kind of ignorant ass question was that and what did she expect me to say? *Oh, why yes, ma'am, I sure do know why you're here. You're here because I like to shop with other people's credit cards and all my associates are hustlers, boosters, and check writers. Of course, I know why you're here. You're here to take me to jail.* Well, honey-boo, bye! If that's what she wanted to hear from me, she was about to be ass out.

Okay, let me get this right. Remember to make and keep constant eye contact, don't fidget, keep my hands still, speak clearly and evenly, use intelligent wording, and lose all traces of that hood mentality. I sure am glad I watch CSI Miami. Horatio damn sure comes in handy.

"No, ma'am, I'm awfully sorry, but I have no idea why you are here," I said, hoping that I came off as innocent as I was trying to sound.

I catch the agent who came through the door first as he nudged Agent Wells and whispered something in his ear.

Agent Wells looked around the house suspiciously and asked me, "Ms. Summers, do you care to tell me what that smell is in here? Were you burning something?"

I almost choked on the cigarette smoke I had in my mouth.

Of course I wasn't about to tell them what I was burning, but I have to tell them something because the house is still full of smoke.

I looked Agent Wells straight in the eyes and in the most soft and humble voice I could muster I told him that I was cooking some hard boiled eggs earlier and forgot them when I went to take a bath, so the water boiled out and the pot was scorched.

Uh-huh, that sounds about right, I convinced myself, hoping he bought that bullshit story.

Agent Wells looked at me as if to say, "Child, please," but instead he asked me if I minded if he opened the back door. I told him to go ahead.

While he was doing that, the officers in the house took turns introducing themselves to me. To my surprise the one who was about to shoot Diva wasn't even a federal agent; he's a damn postal inspector, the Postmaster General to be exact. Ain't that some shit? I didn't even know that people at the post office carried pistols and badges. You learn something new every day.

They suggested that we all have a seat so we could discuss the business at hand. We all sat around my seven foot long dining room table, which had seating for eight people.

Officer Smith commented on the dining room furniture and asked me where I was able to purchase that kind of set. Wow, she must really think I'm retarded or something. Why in the hell would I tell her I bought it anywhere when I'm sure they know that I don't have a job or any other legal means to purchase this type of furniture?

I laughed it off and told her, "No, this particular set was hand made by a friend of mine named Chase. He's a very talented carpenter." I amused myself because I actually did purchase it on-line from Miami's City Furniture and I used a Chase credit card to pay for it.

Agent Wells was up, wandering around my house like he was looking for something in particular. He made his way toward the back door and my heartbeat sped up. *Uh-oh.*

He ended up at the back door looking out into the yard. He motioned with his hand for the other agent, whom I found out was named Garcia, to join him. I realized that they have found the pot I burned those social security numbers and shit in.

I hoped and prayed that it all burned beyond recognition. I know that forensics have made some great improvements on their technology and they had ways to piece evidence back together.

Agent Wells stepped outside the backdoor only to return with the smoldering pot in his hands. His facial expression told me that he was not a happy camper. His cheeks and ears turned a beet red and if I didn't know any better, I would swear that that man was looking at me like he was sizing me up to take a swing at me.

It must have been my damn nerves or the Grey Goose talking because he was an officer of the L-A-W and he would not possibly be considering getting into a fight with me; although I'd swear he'd been thinking about it. I'll tell you what though, police or no police, if he had swung on me in here it'd be on and poppin' because I would've forgotten that he had a badge and either he would kick my ass or I'd kick his, right? I quickly got over that crazy thought.

When I came out of my little fantasy fight with Agent Wells, I saw him standing directly in front of me with latex gloves on as he held the smoking pot in my face. He appeared as if he wanted an explanation. I decided to see exactly how long he would allow me to play dumb, so I sat at the table, smoked another Newport, and looked up at him as if I really couldn't seem to understand what it was that he wanted to know.

Agent Wells peeped my game and decided to switch his game up. He went drill sergeant on my ass by screaming at me and asked, "What the hell is this, Ms. Summers?"

I didn't know if this was a rhetorical question or if I was actually supposed to answer it, so I chose to just sit and look stupid a little while longer. I sure wished I hadn't dropped that bottle of liquor. Hell, I needed a drink or a Xanax or something.

I turned around for a second to find the ashtray and put out my cigarette. When I switched back around, I almost choked because this fool had the burnt pot all the way in my face. I coughed a little from the smoke that was still coming out. I tell you what, I could guarantee that I wouldn't be cooking in that pot anymore since it is burnt all to hell.

Wells continued to yell at me once again, so I figured it was best to finally answer him because he looked like he was ready to pop a blood vessel in a minute. Let me get my shit together. It was time to play my role correctly if I wanted to keep my ass out of jail. I put on a straight face, set my shoulders back and made eye contact.

With all of that intact, I answered very meekly. "Sir, I have absolutely no idea what that is, but it appears to be burning. Where did you get that from?" Oh wee, I couldn't believe I got that off without a smile, an eye twitch, or anything, just perfect delivery. I'm very proud of myself.

Officer Smith was unable to keep a straight face, and even let out a girlish little giggle. Unfortunately, for me, the feds weren't in a laughing mood.

Agent Garcia made up his mind to enter into the game. He turned his attention to me and for the first time I saw how truly fine he was. Hazel green eyes, mocha colored skin with jet-black hair cut short and faded around the temples. I'm thinking if he wasn't trying to take me to damn jail, he could get it.

I was curious as to what nationality he was. I thought about how it would feel to have his huge hands rub all over my body, or have his thick fingers entwined in my hair while he kissed me passionately on my neck and gently bit my ear lobes…

"Ms. Summers, Ms. Summers, are you high on something, ma'am, or are you purposely trying to ignore the questions I just asked you?" Oh Lord, I kept zoning out, daydreaming, and these folks were wanting to give me a life sentence. I had to get my mind right and show them what I'm really working with.

"Sir, by no means am I trying to ignore you or be disrespectful, but you keep asking me questions that I can't possibly answer. How can you go outside somewhere and get a burning pot and bring it into my house and turn around and ask *me* where it came from or what it is, like I would know?"

"Ain't this some shit?" Agent Wells said. I feigned as if I was really shocked by his words and placed one hand on my chest and let my mouth hang open while I fumbled around for my cigarette pack.

Hell, I was sure that more likely than not, I'd be going to jail anyhow, so I figured I may as well have some fun with them. I turned away from them and blew the smoke out the side of my mouth.

With a slight tilt of my head, I looked upwards at the agent and calmly said, "Look. I don't know what's in that pot or where you got it from for that matter. All I know is that you went out my back door and returned with it in your hands. I have a house full of police, both federal and state, and I have a trigger-happy man from the post office who wants to kill my dog. My son will soon be home from school because they have a half day, and I do not wish to have any of you in here when he arrives."

Agent Wells turns to Agent Garcia. "Garcia, take this pot out to the truck and bag and tag it as evidence. Ms. Summers, I hope you understand that I gave you an opportunity to tell me about the contents of that pot. My office has the means to reconstruct evidence that has not burned completely. We can and will find out what is in that pot and then we will deal with you accordingly. All of that aside for right now, I'm sure you wish to know why we're all here. Ms. Summers, may I call you Ra'Quelle?"

I wasn't going to answer that question, but he was sitting there glaring at me, obviously not going to continue, until I answered. "No, sir, I don't mind if you address me by my first name."

Agent Wells gave me a smile so quick, had I blinked my eyes I would have missed it. "Okay, Ra'Quelle, here's my card. I work in the federal building downtown. I work in Homeland Security with the Secret Service of the United States of America. Mr. Garrick here works in Atlanta, Georgia and is the Post Master General for the Southeastern Region. We received a call from him concerning a staggering amount of credit cards from various companies that are being mailed to your previous address as well as this current address, along with other residences throughout the area. We are here to try and find out what if you may know about these fraudulent accounts."

One thing about me is that I have never been a punk about

my shit; I'm true to the game with mines. I've been to jail several times before. Matter of fact, it's how I lived my life. But the situation at hand was some whole other shit.

These people pulled up driving a navy blue suburban with the police tint. Agent Wells had a swag about himself that assured me that he usually gets his man. Agent Garcia seemed to have an anger management problem, and to top it all off, they are the damn Secret Service.

They were not just any ole federal agents. These were the people that work with the people whose job it is to protect the goddamn President of the United of the States. We are in a whole new ball game now. I done up and did it now. Not only were they going to lock me up, but the feds also gave out football numbers, lots of time in federal prison, and they don't even have federal parole anymore.

Man oh man, I ain't never gonna see Isaiah anymore and I was sure that they were gonna take Diva out back and shoot her. I hoped they'd let me get some clothes on. It's cold in the county jail. I was very seriously starting to regret the day I learned to do the credit card scam. But, coming from a family composed of drug dealers and hustlers we were taught to hold our own. I was expected to join the family hustle, instead I chose my own life of crime. One I thought posed less of a risk.

Why in the hell didn't I stop fucking with them credit cards a long time ago? No, I wanted to 'ball till I fall'. Every stupid reason I ever gave myself to continue using those cards came flooding into my mind. My brain was not cooperating. *They can't catch me; I'm the best that ever did it. There ain't no way they can possibly link those cards back to me. I never use my real name nor am I stupid enough to get caught on camera.*

Calm down, Rocky, and think this shit through. I tried to hype myself up for the games to begin. I knew it wasn't over till it was over. I just had to play the hand I'd been dealt. I wasn't new to this; I'm true to this. Just because he had a badge and a gun didn't make him smarter than me.

I swallowed that giant lump of fear that had found its way to my throat and met his gaze head on. "Excuse me, but I don't exactly understand what you're asking me. Can you clarify yourself a bit please?"

Agent Garcia pulled his head back as if I had slapped him across the face. He glanced over at Wells, who was smiling for some reason. "Well, I see we have a smart-ass here who thinks that this is a game and we are here for the fun of it. I hope she understands that I do this shit every day, and dealing with her kind is nothing new to me. Somehow or another things always end up in my favor."

He was just as thrown off as the other one. They made an awesome team. Uptight and tight ass. Okay, now seriously, this wasn't any time for foolishness.

Agent Wells shook his head at me. "Ra'Quelle, first I want you to look over this evidence that I brought here with me. I have laid it out for you so that you can get a clear view of what we are dealing with here. As you see, we have photos and credit card receipts. We also have credit card statements along with print outs from AT&T, Direct TV, Time Warner Cable, and various other accounts past and present listed for your current as well as your previous address. None of these appear to be in your name. "

He continued, "I have ATM withdrawals, car payment receipts, and receipts for furniture we believe is all through this house. I believe this very table we are sitting at is listed as a fraudulent purchase that we are trying to link to you and your friends. I want you to please take your time and decide rather you want to A, go get dressed and we will take you to the detention center for questioning or B, sign this waiver that allows us to talk to you without an attorney present. We expect you to answer our questions as openly and honestly as possible. Now you take your sweet little time and think about what you've done and what's at stake here and decide how you want to proceed from here."

I watched as all of them got up from the dining room table and converged over by the front door, leaving me sitting all alone looking down at my worry stricken reflection that I could see in the glass on the table. Before I could even look at anything that was laid before me, I closed my eyes and said a silent but oh so powerful and heartfelt prayer.

INDICTED / *Keisha Monique*

Dear God, please hear my cry; hear my call. Please, Father, look into my heart. Forgive me of my wrongs, and please have mercy and favor on your lost child. Lord, I know that I have not been living my life right, I know that what I have been doing is wrong, but I don't want to spend the rest of my life in jail. This is a pretty big mess that I have gotten myself into, and these are some very powerful people in here. They are not as powerful as you though, Father. I know that the end result will always be your will. I just humbly ask for the strength and the wisdom to deal with this. I pray that my penance is not more than I can bear. Keep me safe, help me stand and do what's right. In Jesus name, I pray.

Amen.

Chapter 3

Playing My Position

I opened my eyes slowly after calling for a little spiritual backup. I looked around the living room and the feds were still over by the front door conversing about something or another. I don't know, maybe I thought they would have magically disappeared when I looked over that way.

Since spontaneous human combustion is not an option for them, and it was painfully obvious that they weren't willing to just let me slide this time, I decided to go ahead and deal with the matter at hand.

I glanced around the table at the papers that were laid before me and did a double take. Something about this investigation was off but I couldn't quite put my finger on it. I had to admit though, I was very impressed with the investigative skills of the U.S. government. They had a whole slew of evidence on lil ole me. The question was no longer what they know, but what they could prove. Me, I'm old school. I'm not gonna say, "Oh yeah, of course I did this, I did that, and yeah, I did that as well." No, no, no, the game didn't work that way for me. I was always taught that loose lips sink ships and not to volunteer information. They were gonna have to do their damn jobs if they planned to take me down. My entire life has consisted of one hustle after another, and certain things just came to me like a second nature. Being the love child produced by a drug dealer and his trap queen had its pros and its cons.

While thinking of the best recourse to deal with this situation, a couple of the photos jumped out at me and caught my attention. I slid them a little closer to me so that I could get a better view of exactly who it was and what they are doing. I became dumbfounded to see pictures of my sister and my two best friends. All of the photographs were taken at different ATM machines around the city, and they appeared to be making withdrawals.

I laughed quietly to myself when I l saw my sister Michelle's picture. I had to wonder why the hell she was looking a hot ghetto mess. There she stood, at the ATM with a lime green halter-top on and a yellow bra underneath. She was sporting huge goddess braids, Gucci shades, and if my eyes weren't deceiving me, she also had a blunt in her mouth.

I really loved my sis. There would never be anyone else I knew who could tell the whole world to kiss their ass without saying a word. My sister had always been to the left. She didn't take shit from anyone except me and that's only because I was the baby. Any money-making hustle or scheme in our area, she was down with it. She never showed fear when it came to getting her hands dirty and getting paid, not to mention she was loyal to the game. Death before dishonor was tatted on her left forearm, and those were not just words that sounded good; that's the code that we lived by.

I felt some kind of way seeing my sister and my friends on the table because I promised them that they would be straight if they helped me do this credit card thing. That may no longer be the case. Damn, how many times did I tell them that the ATM cameras automatically came on as soon as the card was put into the machine? It's a ritual that I went over with them all the time; knowing what you're doing when using these credit cards could make the difference between staying on the streets or doing fed time.

Your left hand was always used to cover the camera while you inserted the card and typed all the needed information with your right hand. By no means should you ever remove your hand before completing the transaction and removing the card. Now I was wondering why she got caught slipping like that. I'd heard people say that she had been snorting cocaine and taking X pills, but I didn't want to believe that, not my sister.

We were top shelf, designated dimes, and hard-core drugs were not what was happening in our lives. I had to remember to get at her about that as soon as I could clear this mess up. I knew that I had to handle this in a manner in which everyone had the opportunity to walk away from this clean. I'd always been a real soldier and I would not have it any other way.

My best friends Charla and Dream didn't even have an arrest record. They weren't street broads and usually wouldn't involve themselves with criminal activities, but time and circumstance somehow brought about their participation. Their roles were minor so I figured it couldn't be too hard for me to cover for them and keep them home with their families and loved ones. If they stuck to the code and played their cards right, things would go well.

It was established beforehand that if anything ever went down and somehow or another we got caught up, they would remain silent, refuse to sign anything and request an attorney to be present before answering any questions. I was the brains behind the operation so it was agreed that I would handle everything and even take one for the team if it came to that. I was a ride or die chick so I didn't mind claiming all the shit so everyone else could walk away if that's what I had to do. However, if there was the slightest chance that I too could walk away from this, then that was the desirable route for me.

I saw how they had all of the store receipts stacked by location. All of the Macy's receipts were piled up and stapled together. The other receipts were organized in a similar manner. The jewelry store and furniture receipts were separated from the rest. They even had everything grouped by the amount of the purchases, and since the appliances, furniture, and jewelry cost the most, they were grouped with each other.

I cracked a smile and lit a cigarette as I reminisced about the days of me and my girls running through the malls and boutiques, as if we had just won the lottery and money was not a problem. The days that we came out of Macy's and Footlocker with bags so full we looked as if we were carrying sacks of gifts for Santa Claus. Shopping was something we did on a regular. You name it and we had it; Gucci, Prada, Fendi, Coach, Chanel, all that and more. Money ran through my hands like water, that's how I did it. My son drank out of Waterford crystal glasses, and my china cabinets were adorned with Limoges china. Yeah, balling was my hobby.

I was awakened from my little trip down memory lane by someone touching my shoulder and snapping at me at the same time. Who else but Agent Wells? Damn, I almost forgot he was still here.

"Ms. Summers, I would love for you to share what's so damn funny with the rest of us. You're sitting there laughing and puffing on your cigarette like this shit isn't really happening. Let me see if I can help take you down a peg or two. Maybe I can erase that lopsided smile right off your face. Let's take a minute to look over what we have here. Are you willing to talk to us now and sign this attorney waiver, or do you want us to take you to jail and question you later? And when I say later, trust and believe, I do mean later."

After speaking his peace, Wells glared at me as if he expected an answer or some kind of reaction from me.

"Yeah. Later, as in a couple of weeks, or even a month kind of later," Agent Garcia added.

Agent Wells took it upon himself to come and sit right beside me and continue his song and dance as if I really wanted to hear any of the propaganda he was spitting at me. "Look, Ra'Quelle, I know you're waist deep in this mess, but I also know that you're a very intelligent person, and I believe that maybe somebody has taken advantage of you and has you in deeper than you can deal with. I'm sure this situation goes far beyond you or your realm of understanding. What I am offering you is a chance to help yourself and to make something right that we both know is very wrong."

He lowered his tone, and if I didn't already know how they operated, I would have thought he was sincere. "I know you didn't come up with this scheme all by yourself and that you're working with somebody who has access to information. The government is interested in knowing how that information was obtained. We are dealing with over two hundred fraudulent accounts at several credit card companies. We have stolen checks as well as printed checks.

26

Somehow, someone got a hand on a lot of people's personal information and used it to their advantage. You're caught right up in the middle of all of this along with your sister and your road dogs. So don't let this thing take you down alone. If you just cooperate with us, I promise you that we will go after the bigger fish in the pond and try to help you along the way as well." He sounded dead ass serious.

Did he just call my friends road dogs? Who says that? I thought to myself. *This is by far the lamest law enforcement dude I have ever had the displeasure of meeting. Seriously.*

I hadn't a clue what these people had in store for me, but I did know that they had made a grave mistake. They allowed me to peep their game, and I knew for a fact that they did not have all their ducks in a row.

There was no big conspiracy with all that shit and I didn't now, nor had I ever, worked for anyone with access to that information. I was in charge of all my hustles. He obviously had no clue about me because never had anyone gotten the chance to take advantage of me. It was impossible for someone to do that.

I smoked the last of my cigarette and tossed it into the ashtray. I took a deep breath and let the smoke escape my mouth before I asked Agent Wells, "Are you guys going to let me change into something warmer before you take me to jail since I know how cold it is in there? Also, I need to make arrangements for someone to get my son off of the school bus."

What happened next really blew my mind. Agent Garcia came rushing toward me like he was about to bust my shit wide open and all I could think was that this dude has lost his damn mind.

He slammed his huge hand down on the table with so much force, the entire center glass cracked down the middle. Spit foamed in the corners of his mouth and his eyes seemed very dark and dangerous. He was so close to me that I could see the lettuce in his teeth that I assumed came from an early lunch.

He grabbed my chair and spun me around to face him. He pointed his finger directly in my face and yelled, "We are done playing with you, girl! Let me repeat that in case you weren't paying attention. We are fucking *done* playing with you! You're running around town spending hundreds of thousands of dollars! You're in this fancy house with all your handy dandy shit, living like you're some kind of damn rock-star rapper. You're just living la vida fucking loca and you're sitting up in here like your shit don't stink".

He paused, took a deep breath and continued "Well, let me tell you, missy, your shit does stink and if you ask me, it stinks pretty bad. I've seen the damn pictures of all your fucking Gucci, Coochie, Coogi, who gives a flying fuck, whatever you call that shit you have been buying with these credit cards. Now I'm telling you right damn now, I will go back there and shoot that big ass horse you call a dog, and I'll run through this damn house like Hurricane Katrina never could. I will snatch up everything in this house, all your little prized possessions you have here, all your fine clothes, and shoes, all that God-awful jewelry. I'll take all that shit and toss it into trash bags, and load it up as evidence. I'll remove every stitch of furniture from this house, the stove, and the damn refrigerator too."

I chose not to respond to this mad man in hopes that he would calm down. Unfortunately that wasn't the case. "I'll have a truck take all that shit away and I'll go so far as to take the shoes off your feet. I'll haul your ass to the nearest federal building to arrest you, take you to the county jail for holding and leave you there while I lose all your paperwork and take about two or three weeks to find it while you sit there and get to know Big Bertha. I'll bet she will just love a pretty little thing like yourself. By the time, you're able to post bond, I'll have ten more charges to hit you with, and *that* is a promise from me to you. By the time you get out of jail, your son will be graduating from high school. Now why don't you just try me? Try me, you hear?"

By the time, I wiped his spit off my cheek and attempted to calm my nerves down; I came to the realization that he was just a regular ole country redneck. All that backwoods country came up out of him just now. All his professionalism went right out the window. That dude was crazy.

His outburst didn't scare me though. I had dealt with many

fools in my lifetime. All it did was let me know that Agent Garcia wasn't working with a full deck; so therefore, I needed to be wary of him. His behavior was very volatile. There was definitely something wrong with him and there was no telling what he was capable of if I didn't at least respond to him.

On top of that, how would we live if they took all of our things out of the house? Where would we sleep, how would I cook, where would I keep the groceries? No, going to jail today and having the federales remove all my stuff from the house was not a viable option for me.

From my past experiences with the law, I knew that the police just didn't decide, *Okay, hey, I think I'll give her a break today. She seems to be a nice person, so I think I'll give her a pass.* No, shit just don't work like that.

If the police came to your house about some shit that you knew you were mixed up in and they wanted to question you but didn't arrest you; that simply meant that they didn't have the proof they needed to lock you up right at that moment. They couldn't care less about you, your kids, your momma, whoever. They just didn't have all the pieces to the puzzle yet. So they come to interrogate you and if you're not up on your game and you play into their hands and fuck around and start answering questions without knowing where that line of questioning is going, I can pretty much assure you that by the time they leave your house, you are going with them or will be a day or two behind them.

Understanding all of this, I knew that Garcia's outburst wasn't because he was mad at me or that he didn't like me. He was mad at the fact that he didn't have what he needed to take me to jail right now and solve his little case. I knew he wanted to lock me up now, but his superiors wouldn't let him just yet because the whole case was circumstantial.

So I played ball with the feds for a minute just to see how much they truly *didn't* know. The moment I became uncomfortable, I'd throw out my attorney card to stop all of the questions. I asked permission to get something to drink because my mouth was parched. When I came out of the kitchen with a tall glass of orange juice in one of my Waterford tumblers, immediately Agent Garcia recognized the crystal and shook his head in utter disgust. I dismissed his scowl and reclaimed my seat at the table and read over the attorney waiver. I signed it reluctantly and agreed to answer some of their questions.

It felt like with that one simple gesture, half of the tension in the room had dissipated.

Officer Smith was the first one to speak as she asked me if she could pat me down and if I'd agree to a search of the premises. I thought to myself, *what does she want to pat me down for, what is she looking for? I don't have any pockets so what the hell is she talking about patting me down?*

As for searching the house, well, that joke's on them. She could search all she wanted to because the shit they were looking for was in that burnt pot. I was ninety-nine percent sure that I got everything. I had a few social security numbers around the house in my Polo boots but I didn't foresee her taking the insides of my boots out to look in there, so I went ahead and gave her consent.

After I did so, they informed me that they would have been able to search the house anyway because my being on probation. Now, ain't that some shit? I didn't know that I could violate my probation for refusing to cooperate with a law enforcement officer. You learn something new every day.

I stood up and placed my hands on the wall, spread my legs, and assumed the position. I'd been through this several times in the past, so I already knew what to expect. "Do you have anything in your pockets? Do you have any weapons on you? Anything in your pockets that might stick or poke me?" she asked.

"I don't have any pockets, ma'am," I replied while giving Officer Smith the "duh" expression.

Smith stepped behind me and went up on leg and down the other, under my arms, lifted my bra, shook it out, lifted my feet so she could feel the bottom of my socks and lastly, she ran her hand through my hair.

She appeared shocked when she realized I didn't have any tracks in my hair. She must have assumed that there was. She seemed relieved that I wasn't holding a pistol or anything that could have been a threat to them, and so she moved on to the rest of the house.

I joined Agent Wells and the postmaster general at the table while Agent Garcia went outside to call someone.

Agent Wells picked out the photo of Michelle first and placed it in front of me. Then he pushed over the ones of Charla and Dream and turned towards me with a hopeful expression. "Do you recognize any of these people?"

I can't believe he just asked me that foolishness. What does he think I'm going to say? No, I don't know them. Hell, Michelle is my sister. How in the hell could I not know her? He's trying to play me like I'm slow now. That's okay. I'm going to let him have that simple-minded question and just go with the flow.

"Mr. Wells," I chuckled, "you know as well as I do that Michelle is my sister and Charla, Dream and I went to college together at Winthrop University in Rock Hill. Of course I recognize them."

"Very good, Ms. Summers. I was just testing the waters. Well, as you can see, I have several photos from banks in the surrounding area. I have surveillance photos from ATM machines at Wells Fargo as well as Bank of America. Apparently, withdrawals were made with these credit cards that are listed below. Pictures of your friends are stapled to the receipts for their individual transactions. There were two cards that Michelle used with a total of seventeen transactions withdrawing $8,500.00 in cash, plus the bank fees. All being charged to accounts under the names of Ashley Garrick and Kae'Leigh Sumpter."

"Neither Ms. Garrick nor Ms. Sumpter had any knowledge of these accounts being opened. The credit card company is Citibank Visa out of Wilmington, Delaware, and their records indicate that those cards were mailed to this address here where you are the sole occupant aside from your minor son. The postmaster has spoken to the mailman who runs this route and they have observed several cards being sent to this address. They also have given statements to us that you have been receiving a great amount of mail that is not yours and addressed to someone else at this residence."

"Next, we have Ms. Dream Austin, and these three photos

INDICTED/*Keisha Monique*

show her using a credit card that was issued to Travis Young to pay for gas to fill up this GMC truck, which is registered to her. Also, we have her shopping for groceries and household items at the Walmart on Forest Drive. The credit cards were issued from Discover and were mailed to 2524 Windy Drive, which coincidentally, is right next door to you. Hmm, imagine that."

He glared at me and continued, "Last, we have six photos of Charla Harris using a credit card issued to Tevin King from Chase Manhattan Bank. She's at an ATM machine inside of the Publix grocery store on Rosewood Drive. Ms. Harris used this card twice a day for a week, and on three separate occasions, she withdrew cash from the ATMs for a total cash amount of $2,500.00."

"I also had an opportunity to speak with Mr. King, who had no knowledge of this account. Mr. King assured me that the account is indeed fraudulent, and he wants to prosecute whoever is using this card to the fullest extent of the law. This particular card was delivered to your sister Michelle's house at 822 Richmond Street where Michelle has been in residence since 2001."

"Now," Wells continued, "for the moment I'd like to focus on these photos and these three accounts, which are directly linked to you. These card applications were done at the Southeast branch of the Richland County Public Library on Garners Ferry Road, using its internet access. I think that it is kind of convenient that this library is less than three miles from where we are right now."

"I have cause to believe that you have made several trips to this library on numerous occasions and filled out hundreds of credit card applications, having them sent to your house, your previous house, and other houses in Columbia. Some of these houses belonging to your friends and family members. What I'd like to find out from you, Ms. Summers, is how you obtained all these victims information and who helped you to orchestrate this elaborate scheme?" He finished and waited for a response from me.

Damn, I couldn't believe how sloppy my whole damn team got. We went over this shit all the time. I refused to understand how the hell they had gotten caught up like this. There had to be a damn good reason why he didn't have a picture of me in this pile. Not a single picture of me doing anything. I knew how to avoid places that had a lot of cameras and when I went to the ATM, I sure as hell didn't just step in there and place the card in the machine.

I wasn't that stupid. Who doesn't know that the camera on the grocery store ATM machine sits right at the top left hand corner? Those little cameras are just in the right place to get a close up of the face of the person using the machine. If they didn't cover the camera they might as well just have stood there, said cheese and smiled for the camera 'cause they got your picture. Best believe that if it's someone else's card you are using, your ass is going to jail. Point blank.

Who doesn't know that Walmart is a small replica of Fort Knox? What the hell could they have been thinking about? You can't go in Wally World without being caught on one of the hundreds of cameras they have in there.

I explained the rules to all of them at the time I activated the cards and handed them out. I told them how much money I wanted off of each card, how much to keep for themselves, and how to avoid being captured on film. How could they forget the most important part of this whole thing?

I don't even know how salvageable this situation is.

Wait, wait, wait one goddamn minute. Hold up.

I just realized that this dude just said that my sister took $8,500.00 from the accounts I had under the names Garrick and Sumpter from Citibank Visa. I knew that was a fuckin' lie. He was trying to get me to tell him about some shit that he ain't had no clue about, for real. He wanted to close this case bad and attempted to play me bad, but it was obvious that he didn't do his homework. Furthermore, I was much smarter than they gave me credit for and I'd be damned if I fell in their trap.

I clearly remembered those cards that I gave to my sister. They were what I called baby accounts because they had small credit limits and I wasn't going to break the bank. Each of those cards had a credit limit of $5,000.00 for a combined total of $10,000.00. After I did some minor shopping and paid a few bills, I told Michelle that she could have them. I told her she only had to split the cash advances with me 50-50.

A credit card with a $5,000.00 limit only had a cash advance amount of $2,500.00, which is 50% of the credit limit. Therefore, it would be totally impossible for her to withdraw any more than $5,000.00. That was, $3,500.00 less than the amount he just tried to tell me she was on tape withdrawing.

Credit card companies don't allow you to go over the cash advance amount that is preset for each card. Even if there was additional credit left on the cards, they only allow it be used towards purchases. Once you have reached the cash limit, you could still shop, but would not be allowed to receive any cash back from the ATM, bank, or anywhere else until the bill had been paid.

Either Agent Wells had his dollar amount wrong or he was attempting to run game on me and corner me into ratting out my girls and myself. For all I knew, those pictures could be of them at the same stores and ATM machines handling their own personal business. They all had jobs and real bank accounts. Agent Wells was gonna have to bring it a little harder if he wanted to take me and my girls down. I refused to go out like that, for real. Never would I gift wrap this little case and hand it to him on a silver platter.

"Mr. Wells," I said while shuffling the pictures in front of me and stacking them on top of each other. "Sir, I don't quite follow your line of questioning. I don't know anything about my people using anyone's credit cards besides their own. As far as any cards that were delivered to this house, I have not personally seen any. There has never been anything in my mailbox except my own mail whenever I've gone to get the mail out. I can't tell you about my previous address, as I no longer live there and have no idea what may or may not have been delivered there. You'd have to ask my sister about any mail that was delivered to her house because only she would be able to answer that question. It seems to me that if anyone received mail at their homes that didn't belong to them they would just return it to the sender. That *is* the right thing to do."

I really wished I could've been inside Wells' head for a minute. I knew he had some choice words for me. He was probably thinking, *This little bitch thinks she is so smart, sitting here like she don't know nothing about nothing.*

34

When he glanced towards Agent Garcia, I could almost see the wheels turning in his head. Probably thinking that since Garcia tried to shake me up by breaking my table, he might be able to intimidate me into talking. .

Sure enough, Wells had waved Garcia over. "Agent Garcia, I'm going to step outside for a second. I need to make some phone calls and see if I can't come up with some more useful information on these accounts. Maybe I will be able to find something that will help jog Ms. Summer's memory. Meanwhile, will you please continue to go over this information with her while I go out to the truck and see what I can come up with?"

The postmaster general stood up as well and told the agents that he had to head back to Atlanta, but if they needed any further assistance, to please give him call.

Any further? I failed to see anything he did since he'd been at my house besides charging in and threatening to kill my damn dog. All he *did* was sit around taking up space, looking crazy. Goodbye to him and good riddance.

Officer Smith finally re-entered the room and regretfully informed them that she had come up with nothing in her search of the house. She added that although she has found nothing illegal or anything pertaining to identity theft or credit card fraud, she felt that they might find the contents of my bedroom interesting because she sure did.

With that said, she asked them to complete the search by themselves and informed them that she would be patrolling the neighborhood should they need her again.

She looked my way and smiled. "You've got more clothes and shoes than you will ever wear; your son has every video game on the market and more Jordan's than Mike himself. Your home could be put into the Better Homes and Gardens magazine, and you have kitchen appliances that I have only read about. I sure wish that after all these years of busting my ass on the force that I could afford half of the things you have. I hope you enjoy them while you can young lady, because I think that they are going to cost you dearly." She nodded her head at me, pulled her long ponytail through the back of her service cap, and exited the house. She passed Garcia on the way out and they gave each other a cordial nod of respect.

To my surprise, Agent Wells seemed to have calmed himself down a lot by the time he came back into the house. I wondered who he was talking to on the phone that helped him get in a better mood than he was.

After Agent Garcia left, I glanced out the living room window while I waited to see if Wells was gonna tear up my furniture or flip out like his partner did. I noticed that the whole block appeared to be deserted. Nothing will clear the block like the damn police. Especially the feds. Wells and I stared at each other for a minute. It seemed like neither one of us wanted to be the first to break eye contact.

Finally, he blinked and cleared his throat. "Ms. Summers, I truly apologize for the damage caused to your table. Garcia just let his temper get the best of him. We just don't like being played for a fool because we are not foolish. I feel as though you disrespected me as well as the other officers when we first arrived. You were acting as if this were some kind of game to you, when in all actuality this is not a game. This is your life we are talking about here and it's your freedom on the line. I remember you said that your son will be home from school early today, and I don't want you to have to explain to him why the police are at your house. I'll go over this stuff as quickly as possible if you will work with me and be honest and forth coming. I can be out of here in the next thirty minutes or so."

For the first time since they burst through my doors, I was able breathe a little easier. At least I knew that they were not going to arrest me that day. Since I wasn't going to jail , I thought to myself that the very moment they left, I would go all out for the loot.

I understood that just because I wasn't going to jail that day, didn't mean that I was in the clear and that was all good. Whenever they did decide to come for me, my pockets were gonna be right. My son would be straight and I'd be prepared to lay down for a minute if I had to. Trust and believe, as soon as he beat his feet and got up out of there, the turn up was about to be real.

My mission was to see how fast I could get them out of my

house. "Did you just ask me how I obtained the furniture here, Agent Wells, or was it another question?" I asked since I was deep in thought when he asked a question and didn't hear him.

"Yes, that was my question to you, but before you answer that, please take into consideration that I have all the receipts right here. I have almost thirty thousand dollars' worth of receipts for furniture that matches this furniture right here throughout your house, even down to this table we are sitting at. So, before you decide to try and lie to me, know that I have the means to prove that this is the same furniture as well as your fingerprints on the receipts from the furniture store. We can talk about this furniture and then we can move on to the rest of the receipts and purchases that were charged to these accounts. Each one is an unauthorized account and each one is directly or indirectly linked to you, Ms. Summers. Do you care to try and enlighten me on how that is possible?"

I looked at Agent Wells and struggled not to laugh. I was just about to break into a cold sweat. Hell, I almost even shed a tear or two until he came out of his mouth with his second mistake. I, for the life of me, couldn't understand why they kept trying to play me like I was half ass slow or something.

True indeed, I did purchase this furniture online with City Furniture out of Miami. My whole house was furnished that way except for the king sized bed that I had delivered from California King's Bedding, but the thing that I found puzzling was the fact that he just said they had my fingerprints on the receipts that I signed at the time of purchase.

Any receipt he had could only be a duplicate of the original, which I had, and it would not have my fingerprints on it as I have never seen or touched it. Yes, the receipts may show a description of the furniture, but of course, furniture doesn't have serial numbers or bar codes that can prove that these are the exact same items that are on the receipts.

It will show that this is the kind of table that was purchased, but how many tables just like this one have they sold? Now I may have been a bit off, but I still came up with four when I added two plus two.

If the sales clerk gave me my receipt and I burned it in that pot, how is it possible for these geniuses to tell me that they had my fingerprints on a receipt? My grandpa always told me, "You got to know when to hold 'em, know when to fold 'em. Know when to walk away, know when to run. You never count your money while you're sitting at the table. There will be time enough for counting when the deal is done."

I wasn't going to let him know that I had already calculated his every mistake. Instead, I attempted to swallow some of my newfound joy and explained to him that yes, the furniture did come from those stores in question, but the means used to pay for it I did not know since I wasn't in the store at the time of payment.

I went through a whole song and dance about how I was out shopping with my son and I happened to be window-shopping at the furniture store when this guy approached me and offered to sell me some furniture that he had just purchased.

He had caught his wife cheating on him and wasn't going to reward her for that kind of behavior. The store had a no return policy and he was just trying to do some damage control, so he wouldn't have to mark the whole thing down as a loss. I told Wells that I offered the guy $2,000.00 for all of the furniture and he accepted. I paid to have it delivered and that was how I came to have it.

I scoped out the agent to see if he was buying my story or not. He didn't even look at me. He just closed his eyes and started to massage the bridge of his nose, like he had suddenly come down with a headache.

It didn't appear to be a good sign for me. I had hoped he wouldn't hit anything else in my house like his colleague did. I thought to try to sneak over and let Diva out to help me.

I thought Wells was about to cry and wondered if he was fixing to start boo-hooing up in my spot? I have read about good cops gone bad where an officer would just snap and go on a killing spree. Agent Wells made me wonder if he was having a meltdown or something.

I remembered a federal agent that went crazy and killed everybody in the house, and when they asked him why he killed them, all he said was, "They were home." It made me question if Diva and I were about to come up missing. Although I knew he had it in for me, I was curious as to where Garcia was. I wanted him to come back and keep his homeboy company; maybe he would keep Wells from going off on the deep end.

Just as I was about to work myself into a frenzy, the delirious agent spoke. "Ms. Summers, do you have any intention of telling me anything about these credit cards, the shopping sprees, the furniture that I happen to be sitting on, the damn jewelry you're wearing, the clothes that are in your closet, the washer and dryer in the kitchen, or the car payments for the Cadillac outside? Or do you want me to disregard my better judgment and believe you when you sit here and tell me that you know absolutely nothing?"

"You have no visible means to support the lifestyle that you are living, yet you expect me to ignore all of the evidence and accept the ridiculous stories that you have been feeding me? Do you honestly expect me to believe that you have no clue how any of this is related to you?"

For a minute, I wasn't sure if I should have answered him or run for the front door.

When in doubt, do nothing. So, I sat there at the table wishing he would go away, wishing I had another cigarette, praying for him to leave so that I could get my shit together and before my son got home.

Finally, he opened his eyes, but avoided looking at me. I'm sure he was upset with me. Maybe just a tad bit.

"Alright, Ms. Summers, you win for now," he solemnly admitted. "I'm going to go out to the truck and get my digital camera so that I can take pictures of everything in here. I'm closing out this interview for right now, but please believe that this is far from over. Please don't even consider removing any of this furniture from this house. Although I am not going to pack up this stuff and hall it out of here at this moment, don't think that I won't know if you try to move it or hide it."

With that being said, he got up, went out to the truck and returned with a Minolta Edge digital camera.

He took pictures of almost everything in the house, including the 72' Panasonic plasma television in the living room, the 65' Vizio flat screen in my bedroom, the 45' in Isaiah's bedroom, his PlayStation 4, Xbox One, and the Wii. He even took pictures of all our clothes and shoes. He didn't miss shit!

After about twenty minutes, I guess he decided that he'd had enough. He bid me goodbye, promised to see me "real soon," and left with Agent Garcia.

As they pulled away from the curb, our eyes entered that hypnotic dance, and one more time we played the game of who's going to blink first. This time, I didn't win, and Agent Garcia smirked at me as they drove away.

Chapter 4
Family Ties

As if my day needed any additional stress, I received a call from Mrs. Alston, the transportation supervisor from Rosewood Middle School, where my son attended. She called to inform me that I would have to pick Isaiah up from school. For reasons she chose not to disclose, I'd been informed that the bus wouldn't be bringing him home and they had no substitute driver. *Retrieve my child? What kind of shit is that?* They made it sound like I had lost a pet or something, like, *Ms. Summers, we've located your lost puppy and you may retrieve it at the local animal shelter.*

Anyways, I was probably just tripping after all the bullshit I had to endure that morning and being stressed out. Those federal agents had me shook, so I needed to try to shake that off so I could focus and think about how to get my weight up.

I just wanted them to be gone and not sitting out around the neighborhood trying to watch my house because I damn sure didn't have a valid driver's license and I had to get my boy from school.

I called my sister and to see if she wanted to ride with me to go pick up Zay. I needed to talk to her about this fed shit anyway. When I called her cell phone and she didn't answer, I went ahead and got dressed. I figured I would try her again from the car.

I went into my room and picked out something warm to wear since it was chilly outside. I scanned through my closet, passing by several things I liked but, looking for something that would be comfortable as well as sexy. Passing up Gucci, Fendi, and Prada, I settled for a crème colored Polo cashmere sweater that had a plunging neckline. The sweater was form fitting, so it showed off my 36D cups. I matched it up with dark blue Versace skinny jeans, and I grabbed my calfskin Versace boots with the three-inch heels. Not too much heel, but just enough to keep it sexy.

I took a really quick shower and when I got out, I applied my Victoria's Secret body butter so that my skin would feel baby smooth.

I sprayed on a little Chance perfume by Chanel and then I got dressed. I brushed my hair out and let it fall around my shoulders and applied my mascara and some MAC lip-gloss.

I checked myself out in the mirror and was very pleased at what I saw. 5 feet 6 inches tall, 145 pounds, light skinned, with a fat ass that had been turning heads since I was a teenager. I admired my slim waist and plump breasts. Yeah, I still had it.

Twenty-eight years old and wearing the hell out of it! I guess since I had my first and only child when I was 17, I didn't really have to worry about baby fat and stretch marks and all that extra shit that we, as women, have to deal with while trying to keep it sexy. Good genes along with a good diet and regular exercise kept me turning heads whenever I stepped out.

Where the hell are my car keys? I asked myself as I put Diva on her leash and searched for my keys at the same time.

"Come on, Diva; let Mommy put this leash on you so we can go bye-bye. We have to go get Zay. Come on, Diva, damn. Just let me put this leash on so we can go." Diva acted like a big ass kid sometimes. I finally got her leash on, found my keys on the sofa table, and proceeded out the backdoor to my car.

On my way out of the neighborhood, I dialed Michelle's number again. This time she answered on about the tenth ring.

"What's up, sis, what it do?" she asked, sounding like she was smoking what I assumed to be a blunt since I knew she didn't smoke cigarettes.

"Girl, get your ass up and ready. I'll be pulling up in front of your house in less than ten minutes. I need you to ride with me to get Isaiah, and I gotta tell you about this shit that just went down a few minutes ago."

"Rocky, I don't feel like going anywhere. I am trying to relax. And what kind of shit are you talking about went down? I know nobody messing with my lil' sister. Do I need to boot up? What's really good?" she asked, getting all excited and ready for some shit to kick off.

"Yeah, somebody is messing with your sister big time, and they probably going to be messing with you in a minute. It don't look good for the home team, so get up, and come on so we can talk about this shit and I can put you up on game."

"Quit playing so damn much, Ra'Quelle. Who's messing with you? And ain't nobody gonna be doing shit to me, not today. I ain't in the mood for no dumb shit, for real," she asserted with a hundred percent ghetto conviction.

My sister was so shot out, the ghetto in her would be quick to come out no matter what the situation. I wasn't sure if I should I burst her bubble while she was on the phone or in person.

I laughed at her antics and told her, "The Feds can mess with you anytime they feel like it boo, and I think they will be paying you a visit real soon. They just left my house, and they asking about you."

"Oh, hell no," is all I could hear her say before the phone hit the floor and the call disconnected. I didn't call her back since I was only four blocks from her house.

As soon as I placed my cell phone in my purse on the seat, it vibrated, played the ringtone I had set for Michelle. I nodded my head in agreement and sang along with Tupac's "All Eyez on Me."

I couldn't help but laugh when he spit, "The feds are watching, niggas plotting to get me. Will I survive; will I die? Come on, let's picture the possibilities." Yes, sir, I was feeling Pac on that one.

I snatched up the phone before it stopped ringing and before I could put it to my ear; I heard Michelle straight buggin' out on the other end.

"What the hell do you mean, Feds? What Feds? Who they wanna talk to, me? I ain't got nothing to say to no federal people. Who the hell told you they want to talk to me? I'm not a drug dealer; I ain't no criminal. Why the feds looking for me? I keep telling you, Rocky; you play too goddamn much. Why do you play so much? You're a grown ass woman. Stop playing all the time and do something with your life besides trying to make my nerves bad."

Michelle rambled all of that in one breath, sounding like she was having a meltdown.

"Chelle, the feds just left my house asking about you, Charla, and Dream. They had pictures of you all and were asking about the credit cards. They just left my house before the school called and told me to come get Zay. I am not playing with you, I am dead ass serious."

The next words out of her mouth totally caught me off guard and by surprise. At first, I thought I was hearing things, but then it dawned on me who I was talking to, so I have to believe it. I tried to keep a straight face as my sister asked me, "Who is this I'm speaking to? How did you get this number? I have an unlisted number. Who are you and why are you calling my house? There is no one named Michelle here, so I suggest you please check the number that you are calling and try your call again. Goodbye!"

With that being said, that whore hung up in my face. I had to come to the realization that there was something really wrong with my sister. Indeed, she was the epitome of being shot out. Talking about she didn't know how I got her number. Didn't she just call my cell phone? That chick was retarded, for real. She had better be ready when I turned that damn corner.

When I turned the corner onto Michelle's street, I noticed a lot of traffic coming in and out. It was like somebody had set up shop.

As I pulled up to the four way stop sign and came to a complete stop, I saw this old head named Treese that I went to school with about to cross in front of my car. She sure looked bad. She had lost a lot weight and no longer had that hourglass shape that I remembered. She had fallen all the way off. I wanted to holla at her just to see what was up with her, but I really didn't have time. I had to get my lil' man from school. I blew the horn, nodded my head at her, and kept it moving.

For some reason, Diva was acting strange in the backseat; whining and running from one side of the car to the other which made me remember that I had to get Mel-G to check my car out.

For all I knew, the feds may have put some kind of surveillance shit on my car to try and hem me up for real; I didn't trust their asses.

I pulled up to this ghetto superstar's house and she was sitting on the porch drinking a 24- ounce Bud Light Platinum and smoking a blunt. *Lord, have mercy*, I thought, *look at this child.* She had finally gone over the edge.

I gave Michelle a glance over from head to toe and I couldn't help but laugh, even though the shit wasn't really funny. She was dressed like were about to do a drive by or midnight burglary or something. She had on black Seven jeans, a black Timberland hoody, and black Timberland boots. Her hair was tied up in a black and gray bandana and she was wearing full face Kenneth Cole wrap around shades, which, mind you, were black as well.

Before she approached my car, she made a big production of looking up and down the street like she was looking for the police.

Michelle threw on a black Oakland Raiders ball cap and pulled it all the way down so that it was sitting on top of her shades. After peeping around with her paranoid self, she finally decided to get in the car.

Just when I thought she was good, she went and got in the back of the car with Diva and laid down across the seat before telling me to drive. She was worse off than I thought.

"Girl, if you don't get your ass up and get in the front so we can go. I don't have time for this, Chelle. I have to get to the school. Get your simple ass up!"

Speaking barely above a whisper, she instructed me, "Just drive sis. I'm going to chill back here. They might be watching the house. You know you're kind of hot right now. I don't even think I should be seen talking to you."

Oh, no, she didn't! I thought as I looked back at her to see if she was serious. I got pissed when I could see in her face that she was dead ass serious.

"Look, genius, if the feds were watching your house, they would have locked your silly ass up when you were standing out there smoking that blunt dressed like a crack head ninja. You look ridiculous. Hell, we might get pulled over because you look like you have been out doing all kinds of devious shit. Anyway, pass me the blunt so I can get my mind right and you stay right on back there while I tell you about this shit."

After I got my smoke on, I told her the whole situation with Agents Garcia and Wells from earlier today. I asked my sister if she had used any of the cards without covering the security cameras and she assured me she didn't. Just like I thought, the picture of her was of her handling her own business.

I had to school her on how to handle the Feds when they paid her a visit to her house because I knew that they would be seeing her very soon. She assured me that she had it all under control, but I wanted to go over a little Q&A just the same. I asked her, "What do you say when they ask you about the credit cards that were sent to your house?"

I almost ran off the road, as I stared at her over my backseat trying to see why that heifer ain't answer me and acted like she didn't hear me. The girl had dozed off and was just laying across the seat with her mouth hanging open.

"Chelle!" I screamed, loud enough to startle her from her sleep.

"Wha…what?" she replied in a panic, sitting up and looking around.

I was about to catch a serious attitude because I really felt that she thought this was all a game. I grabbed the remote, turned the CD player all the way down, and continued to look at her through the rear view mirror. "Do you or do you not understand that the fucking secret service was at my house this morning? Do you understand that they have *your* picture? Not mine, *yours*. They know about the cards that I sent to your house. What part of this do you think is a game? Do you not know that we could go to jail for a very long time behind this? Personally, I'm not trying to go to jail forever and a day. What about you?"

Michelle kept her game face on as long as she could before the tears started to pour from her eyes.

"Rocky, I don't want to go to jail. I've never been to jail before. You said we could do this thing and get money and no one would get in trouble. I trusted you because this is your hustle and this is what *you* do, so I thought you had everything worked out. Now you're telling me the secret service is looking for me. They came to your house with my picture and shit. What part of the game is that? I don't know what to do or say. I've never been caught with my pants down before. I'm true to mines and you know that, but I need you to handle this like you said you would."

She began to cry again and my heart just broke into pieces. I tried my best to hold back the single tear that fell from my eye, but it didn't work, so I quickly wiped it away because I was never the crying type. But she was my big sister and I loved her. I wished I had never brought her into this. I had to find a way to make it right.

"Michelle, don't cry. Please don't cry. You're my sister and you know that I have your back. Let me work this out and see if I can keep all of us out of jail, okay? But for right now, I'm going to need you to be able to deal with these people when they come because as sure as I am driving this car, they will be there to see you. Just play dumb, which shouldn't be that far of a stretch for you," I said, trying to lighten the mood.

Her crying subsided a bit and I could see a glimmer of hope in her eyes.

"What do you want me to say to them when they come, Ra'Quelle?"

"First of all, don't start telling lies you can't keep up with because if you do, they're gonna catch you and that will make it worse. These people ain't slow at all. Just answer the questions as vaguely as you can without incriminating yourself or me and the girls. Like when they ask you about the cards that were sent to your house, play dumb. Tell them that you never saw any cards in your mailbox. They can't prove that you actually got the cards out of the mailbox just because the credit card company said they were sent there. They could have gotten lost in the mail, or anyone could have taken them out of the box, you feel me?"

Lighting a Newport 100, I inhaled the pungent smoke and blew it out of the corner of my mouth while letting her absorb what I just said.

47

"What else do you think they're going to ask me? What if they ask me about you, Dream, or Charla?" she asked.

"Trust and believe, they will be asking about all of us. Just tell the truth about knowing us but tell them that you have no knowledge of what I do or don't do. Tell them we don't talk about shit like that when we're together. I'm probably going to jail anyway because I'm deep in this thing, and last week I paid my car note with one of them."

"What the hell were you thinking, Rock? Why would you do that?" she cried.

"I don't know what the hell I was thinking, boo. I really wasn't thinking. I was just too lazy to get up and go get the cash from the ATM, so I paid it over the phone with the automated payment system."

Michelle started to question me some more about the dumb move that I had made.

"Hold that thought, I'm about to run in here and get Zay, and then I have to talk to him before I take him to his daddy's house for a week or so until I can deal with this mess and get my money right. I can't have him in the middle of all this or at the house when the Feds come back. That would scare him to death. After I drop him off, we're going to pick up Dream and Charla so we can all sit down and discuss this. Go ahead, call them, and let them know I'll be there in a few. And can you take Diva out to pee before she pisses in my car?"

"Rocky, you know damn well that dog don't listen to nobody. She don't even listen to you if she's feeling some kind of way. By the time y'all get back, she will be dragging me up and down the street."

I laughed because she was telling the truth. Diva could be a handful at times. "I think she'll be alright as long as no cats or other dogs come down the street."

As I walked to the attendance office, my cell phone played "Incomplete" by Sisqo and vibrated in my Coach bag. I knew it was Isaiah's dad since that was the ring tone I assigned to him when we broke up three months ago after he caught me with my ex-girlfriend.

I snatched the phone out and answered it. "Hey, sexy, what's good?" I purred into the phone sounding as sexy as I could.

"What's up, Ra'Quelle, how are you? Where is my little man? He didn't call me when he got home from school like he always does, so I got concerned."

Dude was a trip, but I had to give him his props. He loved his son to death. He was all about his boy and all about me too until he caught me cheating with K.G., my ex-girl. But that's a whole other story.

I took a deep breath and told him everything that transpired that morning, all the way up until I got the call to come pick up Zay.

I asked him if he can keep his son for a minute while I handled my business. The disappointment was so apparent in his voice. He had been trying to get me to stop all the dumb shit for a long time. He always told me that I didn't have to be in the streets like that because he got me and Zay, but I was used to getting my own money and doing me without anyone's help.

"What have you gotten yourself into, baby? How much money do you need to be content? Are they going to lock you up or what? I thought you left all that ill shit alone. Ain't you supposed to be working at the bank? What are you out here doing, ma? What are you going to tell Isaiah?" He fired those questions off so fast, there was no time to answer.

"Of course I'll keep my little man. Just bring him straight here. I just bought him a bunch of new clothes and shoes anyway, so don't worry about him. He's good. What time will y'all be coming through?" he asked.

I smiled as I remembered what a good dude Donnie had always been. He was still the keeper of my heart.

"We'll be there in about an hour. I'm gonna stop and get him something to eat and I want to have a heart to heart talk with him before I drop him off. I've got Diva with me and you know that he's going to want her to stay with him. You cool with that?"

"Yeah, she's straight. As long as that dog don't shit in my house or try to tear up everything. You know she's crazy just like her momma."

"Oh, you got jokes too? Okay, I'll show you what crazy is," I laughed.

"Aye, baby, can I get some pussy too when you get here? I know you said that the last time was it since we ain't together anymore or whatever, but you know I love that thang you got and I need to be hittin' that real soon, ma."

I couldn't contain my laugh and told him that I would see him very shortly. Automatic thoughts of his lean and muscular body and his 10 ½-inch dick had my heartbeat slowly on the rise. As soon as I got ready to get deep into my fantasy about him, I was greeted by Mrs. Alston, the transportation supervisor.

"Ms. Summers, how are you? I am so very sorry we were unable to provide transportation for Isaiah this afternoon. We'll try to prevent this from happening again." She glanced me over and gave me the fakest smile I'd seen in a minute and tried to sound all sincere like I didn't know that Mr. Phillips, the bus driver, was a raging drunk.

I asked her, "How are you gonna do that? Is Mr. Phillips going into rehab or alcoholics anonymous?" Before she could give me some sorry ass excuse, I turned to my son. "Hey, stank, how was your day?"

I looked at my son and couldn't help feeling very proud of him. At 11 years old, Isaiah was an honor roll student, played J.V. football and he'd been the spelling bee champion two years running. Not to mention he was also very well-mannered and just an all-around great kid.

My chest filled with pride when I took in how handsome he was. He had very light colored skin, wavy black hair that was freshly faded twice a week, thick eyebrows, and a smile that could light up any room. Isaiah was neat and well-groomed. He took a lot of pride in his appearance, just like his momma.

Today was no different since he had once again flawlessly put his attire together. He sported a beige, brown, and white striped Polo shirt with black Polo jeans he creased himself. Brown and black suede and leather Polo boots completed his ensemble. He carried his leather Polo jacket across his shoulder and his North-face book bag on his back. I had to admit, he was quite the little fashion statement.

My son was too cute as he looked up at me and said "Hey, Ma."

As I took his jacket from him and pulled him in close to me, I kissed him on the top of his head and told him how much that I loved him. We turned around to walk towards the door and I glances back at Mrs. Alston and mouthed the word "alcoholic" as I strutted out of the office.

INDICTED/ *Keisha Monique*

Chapter 5

Keepin' it 100

As Zay and I walked back out through the front door and entered the parking lot, we encountered something that I would always have a mental picture of. It was definitely a Kodak moment if I've ever seen one.

My sister was sitting in the back of the Cadillac stone cold knocked out, with Diva on the seat beside her drinking all of her beer out of the can. Isaiah and I looked at each other and burst out laughing at the same time.

As we get into the car, I looked over at him. "You know your auntie is crazy right?"

He was still laughing when he responded, "Yes ma'am."

I started the car and pulled out. I told Zay that I had something important I needed to talk to him about and asked him where he wanted to eat at, as if I didn't already know. McDonalds was his favorite spot to eat.

We approached the McDonalds that was right down the street from his school. After ordering from the drive-thru, I drove over a couple of blocks to Hyatt Park.

I parked by the basketball court and we sat there on the bleachers. I stole one of his French fries and got it half way in my mouth before he snatched it back.

I loved that kid to death. I racked my brain trying to figure out how to tell him that I might be going to jail and he'd have to stay at his dad's while I attempted to shut the whole city down?

He didn't deserve to go through all of what I had to prepare him for. He was a good kid and he deserved to have a normal family life, but for some reason I couldn't pull myself away from the streets. I really needed to get myself together, especially for him if for no one else.

After this storm, I intended to get a job and do the right thing for a change. It was definitely time for a change and I had hoped he would understand what I had to tell him.

I inhaled deeply and looked over at my son, my prince and wondered what was wrong with me. I had every reason in the world to get right, sitting here in front of me. I stopped putting off what I knew I had to do and I began the talk that would more likely than not break my heart into a million pieces.

"Zay," I began with a slight quiver in my voice, "you know Mommy loves you, right?"

I had his undivided attention and could tell he sensed something was wrong. I swallowed the lump in my throat and continued. "I hope that you know that from the moment you were conceived, you have been the center of my universe. I loved you with all my heart before you were born and once I gave birth to you and held you in my arms, I loved you with all my heart and my soul. You are a great kid. I promise I couldn't ask for a better son. You've smart, caring, generous, well-mannered, respectful, and just an all-around good guy. I appreciate the effort you put forth in school and how you always help me out at home. I know you're going to do great things in this life. You have all the makings of a very successful man. I am so proud to be your mom, but something has come up that is serious."

Isaiah looked at me and I noticed the tears well up in his eyes, but like the young man he is he tried to fight them back. However, his voice betrayed his brave front as he asked me, "Ma, what's wrong? Please tell me. Are you sick or something? Are you going to be okay? What's the matter, Mommy?"

Every ounce of strength I had went out the window and the tears I had been holding back at bay began to fall from my eyes, saturating my face. I needed to pull myself together because I knew that I was scaring him. He wasn't used to seeing his mom cry, but it hurt me to see that I was hurting him because God knows he deserved better.

I wiped my eyes and continued. "No, sweetheart, I'm not sick, but I have some stuff that I have to deal with. I'm going to need you to be a really big boy for Mama. I've got myself in some trouble and I need for you to go stay with your dad for a little while so I can handle my business. You can take Diva with you for a week or so. I've really got to take care of some things, son, and I want to make sure you're safe and well taken care of."

He began to cry and the look on his face was killing me.

"I'm scared, Mommy," he expressed to me while reaching out for my hand. "I don't want nothing bad to happen to you. Please don't go away, Ma, I'll take care of you. I'll help you get out of trouble. Just don't leave me please."

I prayed for strength. None of what I had done was worth hurting my son. None of the things that I had were worth what I was putting my baby through.

"What kind of trouble are you in, Mommy? Are you going to jail because of those credit cards you use? Mommy, I don't want any more video games and new shoes if that is why you're in trouble. I don't need all the things that you buy for me. I need you!"

Wow, he knew more than I gave him credit for. I wiped the tears from his eyes and pulled him over so that he could sit on my lap. "Don't act like you're too big to sit on my lap," I teased.

Since there was no need to try and sugarcoat the situation and I had always been honest with him, I decided to tell him what was what. "Baby, look, I haven't been doing the things that a good mom should do. I haven't been getting all of our things the right way. I always wanted to make sure you had the best of everything; I didn't want you to want or wish for anything. Somewhere along the way, I got caught up and took things to a whole new level, doing things that I should not have done. And now I have to account for that. You know I always tell you that whatever you do in the dark will come to the light, so try to make sure you do the right thing the first time around. People can't go around breaking the law and not be held accountable for their actions. I made some bad choices, baby, and now I have to face the demons I created. I want to make sure you know that none of this is your fault and no matter what may happen, I will always make sure that you are okay. Always."

I lifted his face towards mine, kissed him on the forehead, and looked deep into his eyes. "Isaiah, I have been doing things the wrong way and not setting a good example for you. What I've done is wrong, and there is no other way to say it. But I want to make you a promise right here and right now, and you know your momma's word is her bond, right?"

"Yes, ma'am, I know that."

"I promise you that as soon as I'm done with this whole situation, no matter what the outcome, I will never ever put anything in my path that will cause me to stumble and jeopardize my freedom again. I won't do anything else that might take me away from you. Now I've got to make some moves and handle some things to try and get money for a lawyer and my bond, if it comes to that. After I'm done with this case, Zay, I will go back to doing the dog thing and we can open a kennel and start breeding pits again. That way you can help with the puppies. We will make our money the right way and still be able to live good without having to worry about me going to jail, okay?"

His whole face lit up and he gave me the biggest smile ever. "Okay, Mommy," he said with joy and excitement in his voice.

"I'll help take good care of the puppies, Ma, I know that you can be good too because you are the one who taught me how to be good. So you can do it if you really try. I love you and I'm not going to cry anymore. I'm gonna ask God to help you and keep you safe and to bring you back to get me fast. And I'm going to make sure Diva don't pee in daddy's house 'cause he will go crazy."

"You got that right, son, and thanks for being understanding. Thanks for just being you. I love you, boy."

As if she knew we were talking about her, Diva came running over barking like she is was taking part in the conversation.

Feeling better about keeping it real with my son and happy that he'd took this a little better than I imagined he would, I hugged him close to me for a few minutes before we finished our food and headed back to the car, where Sleeping Beauty had decided to rejoin the land of the living.

Standing beside the car chewing her McNuggets, Michelle asked, "How long we been here? What y'all doing and where the hell are we?"

I looked from my son to my sister and shook my head, laughing. "Girl, you know that you are shot out, right?" I asked her while entering the car. I leaned across the seat, kissed my baby again, and asked him, "Who's the man?"

He smiled and replied, "I am!"

"You got that right!" I agreed as I pulled out of the park and drove over to his dad's house.

Coasting down Monticello Road, Isaiah must have changed the song on the CD player about ten times until he found what he was looking for. I swore my son was Young Thug's number one fan. I smiled as I watched him sing along and dance to Thug's *Hercules* song.

Michelle leaned up and asked me to stop at the store so she could get a blunt and something to drink.

I didn't really want to stop but she pled her case, "Look, I already know what it is when we get to Donnie's house, okay? Y'all are gonna be playing make the bunny hop, and I'm going to be bored to death or playing a game with my nephew. He never lets me win, so I need something for my nerves while I get my ass whipped on PlayStation by an 11-year-old. You might as well let me get my mind right while Donnie blows your mind."

I just shook my head. There was nothing for me to say because in all honesty, I knew that she is telling the truth.

I turned into the nearest store and shut the car off. I told Michelle to get me fifteen dollars' worth of gas – that should fill it up – and for her to get Zay whatever he wanted while they were in there.

Isaiah was already halfway to the door and Michelle remained in the car looking at me like she was crazy, with her hand stretched out over the back of my seat.

"What the hell are you reaching for?" I asked her curiously.

"Rocky, I'm going to need for you to pay for your own gas because my money is funny."

I know this girl didn't just come out of her mouth like that. I knew damn well she wasn't waiting on me to give her fifteen funky ass dollars for some gas. She had to be out of her rabid ass mind, for real. I cocked my head to the side. "Chelle, on some real nigga shit; if you don't get the fuck out my car and go pay for the gas, me and you are gonna have some problems and complications. And bring me some Doritos while you're at it."

I heard her mumbling to herself as she walked toward the store. "Old cheap ass broad, don't ever want to spend her money. I shouldn't go pay for it and let her go to jail for driving off with these people's gas." She laughed as if that were funny to her.

"I heard that, Chelle. You better pay for that gas, girl. Ain't nobody playing with you either," I yelled in her direction and proceeded to get out of the car.

I nodded my head to the beat of some music coming from a nice Sapphire blue Yukon Denali sitting on 26-inch rims with Pirelli low profile tires.

Cute truck, I think as I got back in the car, remembering that I forgot to flip the gas switch and since it was automatic, the gas tank wouldn't open without it. I got out of the car again and bent over to wipe a small smudge off my boots.

When I stood back up, I was startled by someone standing very close behind me. I could feel their breath on my neck. I automatically tried to gauge the distance between me and my Coach bag, which held my trusty 9mm Ruger.

Sensing my tension and knowing my intentions, this mystery person whispered in my ear, "Aye, lil' mama. Be easy, baby. The god wishes you no harm. I'm all about bringing you pleasure, boo."

I recognized that voice and smile instantly as he kissed me on my neck. I turned around and gazed up at 6 feet 4 inches, 180 pounds of pure sexiness.

Jay-Baby stood before me looking like a bronzed Adonis. When he smiled at me, he revealed a complete set of diamond and platinum fronts. Usually, I thought that shit was whack, but in contrast to his chocolate colored skin, he wore them well. I believe my panties got wet. That nigga was fine as hell and he kept it tight no matter where I saw him. He was always doing it big.

His haircut was barbershop fresh and his jewelry was on point without being over the top and gaudy. Jay-Baby sported a simple but elegant stainless steel Rolex watch, his ears sparkled with 3 carat, flawless round diamonds set in platinum that offset his platinum chain, which hung just on top of his rock hard abs. He had one diamond and onyx ring that glittered blindingly as he place d his hand on the roof of my car.

When he looked down at me, he gave me that that 'I will fuck the shit out of you if you let me' smile.

"What did you do to my dog? She just let you walk all up on me, and now she is sitting there looking like a bitch in heat. She don't ever let people get that close to me and yet you walked up behind me and the bitch didn't even bark, growl, or bat her damn eyes. What's up with that?" I teased.

"Don't be so hard on the puppy, ma. She's just vibing with me, that's all. Real recognizes real and she knows that the god ain't trying to bring no mischief, nor do I have disastrous intentions to- ward her master. Dogs are very good judges of people. Besides, she knows that I've been trying to hit it for a minute. She's trying to tell you to give me a break."

I blushed and slapped his hand down as he tried to pull me closer to him. "How much gas are you getting?" he asked, insert- ing the nozzle into the tank.

"Just fifteen dollars. That should put me on a full tank."

I was glad to see this nigga. Fate must have been on my side today because I was sure going to try and get up with him later.

I peeped Michelle pointing toward the Game Stop store that was next door to the gas station, letting me know that was where they were going. Watching them climb over the wall that separated the stores, made me smile and think about how Zay was gonna get Michelle to buy him every new game they had for his PlayStation 4 and his Xbox One.

I was curious to know if she would still use the credit card or if she was too shook and pay cash instead. Knowing her, she would still charge it. Investigation or not, we still shopped until we dropped.

"Damn, lil' man getting big as hell," Jay-Baby said, bringing my attention back to him. "I remember the night we made that baby. Girl, we was tearing it up!" he said, looking at me out of the corner of his eyes.

"Boy, you better quit playing and shut up with all that crazy talk. That is *not* your boy. Don't play with me, Jay. I'm about to take Zay to his daddy right now. You know Donnie don't know you. You used to work for him, right? " I said in a manner that coincided with my flirtatious yet sarcastic attitude.

"I don't know about all that working for a nigga shit, but yeah he knows the god. We've had some dealings in the past. I still think we should let Maury decide who the daddy is though." Just as I was about to spazz out on him, he calmly said, "Let me stop teasing you before I can't get no more pussy for real. I'm just really admiring how you hold your lil' man down. That lil' nigga stay in some fly shit. Hell, he can out dress me and I'm a grown ass man. He's a trill little dude for real, Rock. Continue what you do for him and guide him on the path of the righteous."

"I plan to. That's my heart right there."

"You might want to keep him away from Michelle though. Your sister is way out there in left field somewhere, but she good peoples though."

We shared a laugh at Michelle because she was truly a trip for real.

I used this opportunity to tell Jay-Baby that I needed to get with him on some real serious shit. I stopped lusting long enough to say, "Jay, I need to holla at you later when you get some time. I've got some problems I'm dealing with and I need your assistance because I trust you and I know that I can always count on you to hold me down. I was planning on coming to the hood later on to see if I could find you."

He replied with the look of surprise. "Damn, shorty, *you* were gonna grace the hood with your presence? You must have some complicated shit going on right now. I know ain't no nigga dumb enough to be laying his hands on you or your she-man either, for that matter. You know I will lay a nigga or niggette to sleep for my future baby mama."

"Honey-boo, bye. That's the least of my worries. I've slowed my roll a hell of a lot, but I will still rock a nigga to sleep if he violated me to that point. Naw, my nigga, this is some whole other shit. I got the damn secret service on my ass about these damn credit cards."

He stretched his eyebrows up and tried to determine if I was serious or not. "Say word, Rock."

"Word is bond, boo-boo. They came to the house this morning with a great deal of shit they trying to throw at me. I know for a fact that most of it won't stick, but you know how the feds do. They will make up a charge just for you, and if that don't work, they come with that conspiracy shit, which is damn near impossible to beat. Since I am still throwing bricks at the penitentiary, I need to try and make something happen before they cuff me up."

"Damn, ma, I feel you, I feel you. You know if it was anybody else telling me they are under a federal investigation, I wouldn't even fuck with them on no business type shit. But you been down with me for a minute, and I consider you a friend. That is a term that I don't bestow upon many. So yeah, Rocky, I got you. Just tell me what you need and you can bank on it to happen."

I knew in my heart that I could count on him and that he meant every word that he said.

Jay-Baby and I had quite the history. We were accomplices first and then we became lovers. I met him when he first moved to Columbia from Brooklyn. He was on the run from some charges that he had gotten up there and decided to move south with his auntie and make something happen here.

Staying low key wasn't in the cards for him because his swagger and his hustle soon brought about a lot of jealousy and envy from the niggas from the south. They was really hatin' on how a nigga from BK could just come to the Metro and not only put the dope game on lock but also have most of the prime females at his beck and call as well.

I had noticed him in passing, but never really had a chance to converse with him. Donnie was my man at the time and he was having a drought on the work because of a drug bust in the city that was hurting everyone. I overheard some of his workers talking about trying to rob Jay-Baby. I went to Donnie and told him that I felt like that was a bitch move and he really didn't want to open up that can of worms.

All the money we had made, we earned it, and I didn't want to take the punk way out just because shit was short for a minute. I told Donnie to let me handle the situation and if he didn't like the results, then they could get it how they liked. I wanted him to understand that they didn't know enough about this dude to be trying to run up on him in the first place. I was a very good judge of character and nothing about Jay-Baby was soft.

I found him at Hot Rods down on Bluff Road. He was surrounded by at least five women, so I went over to him and asked if I could get a minute of his time. He looked me up and down, calculated the way I dressed, and my demeanor, and he surmised that I was about my business and making money was that business.

To make a long story short, I told him that I had some info that he was about to become a victim in the hood and niggas was plotting on how to get him. He had assured me that wasn't what they really wanted because he was willing and able to go to war with the best of them.

I let him know I had no doubt of that, but why risk all that when it was a pretty good guess that several people would lose their lives. Especially when really all niggas were trying to do was eat. I told him that we were looking for a connect and if he could make that happen for me, I could pretty much guarantee him free passage in the hood.

He asked me if I was I woman enough to handle all the power that I obviously had, and I told him, "Even more than you know."

I explained to him that I wasn't really running shit because selling dope wasn't my forte, but my man was a wise man and when I spoke out on his business, he usually listened because he knew I wasn't gonna steer him wrong.

"That's one lucky nigga to have a shorty like you. I hope he appreciates you and all that you represent. Tell your man to come holla at me and we can see about combining the north and the south and get this money. I have all respect for a nigga that ain't too hardheaded to listen to knowledge when it is being presented to him," he had told me as he licked his lips seductively.

Ever since then, he'd been my dude, and when me and Donnie started to have problems and I was going through it with him and needed to get away, we spent the weekend in Atlantic City. The rest was history.

We had remained like that over the years. If I needed a nigga beat to sleep, it was nothing. If I needed a drug connect, I got it. If I needed to get my back beat out, it was all love too. Jay-Baby was a man of many talents and had been involved in everything from pushing weight to making people disappear. He was *that* dude.

We rode on people, partied, even laughed and cried together. It had always been understood that whatever happened between Ra'Quelle and Jay-Baby stayed between Ra'Quelle and Jay-Baby.

I leaned forward and placed a long sensual kiss on his gorgeous plum colored lips and ran my hand up under his shirt to feel the dip in his back that I loved so much.

"Where are you gonna be in a couple hours?" I asked him, thinking that I might need a tune up from him. It had been a minute since we been together and I thought it was as good a time as any.

"Wherever you need me to be, queen," he responded.

"Okay, bet. Let me drop Zay and Diva off at Donnie's house and handle a few more things and I'll be calling you to see where you are so we can meet up and discuss my plans to get this paper straight so I can afford to do battle with these demons."

He leaned over, kissed me on my forehead, and told me that he would be waiting for my call. As he turned to walk away, I stared at his ass in the Rocawear jeans that hung just low enough to make me want some. Yeah, I needed to get some of that. I smiled and caught a shiver thinking about our past sexual escapades.

"Damn, the nigga got you shaking and shit. What the hell are you doing? Having a fuck-flashback or something?" Michelle yelled, scaring the hell out of me as I got back into the car.

Isaiah laughed when he saw me jump because of my sister

and her big ass mouth.

"Oh, so you think that's funny? You think that's funny, for real?" I taunted him as I ran around to the passenger side and began to tickle him until he laughed hysterically. I kissed him on top of his head and closed the door. Damn, I loved that boy. I had to make something happen for real so I could come out of this with minimal damage.

"What games *didn't* you get?" I asked as I looked at the three GameStop bags sitting on the seat beside him.

"We got all the new PlayStation 4 games and all the new ones for my PSP too! Auntie Chelle said I could have them all since I was having a hard time choosing." I watched as his face lit up in anticipation of playing all those games.

I smiled at the bond between my sister and my son; they had their own thing going on. "Michelle, you know you got him spoiled, right? And why would he even try to choose when he knew his auntie would get them all, right, Zay?" I winked at him to let him know that I had peeped his little game from the jump.

"In case you forgot, Rock, you and Donnie made Zay just for me. He has been and always will be *my* baby," she reminded me with a twist of her neck and a roll of her eyes.

"I know that's right!" I agreed, just before me and Zay start to laugh at her crazy ass. I turned the radio up and sang along with Soulja Boy as I drove out of the parking lot.

Chapter 6
Always Be My Boo

Diva jumped out of the car as soon as the door opened and ran towards Dee's front door. It was weird how she remembered and loved him like she did. He was actually the one who bought her. He got her for himself, but I was the one who had to take care of her since he was always in the streets getting money.

Diva and I just bonded like that after a while and after Zay got over his initial fear, the two of them were inseparable. When Donnie and I went our separate ways, taking the dog with him was out of the question.

I watched as Donnie opened the door and greeted Diva with some playful shadow boxing, which she thoroughly enjoyed. My ex walked up to his son and lifted him into the air like he was a toddler instead of eleven. Those two guys had an amazing relationship. They were mirror images of each other. Zay was just a smaller version.

I watched as Dee went over his ritual with Isaiah.

"Who are you and where do you come from?" Dee asked with a hopeful expression on his face.

"I am Isaiah Shakur Sims, and I descend from a rich heritage of kings and queens," Zay responded, looking his dad directly in his eyes.

"Well, why do you have such a funny name like Shakur?" was the next question from father to son.

"It may seem funny to anyone who is ignorant to its true meaning, but the definition of Shakur is 'grateful to God,' which I am every day," my son proudly stated.

Sometimes I couldn't believe how smart, proud & well-spoken my child was. It made my chest swell with pride.

"Well, Mr. Isaiah, what do you plan to contribute to this world in your lifetime?"

"Daddy, you know that I am learning how to become a strong black man who will know where he came from so that it will be easier to find out where he is going. I will take this world by storm, Dad, and uplift and teach those who don't know. Also, I'll be taking the business world by storm! I intend to finish school, college and grad school too! My goal is to get my doctoral degree in business, Daddy, don't act like you don't already know!"

The love and pride that I saw in Donnie's eyes almost made me cry.

"Oh yeah, Dad, I almost forgot, I'm gonna be the PlayStation 4 mega champion of the world!" Isaiah teased.

"I got your PlayStation 4 mega champion alright. But I must admit, son, you are the man. You are definitely the man. Now go take Diva in the house with you and before you even ask, no PlayStation until you have done your homework and read for thirty minutes."

"Yes, sir," was the last thing I heard from my son as he entered the house on the way to his room.

"Come here, baby," Donnie said to me, looking at me like a hungry lion or something. As he grinned from ear to ear, he held his arms open for me to jump in.

"Un-Un," I said to him and slid out of his reach.

"I want to get a good look at you first since I haven't seen you in a minute."

I focused on Donnie and was in awe of how handsome he truly was. I wondered why I couldn't keep it a hundred with him. Why did I have to play someone so smart, paid, loyal, and loving towards his son and I? The sex was off the meter and with him being fine as hell only added to the lust I had for him. I guess I just couldn't do right. Maybe it wasn't in my genetic makeup to be a good girl.

"Damn, baby, you keeping your shit tight I see," I told him as I scanned him from head to toe, taking in everything about him.

I liked the way he carried it today. The white Polo boxers with the black lettering sat right at the base where his wife beater met his baggy black Polo jeans that were pressed but not creased. He sported an expensive looking leather Polo Ralph Lauren belt with a silver buckle, topped off with a black button down Polo shirt that he left open to reveal the wife beater. His Polo boots were identical to Isaiah's except his were all black. I smiled when I imagined how Zay would look in the future.

I was abruptly brought out of my daydream by my sister and her loud mouth. "Look, before y'all nasty ass freaks get into all that extra shit y'all about to get into, can a bitch get something to smoke on and a drink or two so I can sit downstairs all by my lonesome? You know Zay is about to zone out on that game and y'all about to go try to make another bigheaded boy. I need something to occupy my time. I knew I shouldn't have come over here. Y'all are just rude as hell. You really don't know how to treat your guests."

"Why did you ask me to stop you by the store for blunts if you didn't have any weed?" I questioned.

"Shit, I got weed. I got plenty of weed. It's just in here, wherever Donnie keeps the weed at." She laughed out loud at her own silly joke. "Why in the hell would I bring weed to the weed man's house? Rocky, sometimes you ask the dumbest questions. I suggest you go and try to get your own mind right and stop minding my business. Don't worry about what goes on with my brother-in-law and me. Now Donnie, you gonna let me smoke or what?"

She walked off and glanced over her shoulder and told us, "It's always better to give than to receive."

She didn't miss a stride as she entered the house.

I told Dee that he had better go catch her before she found his stash and had a smoke fest. He reassured me that he knew she was with me and he already left her a quarter ounce of AK-47 on top of the bar, which he knew would be her first stop because she was always trying to drink up all his Henny.

I hooked my arm through his and gazed into his eyes. "You know I still love you, right?"

"You always will, lil' mama, you always will," he said confidently, before I snatched my arm from him and chased him into the house.

I went into his bedroom with the intentions of doing a little snooping around to see if I could spot any signs of female companionship of the previous days and nights. I sashayed over to the king size bed and scanned it over with the eagle eyes of a private investigator.

The bed was adorned with a plush green and crème colored Tommy Hilfiger comforter set that I got for him last month. The curtains and the area rug were in the same color scheme. I strolled over to the dresser and smirked at all the pictures of us at Disney World and Six Flags.

I paid close attention to the one of Zay's last birthday party. I really went all out for his birthday. I hired a professional photographer, a DJ, and a magician. I served pizza, hot dogs, burgers, ribs, chicken, mac & cheese, as well as chips and drinks.

Each child left with a gift bag containing a group photo and individual photo of that child, candy, a one hundred dollar Footlocker gift card, and a fifty-dollar Game Stop gift card.

Needless to say, they loved my boy at that party. Later that week, he told me that everyone in the school was talking about how great his party was and how fly his mama was. I giggled at the compliment. I did my best to make that an enjoyable moment for him because he deserved it.

I picked up a bottle of cologne that I didn't recognize and smelled it. That shit was some fire. I studied the label to remember it for a later date; *Dolce and Gabbana Light Blue.* Just as I was about to open the drawer so I can dig a bit further, Donnie came through the door and put a halt to that operation.

I responded by looking as innocent as I could, but it didn't work because I was cold busted. I gave up on my search and asked if he had checked on Isaiah.

"Yeah, he's straight," he responded. "He just finished his homework and is about to read so he can get on that game."

"That's what's up."

"Oh yeah, I almost forgot. He said he wants a little brother or sister while we're up here," Donnie said, giving me a big ass

Kool-Aid grin.

"Boy, you better quit playing with me, he ain't say that. People have to have sex to make babies and he don't know nothing about that," I countered, sounding sure of myself.

"Yeah, okay, right. You keep thinking that."

"What?" I screamed as Donnie turned around and laughed at me.

"Calm down, ma. I'm just saying the boy ain't slow, that's all. He knows more about sex than you might think. We talk about it all the time."

"I know. It's just that he's my baby and I want to keep it like that."

"Rock, I hate to be the bearer of bad news, but he ain't been a baby in a minute. He's a young man. Now if you want a baby, you know that I'm the man for the job. We make beautiful babies, and the fun part is putting 'em up in there."

"Boy, you are so nasty." I laughed and closed the door before I sat on the bed.

"On some serious shit, Ra'Quelle."

Oh, shit, it's trouble when he called me by my full name.

"What kind of shit have you gotten yourself into? Baby, look, whatever you need, I am here for you. I love you boo, from the bottom of my heart, and there is nothing that I wouldn't do for you. I was real hurt when I caught you and K.G. in the bed together; I ain't gonna lie. I really thought about bodying both of y'all, for real. I felt like you disrespected me to the utmost. But my love for you wouldn't allow me to bring bodily harm to you."

"Since we've been apart, I realize that you were really going through it. I was always in the streets and I wasn't keeping my street shit on the low like I should have. I had to take into account all the late night phone calls you got from some chicken head I might have broke off. I wasn't no angel out there and I got caught up in a lot of shit that I should have avoided. So, I had to pretty much charge your indiscretion to the game. I'm over it and I want to give you and Zay the lives y'all deserve."

"I want you to marry me, Ra'Quelle. I want to spend the rest of my life with you and my son. I ain't even gonna come at you with no engagement ring that I picked out because you're a spoiled brat, and I know that you always want things your way. I'm cool with that, so I have a contact person for you at Tiffany's. All you have to do is go over there and pick out whichever one you want, it's already worked out. Price is of no concern. Just don't get stupid up in there. I ain't at million-dollar status yet, but I'm working on it. So, what do you say?"

I couldn't even wrap my head around what I just heard. I didn't even know how to respond to his proposal. I wasn't expecting that at all. I had to be honest with myself and figure if I truly loved him enough to spend the rest of my life with him.

"What about the game, Donnie? What are you going to do about that? I ain't trying to be on nobody's dope case for conspiracy or nothing else. I got enough shit on my plate with my own misconduct. They ain't playing with them damn drug charges, for real. I promised Zay that soon as I'm done with this shit with the feds, that's a wrap for me and all of those credit cards and shit. I'm about to let all this shit go and try to get right. What are you going to do? What are your plans?" I asked, hoping that maybe he'd be ready to change.

"Look, ma, I've got bread, but not enough to retire on so that we can live comfortably. I don't need to be a multi-millionaire, but I do at least need two million to get out of the game with. My connect hooked me up with some Dominican cats that's coming to New York very soon, and I'm about to go up top and get with them for a couple of months and get this money right quick. Then, I'm coming home and I'm out. Can you deal with that?"

I was always taught that you should follow your first mind, and my first instinct was to trust my man. I knew in my heart that this was the best thing for me and that it was time to settle down. I couldn't ask for a better man or father.

"Okay, Donnie, you go ahead and handle your business. I've got a few loose ends to tie up myself. When you come back from New York, I'll have gone to the jeweler, and if you're truly sincere, we can make this happen."

"Rocky, I know that there ain't even no need for me to try and tell you that you don't have to go out in the streets to get

70

money. In your heart, you know that I will take care of everything
you need, but I respect the fact that you have always been a go-get-
ter. I know that you feel the need to hold your own. Just know that
all you have to do is fall back and let me handle everything, and I
got you."

"In your heart, I know you know all that already. If you
can't or won't allow me to do that for you, will you please just be
careful out there and don't give them any more ammunition than
they already have against you. Be smart about your shit and don't
get caught slippin'. My flight to New York is booked for two
weeks from now, but umm, you're not about to leave just yet, are
you?" he asked, looking at me seductively.

"Why not?" I replied, trying to be a being a smart ass.

"For real, Rock, you would leave me like this?" he whined,
placing my hand on his already hardening dick.

"You see what you do to me, girl?" he whispered as he
slowly stuck his tongue inside my ear.

I let out a slight moan and caught myself before my knees
buckled. I looked at him seductively and opened my mouth to say
something but before I could utter a single word, he placed his
mouth over mine and filled my mouth with his soft, warm, wet
tongue.

My heartbeat increased and my head felt kind of dizzy.
Damn, I love this niggga. his shoulders were so broad and his body
was so perfect to me in every way. I stumbled as I attempted to
step out of my boots without unzipping them first. He broke away
from our tongue dual and just to say, "Here bae, let me help you."
He picked me up as if I was weightless and laid me on the bed,
pushing the decorative pillow to the floor in one sweeping motion.

He lifted my foot and unzipped my boots one at a time, removed my socks then tossed them aside before he placed my toes
into his mouth one by one and then all five of them at the same
time. "Oh," I moaned while I watched him devour my foot. He released my foot, reached up to unzip my pants, and took them off
along with my panties.

I shivered from the cool air that ran across my dripping
pussy. He told me to take off my sweater and my bra, and I com-

plied. He took my breast into his hands and massaged my nipples until they were erect and standing at attention. I closed my eyes as I enjoyed the exploration of my body. I almost screamed as I felt his tongue making its way from my belly button down my thigh and into my love box. He grabbed me by my knees and pushed my legs up in the air as he buried his face deep within my walls. I tried to maintain my composure, but that wasn't gonna happen. As my back arched and my body trembled. He took his tongue and licked my pussy from the top to the bottom, kissing and biting his way back up to my swollen clit where he began to lick at a very rapid pace with just the right amount of moisture on his tongue to almost send me over the edge. I squeezed my eyes shut and threw my pussy at his mouth, really wanting to feed it to him.

"Oh yeah baby, baby please, eat this pussy!" I yelled as he inserted two fingers into my soaking wet pussy and flicked his tongue across my clit with lightning speed. He banged his two fingers deep inside and my love tunnel… in and out slowly and repeatedly. Every time he pulled his fingers out, I would press my pussy down against him trying to get his fingers back inside of me where I needed them to be.

All of a sudden, my stomach muscles tightened up, my pussy walls began to constrict and pulsate around his fingers. He closed his mouth around the entire upper part of my pussy and sucks it like a newborn baby on a bottle. He sucked my pussy with such a passion that I lost my breath as I exploded, soaking his entire hand with my juices as I screamed, "Yes, yes, baby I'm cumin'!! Baby please don't stop, I love you Donnie, I'm sorry, I'm sorry."

After the most intense orgasm I've had in a minute, I laid on the bed spent; yet, I wanted more. I looked at Donnie through slanted eyes. He rose from the floor and stood back so that I could see him as he kicked off his Polo boots and removed his wife beater. He peered into my eyes and unbuttoned his jeans and stepped out of them. His dick was so big and so hard that it popped out of his boxers as soon as he removed his pants. I licked my lips as I stared with pure hunger at his dick while he removed his boxers. I was literally begging him for some of that dick with my eyes.

"What's wrong Ra, you see something you want?" he teased me snickering as I sat up on the side of the bed and pulled him closer to me. I grabbed him by his ass and began to lick my way up and down his big, brown dick that I knew had to be at least ten inches long. I kissed the head of his dick and circled around it with my tongue. I heard him let out a sigh and take a deep breath. I put the head of his dick into my mouth and locked my jaws around it as I danced my tongue across it and sucked it at the same time.

"Oh shit, damn I missed this neck girl, you like daddy's dick in your mouth don't you baby? Oh shit, yeah suck that shit just like that ma, suck this dick baby," he moaned through clenched teeth. I began to deep throat his dick; I couldn't take all ten inches into my throat, but I damn sure wasn't leaving out much. I closed my eyes to concentrate as he started to beat my throat out. He pulled my hair hard enough to tilt my head upwards so that I was looking directly at him as he fucked the shit out of my mouth. I hummed deep in my throat because I knew that he loved the way the vibration felt against his dick. I cupped his balls in my hand and massaged them. He began to pick up the pace as he pushed even more of his dick into my mouth harder and faster. I could feel his nut building up from the base of his dick. Suddenly, he pulled completely out of my mouth and said, "Uh-uh, hell no! You ain't running this shit, bend your ass over, and let me feel my pussy girl!"

Before I had the chance to respond, he took me by the arm, yanked me off the bed, turned me around, and made get on the edge of the bed on my knees. As soon as I assumed the right position, I felt him slap me on my ass with his dick and I heard him mumble, "Damn girl." He used his hand to guide his huge dick to my pussy, which was soaking wet and dripping. He ran the head of his dick up and down over my clit and I pushed my ass back against him trying to get him to enter me. He played with my joy button for a minute before snaking his long dick into my pussy inch by inch.

I inhaled deeply and my head fell forward as he filled me with his thickness. I could feel my walls stretching all the way trying to expand enough to give him full access.

"Damn, this pussy still tight as hell ma, you know you've got some fire ass pussy baby," he whispered as he began to slowly stroke my pussy passionately. He pulled his dick all the way out and entered me again, a little more forcefully.

"You love me girl?" he asked as he picked up the pace of his strokes.

"Yes, baby," I answered.

"I can't hear you, Rocky. Do you love me?" he questioned as he slammed his dick into my pussy and started to pound it harder. I could feel his dick all the way up in my stomach. I attempted to answer him but nothing but deep breaths escaped my mouth. He grabbed me by the back of my hair and slapped me on the ass as he dug my pussy out like a mad man. He almost had the whole ten inches inside of me and it felt like he was gonna kill me. He pounded against my cervix and I yelled out in pain as he slammed his dick into me repeatedly.

"Whose pussy is this, huh?" he asked while he continued to fuck the very taste out of my mouth. My whole body started to tremble.

"It's yo…Yo…YOURS." I stuttered as he gave me every bit of it. I felt my pussy juices flow right down my thighs as he entered me over and over again. Just when I thought I couldn't take anymore, I found myself begging him, "Please Donnie, please stop. It's too much; I can't take it baby please," I cried.

"You want me to stop. Huh, you want me to take this dick out baby; you can't take all of daddy's dick up in this tight pussy?" He switched gears on me and sped up and started to fuck my pussy like he had hydraulics. He was fucking me so hard and so fast I could barely keep up with him. I opened my mouth to let a scream escape and he used his hand as a muzzle. I bit it and he slammed into me real hard. I yelled but it only made a muffled sound because he still has his hand over my mouth.

All of a sudden, every nerve in my body came alive and my pussy started to convulse, the room seemed like it got hotter and smaller. My pussy began to leak like Niagara Falls. I felt a heavy sensation in the bottom of my stomach and I just threw it back at him with a passion to match his own.

"That's my baby, that's right girl throw that pussy back at me. You wanna cum for daddy, huh, you like how I fuck you Ra? You gonna cum on this big dick?" he taunted me and I all I could was nod my head in response.

He removed his hand from my mouth and I said, "Yes, yes fuck me baby. Oh shit, you fuck me so good baby DAMN!"

My arched back and the swelling of his dick as he prepared to cum was all I needed to drain all my nut out. He slid his cum covered dick in and out furiously; he hit it faster and deeper. "Oh shit baby, I'm bout to cum. You ready for me to cum; you want this nut girl? You loving this dick ain't you boo?" he asked as he pushed the very last inch inside of me and filled me with his creamy, hot, thick cum. I laid flat on my stomach and he pulled slowly out of me after a few last strokes to ensure his seeds were where he wanted them to be. He kissed me on my ass before he pulled me over into his arms to hold me as I shook uncontrollably. He pulled the comforter to one side and covered us with it. I laid in his arms with my ass against his stomach and my knees pulled up in a fetal position and allowed him to hold me tightly.

"Are you okay baby, did I hurt you?" he whispered in my ear. I didn't even respond; I just cuddled up against him. "I love you baby," was the last thing I heard as I drifted off to sleep.

INDICTED/*Keisha Monique*

Chapter 7
Am I Dreaming?

"Who in the fuck is this, and why do you keep playing on my motherfucking phone?" I yelled after answering the phone three times in a row and being greeted with only silence on the other end.

I didn't really expect a response. For the past week, ever since Donnie had been staying home to chill with me and Zay, the house phone has been on fire.

Whenever I answered the phone, some idiot just sat there and said nothing; just holding the line open. Sometimes, they'd play music in my ear, like today.

I had a feeling that some shit was about to jump off when I picked up the phone again and hear Aaliyah's voice. "If your girl only knew... If your girl could only see how you be dissin' her trying to get with me. She would probably leave you alone, curse you out, and unplug the phone."

Oh, this chick wanna sing to me? Okay, that's what it do.

Let me check this hoe right now. "Okay, simple bitch, I'll tell you what. Since you obviously want me to know something and you singing and shit, why don't you be a woman about it and keep it one hundred. It's childish to keep playing on my phone. You must be desperate or fucking lonely. Do I have something or someone here that you want? Shit, let me know. Hell, I might be able to help your ignorant ass out," I said into the phone hoping to trigger her into talking to me.

"I might be a bitch, but your man likes it," she retorted.

The bitch had big balls which I found hilarious. "Really

now? And how in the fuck would you know what he likes? Just 'cause he fucked you, you dumb bitch, that doesn't mean he likes you. You're not the first trick ass bitch he fucked and I can promise you that you won't be the last. I'm glad you're fucking him. The more y'all fuck, the less I have to and I'm still getting laced up righteously," I informed the mystery chick, trying to hide the hurt in my voice.

"You can save that shit for the next bitch, Ra'Quelle, because you and I both know that you be all up in that nigga's shit. When he stayed with me Thursday night, how many times did you blow his phone up? If I'm not mistaken, you called like ten times and not once did he answer, nor did he come home that night, so don't try to front like you don't care. As far as getting laced up, shit, he just gave me three hundred dollars to go get some clothes with. So, bitch, don't get it twisted, okay."

I counted to ten to keep from blowing my stack. There was no way in hell I would let this trick know that she was getting under my skin.

Calm down, Rock, you are still the baddest bitch. Don't let this motherfuckin' hoe get the upper hand. Take a deep breath.

Okay, time to go ahead and cancel this bitch. "Three hundred dollars? Did you just say that he gave you three hundred dollars?" I asked, making sure I heard her correctly, not knowing where I was going with that question.

"You damn right. One, two, three hundred dollars for *my* clothes, not yours. And he said I might get some more if I play my cards right," she boasted.

This broad was silly as hell and stupid on top of that. Was that the best that he could find out there to fuck with? If he was gonna cheat on me, I would have expected him to get a classy bitch. Well, at least he wasn't really breaking bread with the hoe.

"Damn, girl," I countered as I laughed into the phone. "Not only are you a dumb ass bitch, but you are a cheap ass one too. What the fuck can you buy for three hundred dollars? My motherfucking shoes cost twice that for a single pair, and you talking about buying clothes with that pocket change. Bitch, bye! Like, where do you shop at, Citi-Trends?"

I laughed even louder. "Oh, I get it, you the Citi-Trends bitch. Oh, okay, that's what's up. By all means, please continue to do you. But FYI, I wouldn't even let a nigga say my name in the same sentence as fuck or pussy for three hundred dollars. And just so you know, I wasn't the one calling his phone Thursday night. That was his homeboy Twan, who came by here looking for him. If you had access to his voicemail you would know that, you semen throat whore."

"I don't have to call around looking for my man because at the end of the day when he's tired of getting his dick sucked and making you swallow his babies that you will *never* have, he is gonna always come home to me. And bitch, I do mean always 'cause I'm that bitch. I'm wifey, bitch. I'm where your tired ass wants to be! And now that you chose to play your cards the wrong way and you're telling me that you're fucking my man, I promise you that you won't ever fuck him again and I mean never, bitch. And you can put that on boss," I said, letting her know what was really good.

As if she wasn't embarrassed enough, she asked for more. "How do you know that I won't fuck him again? I bet you I –"

"Broke bitch, I bet you that you won't!" Donnie interrupted her. He must have picked up the bedroom extension when he heard me going off.

"I don't know how the fuck you got my home number, but, bitch; you are fucking with my home now. Bitch, I will body your ass before I let you bring this bullshit to my wife. And what made you think it was about you? Bitch, I felt sorry for your raggedy ass kids and gave you some change out of my pocket so that they could be decent for a change. And you gonna call my motherfucking house and disrespect my wife with your bullshit? I'll tell you what, Marissa Jackson – and yeah, I said your name so my boo knows who you are now and will fuck you up on sight. But if somehow you are able to dodge her, just remember that if you ever even look at me hard again, bitch, I will fuck your whole world up, and you know that I mean every word I just said. Now try me if you think I'm playing. Try me, bitch!" he screamed.

After a short silence, she shocked the shit out of me by saying, "Okay."

Marissa Jackson? From 48? Marissa with the dirty ass kids? *Damn, he shooting bad*, I thought.

She started crying into the phone and tried to apologize as he slammed the phone down so hard, I was sure that he broke it. Being that she was still on the phone, I just had to say something else. It just wouldn't be me if I didn't.

"Marrisa," I called her name and waited for her to answer.

"Huh?" she said timidly.

"You feel stupid as hell, don't you, bitch? Ha-ha, the jokes on your dumbass. Oh, and do something about those damn kids? You have cute kids and they deserve better than your stupid ass. Matter of fact, I'm gonna send some of Isaiah's clothes that he has outgrown over there with my sister since y'all so cool with each other. Next time you decide you wanna play yourself and fuck somebody else's man, keep that shit to yourself before you get more than your heart hurt, beeeeaaatch!"

I hung the phone up and looked over to see Donnie standing there looking at me like he was stuck on stupid and didn't know what to say.

He started to walk towards me and I stopped him in his tracks. "Don't!" I said heatedly. "Just don't, Donnie. I'm sick of your shit, for real. On some real nigga shit, Dee, that shit was foul as hell. You got bitches calling the house telling me you fucking them? You 'bout one lame ass dude, for real. It ain't even about what you do, Donnie, because you are a grown ass man. It's about you getting caught up and your shit following you home. I know that you're a nigga and niggas do nigga shit, but this is out of line. I shouldn't be confronted with the shit you do in the streets. You know what? Don't even bother to try and respond to that. There ain't nothing for you to say. Fuck you, Dee, and fuck your little cheap ass three hundred dollar bitch too. I'm 'bout to dip, I'll talk to you whenever I get back."

I snatched some Givenchy jeans out of the closet and threw them on with a baby blue silk camisole with t-straps. I laced up my four inch heels by Jimmy Choo and pushed past Dee, not trying to hear nothing that he had to say.

I grabbed my Gucci bag and dumped the contents into my Prada bag, ran a brush through my hair, put on a little MAC lip-gloss and some mascara, sprayed on a little bit of Jador'e, and prepared to haul ass.

He watched me showing his uncertainty. The only thing he could think to say was, "Where you going?"

I didn't even answer his simple ass.

"Where you gonna be, Rock?" he questioned again.

"I'll be wherever the fuck I'm at," I responded back.

"Where are you going, Rocky?" he demanded like he had that right.

"Out."

"Out where?"

"Outside, motherfucker, damn. Leave me the fuck alone. Go get your dick sucked again!" I yelled, pulling out three one hundred dollar bills and tossing them in his face. I turned and made sure my ass was swinging from side to side as I walked out the door.

I stopped at Rickenbaker's party shop and went inside to buy me a six-pack of Corona and some grape Philly wraps. I made my way to the back of the store, ignoring all the whistles and cat-calls I heard from the D-boys that hustled out there on highway 48, otherwise known as bloody Bluff Road.

I approached Rico Montgomery and yelled at him, "Let me get an ounce of dro!"

"Damn, ma, what's wrong with you? You've got smoke coming out of your ears. Whatever it is, I didn't do it."

"My bad, Freak," I said, calling him by the nickname I gave him.

"I'm just going through it right now and I'm trying not to catch a case, boo, that's all. Anyway, how you been?" I asked, feeling bad because I had yelled at him.

"Ma, I ain't even got no wood. I'm out here trying to move this hard, and I know that you don't fuck with that."

"Hell no, nigga."

"Hold up, let me go check with my cousin, K.G., real quick and see if that nigga got dro. That nigga got all kinds of shit to smoke on, but I don't know about dro..."

I reached into my purse and gave him four hundred dollars. I almost dropped my purse and had to catch my beer from falling out of my hands as well.

"Damn!" I yelled at no one in particular. I hated it when I got this mad. I was so heated my hands were shaking.

I watched as he walked over to a pearl white Cadillac Escalade the same color as my DTS. He said something to whoever was in the truck and pointed in my direction and then the truck started up.

I thought, *please don't tell me I'ma have to unload on this damn truck about my money.* As I prepared to set my beer down and pull my Ruger from my purse, the Escalade didn't pull out of the parking lot but instead drove over to where I was standing.

The window rolled down and the driver waved me over to the truck. All I could see was a light brown-skinned dude with braids in his hair wearing a Boston Celtics cap.

"Naw, I'm a Lakers fan, and y'all stole our damn championship last time," I said, trying to see if I could recognize this dude.

The door opened and he stepped out wearing a Paul Pierce jersey with a white t-shirt under it with a pair of baggy Levis. He had on nubuck colored Timbs with the laces undone.

He looked at me, licking his lips, and walked toward me and the only words I could muster up were, "Oh, shit!"

I was shocked as hell to see that he was not a him; he was a she. This girl was fine as hell and I wasn't even gay!

It felt like her eyes were staring through me into my soul or some shit. I looked at her flawless skin and emerald green eyes and wondered what she was mixed with.

"S'up ma, how you doing? I heard you were a bit stressed and you wanted something to soothe your nerves. I don't have any more dro, but I've got some Sour Diesel you can get if that's alright with you," she said.

I stood there in the parking lot trying to figure out why this broad had me stuck on stupid. She had me on pause, like I didn't know what to say or how to respond to her. All I could come up with was, "Yeah, that'll work."

I could feel my cheeks burning because she had me blushing. She handed me the weed and I turned to walk away and heard her say, "What, you gonna leave your change? You got money to throw away like that?"

She smiled hard at me as she handed me my change. I counted the money and asked her why she had given me five one hundred dollar bills. "I don't take money from damsels in distress, ma. It would be out of my character for me to profit from your misfortune. So the smoke is on the house. I will never let money go from your hand into my pocket. I am more of a gentleman than that," she said, trying to calculate my reaction.

"Okay, I hear you, Mr. I'm-Too-Much-of-a-Gentleman, but this is a hundred dollars more than I gave you. I only sent four hundred dollars for the weed."

"Yeah, I know that, gorgeous. The other buck is to pay for the drinks we are about to go have. You need a friend, and I'm in a friendly mood," she said, as she reached for my hand.

Since apparently I was going to have drinks, I gave the beer I bought to my homeboy, Migo. I set the alarm on my car in hopes that no one would break into it.

I took her hand and she walked me around to the passenger side of her truck. She opened the door for me and I could feel her staring at my ass while I climbed into the truck. She ran around to the driver's side and climbed in. After throwing deuces up at her peoples, she pulled out of the parking lot.

I looked over and watched her while she drove. She put in a Maxwell CD and began to groove to the music. Everything about this girl screamed for me to run like Forrest Gump. Her whole swag was about sex, money, power, and respect. I thought that I had bitten off more than I could chew.

"Don't you even want to know who you've got riding with you? You haven't even asked me my name yet," I said.

"Baby girl, you're kidding me, right? Who doesn't know the infamous Ra'Quelle Summers? Shit, I knew who you were the minute you stepped out of the car."

What the hell? Is this chick the police? Are they really try-

ing to set me up like that? How in the hell does she know who I am? I hope I don't have to kill this bitch. I should have just stayed my ass home and dealt with Donnie's shit.

I could tell she sensed my discomfort when she mentioned, "Peanut is my cousin, and I saw you a couple months ago walking the dog. I thought you were sexy as hell, so I asked him who you were."

"Oh, tell me something. For a minute I was starting to think that you were a stalker or something." I laughed.

"Oh, never that, boo, never that."

We drove to the 555 Club on Farrow Road and went inside. We sat and talked for hours and had gone through two bottles of Moet and plenty shots of Hennessy.

I got to know a lot about her and what she was trying to accomplish. I realized that I had a serious girl crush on her.

She shocked the shit out of me when she asked, "Have you ever been with a woman before?"

I spit half of my drink across the table and had a coughing fit. She grabbed a napkin and wiped my mouth and laughed at me because she knew that she had caught me off guard with that one.

I sat there looking at the table saying nothing. I couldn't get my shit together. For the first time in my life, I didn't know what to say.

She leaned closer to me and I moved back but my body wouldn't cooperate with what my mind was telling it to do. She called my name, "Ra'Quelle." I looked over at her and as soon as I raised my head, she kissed me with an open mouth; a kiss that almost mad me bust one in my panties. I kissed her back with a passion I hadn't exhibited in a minute.

For whatever reason, I felt at home with K.G. She made me feel safe and wanted. I felt close to her, it was like we had instantly bonded.

"I'm confused," I whispered to her as I broke the kiss and stared into her eyes.

"It's okay ma, I got you," she reassured me and took my hand into hers and kissed the back of it before licking it and smiled at me devilishly.

"Do you want to get out of here and go somewhere where we can spend some real time together, or do you want me to take you back to your car?" Damn, I hadn't signed up for all of this. I didn't want to go home, but I didn't know shit about being with no woman.

"K.G., I ain't in no rush to go home to Donnie, fuck him. A fair exchange ain't never been, nor will it ever possibly be a robbery. Take me with you." Damn, I couldn't believe that I had said that. Okay Rocky, you done put that shit out there like that. Now what you gonna do about this? This girl is going to think that I'm slow or retarded or something. What in THE hell am I gonna do with her? I sure hoped she didn't want me to give her no head since I hadn't a clue as to what exactly two women did together anyways. Well I guess I was due to find out. As if she were reading my thoughts, K.G. said, "Baby, don't worry. I got you. I won't ask you to do anything that makes you uncomfortable. But I have to keep it real with you; I think that you are sexy as hell ma. And I'm feeling you on da real. If you'd let me, I'd love to be your ace in the hole. I can't promise you that I can fix all your problems, but I can damn sure promise that I won't add to them. Give me a chance to show you what my world is all about."

Shit, I grabbed my purse and told her to pay the tab and led the way to the truck. If she was running game on me and only wanted to get me in bed, oh well ring the bell... Ding, ding, we have a winner! I'm was with it. We hopped back into the truck and headed over to the Fairground plaza hotel downtown. She secured a room, came back to get me from the truck and we entered the hotel and went right to room 345. I was so damn nervous; my hands were sweating. I couldn't be still, my breathing was fast like I'd had a panic attack.

"Come here baby, I ain't gonna hurt you, I promise." She patted the bed right beside where she was sitting and I thought she wanted me to sit right next to her. *Okay, here we go*, I thought to myself. I took a deep breath and tried to get my mind right. I couldn't let this girl know that I was intimidated by her. I sucked all that shit up and decided to take control of the situation. Although I had never been with a woman, I did know how sexy I was. I knew how to make a nigga drool so I figured that I could do the same to her. I knew that she was feeling me just as much as I was feeling her. I considered myself to be a dime all the time so I knew what the deal was. I was glad that I wore my sexy lace thong set. I tried giving myself a little pep talk and began to undress. I made a show of bending over to unwrap the straps on my heels from my ankles. I felt her eyes all over my body. Yeah, I was about to show her ass something. How different can this be from being with a man? Yeah okay, hold that thought.

I finished undressing and stood in front of her with my hands on my hips and my feet spread apart. Before I knew it and before I ever had a chance to open my mouth to say anything, she surprised me when she jumped up off the bed and took me by the back of my neck and damn near stuck her tongue down my throat. With her other hand, she tore my panties off and threw them across the covers back on the bed. She just laid me across the room without breaking from the kiss. She didn't bother to pull the covers back on the bed; she just laid me across the bed and said, "Do you know how bad I want you? How many nights I've went to sleep wishing I could have a chance to touch you? How much I've waited for the chance to be near you?"

I couldn't answer any of those questions, so I just shook my head no. "Let me show you then."

The next thing I felt almost made me jump off the bed and I screamed out loud, not giving a damn who heard me. The feel of her full, warm lips separating the flesh of my pussy before entering me with her tongue was more than I could bare. I knocked her Celtics cap to the floor, spread my legs as wide as I could get them, and grabbed the back of her head, filling her whole face with nothing but pussy. I couldn't believe it when less than three minutes later I was loading her mouth with my cum. I could feel her smiling in between my legs, but she didn't stop or come up for air. She threw my legs over her shoulders and proceeded to do things to me that I couldn't begin to explain. I never had my pussy sucked like that, never. Shit, maybe I needed to be gay, 'cause that shit was fucking amazing. I closed my eyes to savor the moment and wait to see what she would do to bring the next nut, it was then that my whole world seemed to come crashing down around me.

POW, POW, POW! I hear the gunshots hit the wall in rapid concession.

"What the fuck?" K.G. said, as she got up and reached for her pistol, which rested on the nightstand in plain sight. Before she could even take a step, someone completely kicked the door off the hinges.

To my utter disbelief, Donnie stepped into the room, pointing his 45 magnum at K.G. "Bitch, I wish you fucking would! Try it, bitch. Go for your gun, so I can murk your ass and not feel bad about killing a bitch."

He looked at me and shook his head in disgust. "Rocky, you got bitches eating your pussy now? That's how you carrying it? You bulldagging now?"

"What are you doing here, Donnie? And put that damn gun away!" I yelled, trying to sound braver than I felt.

"Get the fuck up and get dressed and let's go! You better not say shit, nothing! Just bring your ass before I fuck around and kill both y'all bitches in here," Donnie screamed, damn near foaming at the mouth.

"She ain't going nowhere, nigga, so you might as well bounce. Chuck this shit up as a loss," K.G. argued.

Aww shit, she should have kept that shit to herself. Donnie was about to go ham on her ass for real.

"What, bitch?" Donnie put his pistol in the waist of his pants and turned to face K.G. before he drew back, punching her in the face.

"Donnie, no!" I yelled, knowing how crazy he could get when he felt he'd been disrespected.

But shit, true to her own, K.G. gave it to him just like she got it. They went blow for blow for a few seconds before Donnie started to fight her like she was a man for real.

"You wanna be a man? You round here eating *my* pussy and shit? Okay, I'ma treat you like you a man, you stankin' ass man butch bitch!"

He drew back and I knew that this would be the punch to knock K.G. all the way out, so I jumped up and grabbed his arm.

"Please don't. Please stop, Donnie. I'll go with you, just stop! Stop hitting her please."

"Let's go!" he yelled.

As I put my clothes on, I could see Donnie's homeboy come into the room and take K.G.'s gun off the table. Now I knew how he had found me. I saw this dude earlier when we first came in, but at that time, I didn't know who he was.

I walk over to K.G. and told her that if I didn't go with Donnie, he was really gonna hurt her. I gave her my number and told her to call me when she got a chance. I also told her that I was really sorry about everything that happened. She assured me that it wasn't my fault.

I tried to make a joke and say, "Alright, Mayweather, I'll be waiting to hear from you."

"You can count on that, ma, and please be careful. Don't let that nigga hurt you," she said, showing concern for me.

"He ain't that damn crazy. He didn't kill me when he came in, so I know I'm good."

"Bring your ass, Rocky!" Donnie yelled venomously from the hallway.

I looked back at her one last time and left the room.

Chapter 8

Back to Reality

"Rocky, Rocky, get your nasty ass up! Come on; let's go. Y'all are really shot the hell out and y'all don't know how to treat company. I've had to keep myself company, cook for the baby, take the dog out to shit, and y'all laid up in here like the king and queen of Sheba. I've got other shit to do!"

I was awakened from my dream by my sister's rampage. That dream had me all upset and shit, I couldn't believe how vivid it was. I still recalled everything about that night as if it were yesterday. I'm lucky Donnie didn't kill her and me. I had never seen him so pissed off and hurt.

Of course, we argued and fought all the way home. Matter of a fact, we argued for days until finally we both had enough and we decided to go our separate ways while remaining friends and raising our son together. I didn't think he would ever get past that, but obviously, he did.

The cold air that hits me as Michelle snatches the covers off me and Donnie brings me back to the present.

"Girl, you gonna make me fuck you up. Keep playing and see what I tell you. Keep playing with me, Chelle, and you're gonna catch it," I told her, trying not to lose my cool and hurt her feelings.

She looked down at my boo who was just opening his eyes, and her face showed her surprise as she smiled. "Damn, brother-in-law, you working with all of that? I see why my sister be walking bow-legged. Do you take those Extend pills that make your dick grow, or is that all you?"

INDICTED/ *Keisha Monique*

She just stood there gawking at his dick. He reached over, grabbed a book from the nightstand, and threw it at her, almost hitting her in the head.

"Get your nasty ass out of here, Michelle, before I beat your ass!" He got up and stepped into his boxers.

Michelle being Michelle, didn't even move. She didn't care that he was mad as hell. She looked from him to me and back to him. Then she has the audacity to say, "I'm out of weed. Can I get something to smoke?"

Donnie looked at me and shook his head. "Yo, ma, you sure this is your sister, for real? Where y'all get this character from? She funny, for real."

I told my sister that I would be out after I took a quick shower and got dressed. I laughed to myself because she really was a trip. She was good people and I loved her to death, but normally, she was not!

I entered the bathroom and got a face cloth and towel from the closet. I saw that Donnie had left his bathroom the same way it was when I put it together for him a couple months ago.

It was done in black and gray with lots of mirrors. I thought it was sexy. His bathroom was almost as big as the bedroom. It had dual sinks and a walk-in linen closet, which was filled with Ralph Lauren towels, sheets, and bathroom supplies. The shower was separate and located to the right of the sunken Jacuzzi tub. The tub looked really tempting I really wanted to use the heat and the pressure from the jets to bring some relief to my twat.

I'd swear on everything I loved, it felt like I had given birth to an eight-pound baby. Donnie puts in work. Overtime, for that matter.

Before I jumped in the shower, I finished the snooping that I had started earlier. After examining the medicine cabinets and under the sink, I came to the conclusion that if he had a girl here, either she didn't stay there often or he was very good at cleaning up behind her.

I hopped into the shower and tried to hurry up before he could come in to molest me. I was good for nothing at that point. I couldn't take no more dick if I wanted to, which I didn't.

90

INDICTED/ *Keisha Monique*

After I showered, dried off, and put my underwear back on, I went back into the bedroom and sprayed on some more Dolce and Gabana perfume, and I got re-dressed. I looked around for Donnie and found him sitting by the window overlooking the back-yard, where Diva and Zay were playing fetch. I never understood how he could get her to release the ball to him. Whenever I threw it, she'd go get it, but damn sure never brought it to me.

"What's wrong, baby?" I asked, sensing that he had a lot on his mind.

He turned to me with an intensity on his face that I hadn't seen in a while. "I hope you realize what a precious gift from God we have in that boy back there playing in the yard. We need to get right, Rock. We need to get our shit together and make sure he has both of his parents to guide him on the path of righteousness. I want you to think about what I said and really consider coming out of them streets. Shit done changed out there, boo. You got niggas doing paperwork on motherfuckers because they too scared to bid."

"Then you got grimy ass niggas that would rather steal your wealth than get out and get it on their own. It just ain't worth it. I'm dead ass serious about what I said about getting to the point where I am out of the game. I want to wife you and take care of you and my son. I'm going to hit Brooklyn real hard and real quick. I'll be in and out within a couple of months if all goes well with these Dominican cats. So you go ahead and do you. Do what you feel you must, since I can't persuade you any differently. Just be careful out there, ma. It's a dirty game, and I'd hate to have to body a nigga because they violated you."

"Thanks for understanding, baby. I'm gonna be M.I.A. for a minute. You know how I get when I really have to get my grind on. I can't have any distractions that could cause me to slip up. I'll get back at you when I'm done."

Damn, I didn't understand why I couldn't just stay there and let him take care of me. It was just that I had always held my own and I didn't know how to depend on anyone else. 'Hold my own', had been my motto since I was a teenager, and it carried over into my adulthood. That was the only way I knew.

91

I bent over and kissed my future husband on the forehead, then on his lips and hugged him around his neck. I expressed my love for him, but that I still had to do me. I did promise him that I would be going to Tiffany's before I came back to pick up Zay.

His eyes lit up as he comprehended that I'd accepted his proposal of marriage. He stood up, wrapped me in his arms, and held me tight. He whispered how much he loved me into my ear and gave me a kiss before breaking the embrace and informing me that he was going to find Michelle because she was entirely too quiet and may have found his stash.

I told him that he'd better hurry up as he raced downstairs to look for my sister. I followed behind him and went outside, where my son was still playing with the dog. "Hey, stank, come here," I yelled for Isaiah, so I could tell him that I was leaving.

He and Diva took off racing towards me and of course, she got to me first and waited for some attention.

I looked at my son while scratching Diva behind the ears. "I'm about to go, baby. Your daddy has some clothes and shoes for you in your room already. Y'all have to go to the store to get some dog food for Diva. Don't feed her any table food 'cause if she poops on your dad's carpet, he is going to beat her butt. I want you to be good and listen to your dad. You have my cell phone number, and since you and your dad have the same cell phone, you can use his charger to charge your battery.

"Make sure you bless your food before you eat and say your prayers every night. I'll be back in a couple days. I love you so much, Zay."

I tried to keep my tears from falling and give him a big smile. I wished I could stay there, but I couldn't. Something had to give sooner or later and I couldn't keep doing what I was doing. It was hard and I loved that boy beyond life. I wanted to give him the normal life he deserved, but I was so caught up in the streets that I couldn't stop.

"Okay, Mommy, and you say your prayers too, so that God will take care of you until you come back home to me. It's going to be okay, Ma, and I'm going to be good for you, okay? I love you, and Diva is not going to use the bathroom in the house this time."

I laughed and kissed him on top of his head. I hugged him so tightly that he yelled, "Ma!" to get me to let go of him. He giggled and waved at me as he ran back in the yard chasing Diva.

I went back into the house to find Donnie and Michelle in the middle of an argument about why she wasn't getting any more weed. I just stood off to the side and watched the comedy unfold.

"Look, Chelle, I just gave your ass some weed. I gave you a quarter ounce. That is seven fucking grams. You only had three blunts, but now you are trying to play me like I'm stupid while you cuffin' my weed and standing in my face asking for more. Get your mind right, girl, 'cause I ain't giving you nothing else." He stood there and looked at her like she had two heads or something.

"Donnie, now you know you're my number one dude. You and me have always been cool. You know that I have bad nerves and I'm bi-polar. Why are you trying to hold on to all that good weed? You see me over here having withdrawals. How could you be so cruel to me? I thought we were better than that." Dee stepped back to get a good look at her, taking in the sad face and the watery eyes that Chelle was laying on him.

"Chelle, how in the fuck can you tell me you're having withdrawals and you still smoking? You still got the blunt in your hand. You blowing smoke out your nose like a dragon. Man, you got it bad, for real. There is something seriously wrong with you. You need to see somebody bout that shit. Why don't you finish what you have before you start begging for more? Better yet, smoke the rest of the weed you have in your pocket and leave me the fuck alone."

I couldn't help but to laugh. Those two were crazy.

Michelle was not finished with him by a long shot. "Brother-in-law, I understand that you are a business man and I respect that, so I have a business proposition for you."

She reached into her pocket and pulled out a ten-dollar bill.

"Let me get ten grams of Cush for ten dollars. Since it's cheaper than the AK-47, this ten dollars should just about cover the cost. See, that way it will be a win-win situation. You'll make some quick cash and I will get my medicine. I know that your momma told you that an even swap ain't never been a swindle. I don't mind spending money to get what I want."

"Bit..." he started before catching himself. Chelle was about to bring the man all the way out of his character and make him call her something ugly. Instead, he screamed, "Rocky! Rocky, you better come get this damn girl before I hurt her in here. Get her out of my face before she feels it."

I believed it was time to make my presence known, so I walked into the kitchen. Michelle was standing there with one hand on her hip and smoking a blunt. I wondered what was really wrong with this girl.

Donnie gave me a kiss and left the room mumbling to himself, "Ten grams for ten dollars, that ma'fucker must be crazy. What does she think this is, gimme, South Carolina?"

I watched my boo go into the backyard with his son.

"What's his damn problem?" Michelle asked like she truly didn't know.

"You are his damn problem, crazy! Now, come on, let's go and tuck that damn weed back into your pocket, I can see it."

"Oh, for real?" She stuffed the weed down in her pants. "Do you think that Donnie seen it too? You think that's why he wouldn't give me anymore?" she wondered aloud as we walked out the front door, got into the Cadillac, and pulled off.

Chapter 9
Riding Out

I handed Michelle my iPhone 6 and told her to call Charla and Dream so we could see where they were. While on that side of town, I wanted to go scoop them up and finish talking about this fed shit. I lucked up because Charla was at Dream's house, which wasn't too far from where Donnie lived. I took a couple tokes off the blunt and changed the CD to Jaheim as we rode out.

We pulled into Dream's yard, I spotted Charla first. I couldn't help but to wonder how it was that those two were best friends, when in reality they're like night and day – literally.

Dream was sitting calmly on the swing she had on her front porch. She was tastefully dressed in a pink and white Juicy Couture thin sweat suit with her hair pulled neatly back into a long ponytail. She rocked pink and white Air Max with the bubbles on the sides and back. She appeared peaceful and serene as she enjoyed the sun setting beautifully in the sky.

Charla, on the other hand, was a whole other story. She danced in the middle of the yard singing that Gwen Stefani's "Holla Back Girl" song. I studied her crazy movements as she mis-stepped and damn near fell over, wearing five-inch stilettos and a gray cashmere Michael Kors dress. Her hair was styled in a Mohawk, and I wondered if she had it gelled down or if she really cut her hair into a Mohawk.

When she regained her step and noticed that we had pulled up, she yelled, "Rocky, I heard the feds were at your house! That shit is bananas, B-A-N-A-N-A-S. I hope you don't holla back girl, you better not holla back girl!"

She laughed at her own little joke and assured that she was just teasing. We greeted with a sisterly hug and she asked if I was okay and where Zay was as we all got into the car to leave.

Driving down the street trying to decide where to go and get some drinks, I became shocked to hear Dream taking the initiative to ask me questions.

Dream was the quiet one, so we were all surprised when she asked, "Rocky, are we going to jail? Do you think the feds are going to take all of my things? How long will it be before they come to my house? Do they put the handcuffs on real tight? Will they let me call my mom? Where are they going to take me?" Her nerves were so shook for her to rattle all of those questions off before I could even answer the first one.

"Dream, Dream, baby, slow your roll. Take a deep breath girl and breathe. Don't start hyperventilating on me. Hold on, we're going to get to all of that. Let's go by Ruby Tuesday and have a few drinks and get something to eat and sit down and talk about all of this."

I had to calm her down because she was the baby of the bunch and my heart really went out to her. I would do everything in my power to keep all of my girls on the street, and that's my word. I loved my girls and didn't want them to get caught up in my affairs.

Charla started sniffing around the car like a bloodhound. "I smell it, that's AK-47. Y'all been up in here smoking the good shit. Let a nigga get something to put in her lungs."

Michelle glared at her with a very serious expression and informed her that she was not now, nor would she ever be a nigga because she was white; Charla needed to sit her ass down somewhere. We all fell out laughing. Michelle was always good at diffusing any situation.

Michelle rolled up a blunt and we all smoked. We only allowed Dream about two tokes off the blunt because she wasn't really a smoker, and her job performed random drug testing. But for the rest of us, we got our puff, puff, pass all the way to Ruby Tuesday.

I parked the car while everyone checked their make-up and

sprayed a little perfume so that the public didn't know what we had been doing just minutes beforehand. We always double-checked and made sure we were twenty-one sharp before we entered any public domain. I ran a brush through my hair and applied a bit more lip-gloss, and Michelle took the opportunity to tell the girls that my hair got messed up when Donnie had me upstairs in his room crying like a baby.

"Please, stop, ouch Donnie, please...please," she teased. "I heard your cry baby ass."

"Shit, you made it your business to see his dick, didn't you? Okay, then. Your ass would be crying too. My man is packing and he puts it all in there, like Prego!"

"True, true," she co-signed.

"Y'all are nasty" was the only comment Dream could come up with, looking like she was high off that little bit of weed she had.

We get out of the car and walked to the door of Ruby Tuesday, where we are greeted by a ten-foot tall giant, who introduced herself as Tammy.

I did my best to keep a straight face. Not wanting to be rude and laugh in the lady's face. We followed her to the table that she had picked for us in the smoking section. After taking our drink orders, she left us with four menus and let us know that Brad would be our server. I thanked her and waited for her to leave before proceeding with the meeting.

"Okay, ladies, as you all know, the feds came to my house this morning. They were there about the credit cards we have been using. They are just starting their investigation and they think that we are all involved in some way or another..."

I glanced around the table to be sure that I had everyone's attention before I continued. "When I brought all of you into this thing, I told y'all that we could make some easy cash, buy the best clothes and almost anything that we wanted. I told y'all we would ball out and live the good life. I thought that I had planned everything to a tee, but I was obviously mistaken."

"Are we going to jail, Rocky?" Dream asked the question that I'm sure they all wanted an answer to. She sat there not even looking directly at me and twirling her finger around the rim of her glass.

I was most concerned about Dream because she's the one who stood to lose the most. She had a great job at the bank and she got back into school for her Master's in finance to climb the corporate ladder. I prepared myself to answer her, but stopped when a tall young, handsome fellow approached the table.

I nodded my head in appreciation of the blond haired, blue-eyed man who I assumed to be Brad. "Hi, I'm Brad. I'm going to be serving you fine ladies tonight. Are you ready to place your order?"

Okay, I see that Brad had a little bit of game with him. That's what's up. You can never go wrong with the compliments, especially when they are due.

"I'm not really hungry. I just want to put something on my stomach so that I can hold my drinks," I said, still looking at Brad.

He was kind of fine for a white boy. I thought about getting his number before I left. I could find plenty of use for him. He would be the perfect decoy whenever I had to deal with older white women. Yeah, he would throw them off their game completely, and I could charge millions of dollars' worth of stuff with this one right here on the team.

He caught me staring at him and gave a smile that let me know that I could get it if I wanted it. I laughed to myself, *"He got game."*

As always, Dream didn't want her own food, but instead she wanted to "pick" a little something off of everyone else's plates, which meant that she would eat all your food before you got the chance to.

Michelle, of course, had the munchies and ordered damn near a three-course meal and then had the gall to turn to me and ask, "Who's paying?"

I didn't even respond to her dumb ass question. What difference did it make? We all had credit cards in our purses. Charla and I agreed to split three appetizers and that would be enough for Dream to eat off too.

I told Brad to make sure the wings were well done and to

leave the guacamole off the nachos. As soon as he left to place the order, the conversation picked back up.

"Now," I began, "y'all know that I love each of y'all like my sisters."

"I am your damn sister, so what do you love me like, a friend or cousin?" Michelle asked, leaving me once again to wonder about her bloodline. Where did she come up with these notions? Better yet, when the thoughts popped up, why didn't she just let them stay in her head instead of letting those crazy thoughts come out of her mouth?

Slamming back her drink, she looked over at me as if she was expecting an answer. I had to remember to ask my mom about that chick, for real. Maybe momma was on drugs when she was pregnant with Michelle or something. There was something very seriously wrong with her, and of that, I had no doubt.

"Shut up, Michelle." I said firmly. The look in my eye dared her to say anything else.

"Like I was saying before I was rudely interrupted, we are being investigated by the secret service. I believe that I am the main focus of this investigation. I'm sure that you guys will be questioned very soon. They do not have all their ducks in a row. They don't have the evidence to prove anything really, so just be careful and don't let them trick you into telling them what they don't know. They may be able to pin one of these cards on me because I paid my car payment with it. We all know that snitching or signing statements are not optional and they would only bring about more problems for all of us. We are true friends indeed, but we all don't need to be on this indictment if we can avoid it."

Before I could complete my thoughts, Charla interrupted me and went into her ride or die chick persona, which I personally knew was not an act. I trusted Charla with my life. Charla and I have done way more dirt than some credit cards and nothing had ever came back because we both knew how to keep our mouths shut.

"Shit, Rocky, we all are in this together. I ain't no snitch, so the feds don't need to come asking me nothing about nothing. It's their damn job to find out who shot John and who did what."

"Who shot somebody named John?" Michelle asked. "Who the hell is John? Are they gonna ask me about shooting John too? I don't know anyone named John. Rocky, did you shoot John?"

I guess she never heard that saying before.

"Shut the hell up with all that stupid shit for a change, Michelle. Our lives are on the line and me personally, I don't want to go to jail if I don't have to, so please let her finish!" Dream not only stood up to Michelle, but cursed too? Now, that would go in the record books.

"Chill out, y'all, and let her talk," Charla chastised them as if they were kids that had gotten on her last nerve.

"Okay, well, if you all listen to me and play your cards right, you won't have to go to jail. Just remember, don't admit to anything, and don't sign anything. Don't even tell them that the cards came to your houses. Tell them you that you never saw any credit cards besides your own. They can't really tie you guys into this whole thing without you telling on yourselves. You all know how I am going to carry it. It was my idea from the jump, so if push comes to shove, I'll take one for the team."

"Hopefully, I'll be able to minimize the damage. I want all of you to pretty much be honest with them so you don't get caught up in your lies. Just don't tell them more than they ask and play dumb as much as you can. I never told y'all where I got the information from to order the cards, so you don't have to worry about that part. When they ask you if we know each other, of course, you tell them the truth. They already know that we went to school together, and that way we all will have the same story. Just leave out all of our criminal activities. Are we clear on that part?" I questioned the girls, making sure that they were all on the same page as I.

They nodded their heads in agreement so I continued, "Now that we have gotten that out of the way, I have about twenty more credit cards that I'm about to activate in a minute. I'm not going to apply for any more cards right now. I'm too hot. I'm going to activate these cards though and max them out so I can get my money right for my lawyer fees or bond, whichever comes first. And to ensure that I eat good in case I have to go lay down and do a small bid."

"I'm not going to ask you all to help me with these cards. I'll just do the best I can with them in the time that I have. If you guys need anything or want anything, let me know and you know I will get it for you."

I took a sip of my drink and drifted off into deep thought, wondering if I could max all of these cards out by myself. If I couldn't, I'd sure as hell have a good time trying.

"Rocky, how in the hell you gonna try to play us like we are soft or something?" Charla asked. "The only soft one here is Dream, and even she is willing to help you do these cards. You are our girl. We love you and we are riding this thing out with you. We are gonna ride this damn thing like we screaming, 'Fuck the feds.' We know how to be careful, hell, we learned from the best. You ain't in this shit alone, so stop acting all crazy. We got you, girl. We all knew what this shit was when we got into it and we all have been eating real well. We can't bail on you now just because there might be trouble. Fuck the feds!"

"Yeah, sis, we are bout it-bout it, fool! We ain't scared of the police. We riding with you!" Michelle adds, looking all crazy.

Now, she wasn't saying that earlier when I picked her up and was laying on the backseat of the car so the feds wouldn't see her with me. But I ain't gonna call her out on that. It can be our little family secret. I guess a few blunts and some alcohol have given her big balls. I sipped some more of my Goose and juice and smiled.

"I'm with you too, Rocky," Dream said, letting me know she was still on my team. "I trust you and if you say that we can do this and get away with it, count me in. Besides, I need that new Fendi bag they have at Sacs, and it's over four thousand dollars. How else would I get it?"

"Seriously, Rocky, you are my baby sister and I would ride with you and for you any day of the week. I love you, girl!" Wow, that was the first sensible thing that Michelle had said in a minute.

"I may not be your blood sister, but me and you go way back like little red balls and jacks. You took me into your home when I was getting my ass beat every day while we were in school.

You showed me how to carry myself like a lady so that I would be treated like one. You really helped me get my shit together, and I love you for that," Charla words poured out of her mouth with tears flowing freely from her eyes.

I got all emotional because I loved my girls and the love they had for me was genuine. After giving myself a moment to get it together, I wiped my eyes and looked around at my crew and smiled. "That's love for real, y'all. Let's make it do what it do. We are in this thing to win it. I'm going to divide the cards up amongst you all, and I'm going to let you handle that while I get in the streets and make some moves to get some bigger cash. As you know, no matter what I'm hustling, I always break bread with y'all. I'll give y'all the cards when we get out to the car, but for right now, let's toss back a few drinks and eat this food 'cause here comes Brad, right on cue."

"I wonder if he wants to put a little cream in my coffee," Charla blurted, trying to sound all sexy.

"What damn coffee, Charla? You are the cream. I keep trying to tell you that you are white!" Michelle added and we all broke out in laughter, even Brad.

He asked if we needed anything else and I told him no. He handed me the ticket. I wondered what made him think I was paying for this food when I noticed that he slid me a folded sheet of paper. I opened it up and he had given me his whole damn personal profile: his name, number, email address, likes and dislikes, and his class schedule along with a note that read, *I am the one.*

What? Let me find out Brad got a little bit of thug in him. Trust and believe; I would be calling him as soon as I found something for him to do. We got our grub on, laughed and talked with each other as if we didn't have a care in the world.

We left the restaurant after we were done and I dropped Dream and Charla off where I picked them up from. I gave them five cards each along with the pin numbers for them. I advised them to be careful and explained that the cash would be divided seventy for me and thirty percent for them.

I allowed them to keep whatever they purchased as long as they left my half on the cards. For example, one of the cards I gave

INDICTED/ *Keisha Monique*

Dream was a Discover card with a twenty five thousand dollar limit. So she could pull half of that – $12,500.00 – cash from the ATM machines. She'd owe me $9,500.00. That left $12,500.00 left on credit on the card that could not be used for cash advances. She can have half of that, leaving the remaining $6,250.00 for me to shop with.

I always bought clothes, shoes, and purses with mine, which is how I stayed in nothing but designer wear and why my son was the best-dressed kid at his school.

I gave the last five cards to Michelle and got ready to take her home. Not surprisingly, she didn't want to go home. She informed me that she wasn't going to start working her cards until tomorrow and she didn't have anything to do at the house, so she preferred to roll with me. That was cool with me. My sister kept me laughing and she helped keep my mind off my troubles.

"Where are we going?" she questioned as she proceeded to roll another blunt. I wondered how much of Donnie's weed did she take.

"I've got to go holla at Mel-G about some business and FYI; you smoke entirely too much weed. You've already killed most of your brain cells."

"So what! I guess that means that you don't want to smoke none of this right here then?" she held the blunt under my nose so I could smell it.

Of course I couldn't let her smoke that good-good by herself. I'd be dead wrong. I shared with my kinfolks. "Michelle, you better light that shit and pass it to me before you have to beat your feet to get home!"

"This is the last of the weed that I got from your baby daddy. Oh, and by the way, since we are over by where K.G. hangs out at, why don't we stop by there and buy some more? She always has good smoke."

"Michelle, don't try to play me. I can see right through your little tired ass plot. You only want to go see K.G. because you know that she ain't gonna make me pay for no weed. You wouldn't give a damn if we had to go to the other side of the moon. As long as you could smoke for free, you'd be with it. I know how you are."

I never understood why she always thought she was so much smarter than everybody else. You couldn't tell her that her game wasn't on point. I smiled at the thought of seeing K.G. again. My flashbacks were quickly interrupted as she added, "Fuck all of that. Are we going to see her or what?"

She looked at me and laughed out loud. "You know you want to see your girlfriend anyway. Shit, you better be glad that I don't do women 'cause I might have to fight you for that one. She is fine as hell!"

"It wouldn't even come to that, boo. I've got that on lock and you can best believe that, so remove all those thoughts from your head and stick to your own cut buddies and stop jacking mine. Now, pass that blunt. Damn, you try to smoke up everything."

As I pulled into Columbia Gardens where my boo held her court, I saw more black folks than I had ever seen in one place in a long time. Some of them were shooting C-low against the wall. The young fast ass lil' girls were doing some dances that make me wonder if they ever worked a stripper pole. The dope fiends were on the prowl looking for a come up or the next hit. Either one will do as long as they get high.

A few of them caught a glimpse of my car and probably wondered if I was a new dope boy coming to set up shop. Some of them knew me and waved.

I laughed when I saw Christine. Christine was the number one dope fiend, a clown ass lady. Sometimes, we paid for her crack just to laugh at her silly ass jokes and the crazy shit that she was always saying. Approaching the back parking lot, it looked like a car show. The Benzes and Lexus coupes and the Caddies were showroom clean, each competing with the other in rim size and the gloss in the paint.

I saw K.G.'s money green and chromed out Kawasaki Ninja 1100, with the seat extender on the back. That bike was by no means intimidated by all the luxury cars that surrounded it. Just like its driver, the bike was in a class all its own. I pulled up beside the bike, cut the car off, and realized that I was once again the center of attention. Looking good and feeling even better, I emerged from the car like the double dime that I was. Michelle stayed content to sit in the car and finish her blunt. She didn't crave the attention the way I did.

"Go get em', tiger!" she yelled when I told her I'd be right back.

A young hustler, who was obviously new to the block, put his game face on, approached me, and attempted to put his mack down. He got his swag right and looked me up and down.

"Damn, girl! What's up with you? Who are you and how can I get to know you a bit better?" he asked, feeling pretty sure of himself.

"Aye, yo, little man!" I heard K.G. yell as she approached us. "Fall back, young'un. That's too much woman for you right there. Only 'cause you are new around here, I'ma let you slide with that shit. But son, don't ever push up on my girl again."

K.G. walked up to me and kissed me passionately on the mouth. I kissed her back and got lost in her embrace.

"That's some cold hearted shit right there." He shook his head in disbelief. "Man, K.G. got all the bad bitches. No wonder all the fine girls are missing in action. They all bulldaggin'. All that's left for the rest of us are the fat and ugly girls." The little fellow appeared as though he was gonna cry a river as he walked away.

I stepped back to get a good look at my baby. She was too damn fine at 5'9, light brown skin and those beautiful green eyes that could see your soul. Her long hair stayed braided and kept in the latest styles. She loved to floss, and that day was no different. She sported four platinum chains, 4-carat flawless diamond studs, a Rolex watch, and two wide platinum bands.

I admired her clothes. She always put her shit together real tight. She wore a green and white Dolce and Gabbana sweat suit with green and white old school Charles Barkley's. Her white on white Yankees cap was cocked at an angle; it wasn't hard to see that her swag was on super-swole.

K.G. caught me staring at the ring on her finger and grinned. "I never take it off, Rock. This is my most prized possession. I will always consider you my wife, and this ring that you bought me solidifies the love I have for you," she confessed, sounding smoother than smooth.

I would have fallen for that line if I didn't know her. She was a big flirt and had cheated on me several times. I didn't worry about it anymore because I broke up with her a while back, so she was free to do whatever suited her.

"So, you wear my ring while you are fucking other people, K.G.?" I quizzed. I didn't want to go there, but I guess I was still a bit jealous.

"There you go with your bullshit, Rocky. Damn, give me a break. I made some mistakes in the past. I told you that I was wrong for hurting you, and that it will never happen again. Do you have to go there all the time? Can't you just be happy to see me? I can't change the past. If I could, I would. I do still hold true to the promise I made you. I will never hurt you again, and I will wait for you as long as I have to until I gain your trust back."

I looked into her eyes to see if she was sincere and it seemed that she was. However, I knew that I couldn't commit to spending the rest of my life with a woman.

"Anyway," I said, leaning back on my heels and putting my hand on my hip. "I've got a problem with the feds. I might need some money later on this week."

"It's already in the works, ma. I heard about your problems earlier. You know that I have someone watching you, right?"

"Yeah, right. Peanut is your cousin, and we both know that he can't hold water. But good looking out. I knew I could count on you."

She smiled and winked at me. She had a spell on me or something! I felt like I couldn't think or breathe when I was around her. She knew the kind of power she had over me too. It showed in her attitude. I often wished that things could of been different between us, but that was only wishful thinking.

"Come here, papi," I cooed in a seductive manner and held my arms open for her to come close to me. "You love me right?" I asked.

"Yes," she replied.

106

"Give me a kiss, papi, come here."

I wrapped my arms around her neck and buried my tongue into her mouth. She tasted so good; just like watermelon Now & Laters. Her wet and warm mouth welcomed me and the way she gripped my ass got my juices flowing. I wondered if I would ever be able to leave her alone. I knew that I should, but all reasons goes out the window as I lost myself in her embrace.

"Get a fucking room. Why don't you just pull her pants down and start munching right here. K.G., damn, get off my sister," Michelle spit as she tried to pull me away from her.

"See, that's why I don't do no dyking right there! I don't know what kind of spell you have over my sister, but it ain't cool. Ra'Quelle gets all goo-goo eyed whenever she is around you, and she acts all stupid and shit." She looked at me and shook her head like she felt sorry for me or something. I knew damn well that crazy ass broad wasn't tripping on me for real.

"What's up, Michelle? I see that you are still cock-blockin'." K.G. laughed at Michelle and her wild ways.

"Yeah, okay, whatever K.G. Anyway, what's really good? What have you got for your sister-in-law? Let me get something to smoke, and I might not tell Donnie that we were down here and make him beat your ass again!"

I have never really been shocked by the things that come out of my sister's mouth, but sometimes she threw things out there that were so far off in left field that even I would be amazed. That day was one of those days. Michelle was in rare form. She was too simple minded to realize that she was insulting K.G. and asking her for weed at the same damn time.

I prepared myself to play the peacemaker because I knew that K.G. was about to spazz on her, so I intervened and tried to get her to focus on me instead of Michelle's silly behind. "Baby, look, I stopped by here to get a little something for my nerves. I need to relax and get my head right, plus I'm thinking about going out tonight. What have you got planned for tonight? You want to meet me at club Levels or what?"

"Yeah, baby, that's what's up. I can do that. I'm only going to be out here for a little while longer and I'm about to head out.

What are you talking about on the wood, how much do you want? You want something just for your own use or do you want some weight?" she asked me while she walked over to her bike to lift the seat up.

I sauntered over to where she stood and told her I only needed enough for myself, like an ounce or so. She pulled out a bag and handed me the goods. I peered down at it and was impressed as always. I knew purple haze when I saw it and tried to guess the weight by just holding it. It felt like a quarter pound which I could definitely work with.

I expressed my delight and batted my eyes at her. "Thank you, boo-boo!"

I gave her a big kiss and gazed deep into her eyes and back away from her shaking my head. I had mad love for that girl, but I had to tread carefully since she was the reason Donnie and I broke up in the first place.

"Love you!" I told her and walked away before I heard her response.

When I returned to my car, I couldn't hold my peace any longer. I turned to look at Michelle and rolled my eyes at her. "You are about one simple ass broad; I hope that you know that. Why do you have to fuck with everybody that you come across, Chelle? Damn. Your mouth is really gonna get us both in trouble one day. You are going to cause someone to beat your ass about your mouth, and then I'm gonna catch a damn case because I just can't let nobody hurt you. You need to chill out sometimes, for real!"

"Shit, whatever, ain't nobody beat my ass yet, so don't stress that. Later for the lesson on manners and proper public conduct, you got the weed, right? Why didn't you tell her to give you some blunts too?"

Lord, bless this child. She needed some therapy. I had to see about getting her some help if it wasn't already too late. My momma should have taken care of that years ago.

"You know what, you might be crazy as hell, but you're my sister and I love your crazy ass just the same."

Chapter 10
Get Ready to Shine

"Chelle, handed me my cell phone out of my purse. I needed to call Mel-G and see what's up with him and if I can get with him later on about some business." I dialed his number and waited for him to pick up.

"Yo, what's good, sexy? Where have you been hiding at?" Mel-G answered the phone as if he'd been waiting for me to call him.

"Hey, boo." I tried to sound as sexy as I could without being over the top.

"You alright, ma? Are you straight? I heard them boys were on your ass hard earlier today."

Damn, news sure travelled fast. I was curious if there was anyone who didn't know how my day had started?

"Yeah, I'm good. But I really need to get with you about some business I'm trying to handle."

"No doubt, no doubt," he said. "I feel you on that. What time are you trying to see me? What about now? I'm at the shop."

"No, I'm about to go to the mall and do a little shopping. You know how I do. I'm going out tonight. Why don't you come through Club Levels tonight? I'll be there. You can bring your girl if you want to. All the drinks are on me," I countered, trying to convince him to come since he really didn't do the club scene.

"Stop playing with me, girl? Why are you trying to play me like I'm soft? Why would I bring my girl or any girl, for that matter, when I know that you're going to be there? You know that you're the love of my life," he told me, sounding like he'd been running game for years.

"Yeah, okay, whatever you say." I see that you are still full of shit, boy. I'll see you tonight. I know that you can get us in the VIP section, right?"

"Of course, anything for you shawty. I'll see you there, and please be careful out there."

As I hung up the phone, I caught Michelle looking at me all crazy and giving me attitude. Why in the hell would she be mean mugging me? Sometimes I forgot how bi-polar she really was. What had her panties in a wad?

"What's your problem now, crazy?" I inquired, preparing to hear some of her foolishness.

"So you're not going to invite me to go out with you, Rocky? You don't think that maybe I'd like to go to the club too? You got your little bulldagger man looking girlfriend meeting you there, your car stealing ass ex-boyfriend is gonna be there, and Lord only knows who else. I'm sure you taking Charla and Dream as well. So what about me? I ain't good enough to roll with you? I don't know why you treat me so bad. Why do you treat your own sister the way you do? Why do I have to go home and be by myself? Maybe I want to go to the club and drink some drinks and smoke on a little something-something. I just don't under –"

"*Shut up!*" I yelled, cutting her off in the middle of her rampage. "You with me, right? Aren't you with me right now, crash dummy? Why would I need to invite you to go when you are right here with me? You're always with me. Stop being so damn dramatic. You're about to give me a headache. Calm your nerves, girl, I got you. We are gonna run into this mall real quick before they close and get some fresh gear for tonight, then we'll go back to your house to change and hit the club. Okay?" I said as I pulled into the mall parking lot.

"Why do we have to dress at my house? Are you afraid the feds are going to be at your house waiting for you? Are you scared to go home or what?"

Michelle was really working my nerves at that point. I closed my eyes and massaged my temples, attempting to regroup. I really couldn't believe that we were even related by blood. I wanted to see some paperwork on her, for real.

"Man, put that blunt down and come on," I yelled once again

The first store I stopped in was Foot Locker. There was a young guy that worked in there and he never asked me for identification when I shopped. In return for that, I always bought him two or three pairs of whatever kinds of shoes he wanted.

I noticed that the store manager was working up front as well, but that wasn't gonna stop anything; business as usual. In a situation like this, he'd ask to see my ID, but only for show so that if anything came back, he'd be on camera following procedure. The ID I showed him was mine and not related to the credit card I used. But they will never know that the ID and credit cards don't match since there is nowhere on a credit card receipt to write any information.

He'd just look at it and hand it back to me, pretending that it was the correct identification for the credit used. He'd also pick out his shoes, only I'd take them with me and wait for him to call me on my cell phone to meet him somewhere for him to pick them up. It all worked out pretty well for the both of us and we've been doing it like that for a minute.

Jermaine greeted me as soon as I entered the store. He schooled me on the new Jordans that came in and he'd put two pairs away for Isaiah and two other pairs of new releases for himself. I liked to buy Isaiah two pairs; one clean pair for school and the other pair for play.

I also grabbed him a pair of red and white throwback Charles Barkley's and some all-white Forces because you can never go wrong with all white Forces. Jermaine brought me some black Timberland boots to look at for Zay, and of course, I got them. My son stayed fly all the time.

Michelle brought over some gray and white Nike Shox that she wanted, and I choose an all-white pair of leather Air Max.

As usual, I purchased more than I could carry, so while Jermaine was over at the register waiting for the credit card receipt to print, I asked his boss if someone could help me carry all of the bags to the car. He instructed Jermaine to help me and I smiled because that was exactly who I wanted to help in the first place. That way he could put his bags in his own car and I wouldn't have to meet him later.

After securing the bags in my trunk and setting the alarm, we got back into the mall. My time was running short since I only had an hour before the mall closed.

I ran into Macy's real quick and copped Isaiah five big faced Polo shirts and some Polo boxers. I peeped a leather Ralph Lauren jacket I wanted him to have, but didn't have time to do all of that. I stopped at the perfume counter to grab a bottle of Giorgio Armani Si' and some CoCo Chanel and headed on out the door.

As we walked through the food court on the way to another store, Michelle nudged my arm to get my attention. I looked to see what she was trying to show me and saw Jay-Baby in the line of the Chinese food place. He was with some chick in a skintight cat suit and a body to die for.

I could see Jay-Baby was still keeping it one hundred. I smiled to myself, giving the girl her props, but by no means did I feel threatened. He saw us and walked right over to me, leaving ol' girl all alone in the line.

"Jay, are you treating on the food today or is that privilege only for the girls you intend to dick down?" Michelle asked, hoping to cop a free meal.

"You good, Chelle. Go over and order whatever you want. Tell Armani that I said to handle that," Jay-Baby instructed without taking his eyes off me.

"You better not get my sister caught up in no shit and make me shut this whole mall down. Don't get little Ms. Armani beat the fuck up!"

"Naw, ma, it ain't even like that. She works for my escort service. I just picked her up from a call, and she wanted to stop and get something to wear for work tomorrow," he informed me, looking all innocent.

"Damn, Jay, so you pimpin' people too?" I inquired, trying to find out more about this escort thing. "So, are you more like Goldie from The Mack or are you like Magic Don Juan?"

I was curious if he beat his women too. Probably not. I don't think the pimp game plays out that way anymore. Women have learned how to fight back, and people ain't going for all that crazy shit they used to a long time ago.

"It ain't even like that, Rocky, but you know that I have to eat too. I deal in supply and demand. There is a demand for women at an hourly rate, so I supply it."

"I'm sure you do, Jay-Baby, I'm sure you do." The way he put it down in the bedroom, I could pretty much see him having things whichever way he wanted them.

"Jay, be looking for a call from me sometime tomorrow. I have a little business proposition for you. It might even help with one of your supply and demand jobs."

"That's what's up, ma. I'll be waiting to hear from you. I hope you know that you can all me for more than business. You can feel free to call me on a personal note at any time, night or day."

"I'll be sure to keep that in mind, boo."

Michelle walked up with Armani. They seemed to have gotten along pretty well. Two hoes from the Metro. I giggled at my own inside joke. We bid them farewell and as we walked off, I watched Michelle devour two egg rolls as if she hadn't eaten all day.

Walking through the doors of yet another store has always made me feel like I was on top of my game for real. It felt great to be very well known by most of the sales clerks and treated with much respect. It was nothing for me to stroll through and spend thousands of dollars on dresses. Of course, if I got the dress, I had to have the matching shoes.

My favorite sales clerk was Jenea', a young girl from the projects who decided that she was not content with her life the way that it was and did something about it. She was a full-time student at the University of South Carolina, and I always gave her as much commission as I could whenever shopped at her store. It made me feel good to see young people be accountable for their lives and not fall victim to the streets.

"How is my favorite sales girl doing today?" I asked cordially.

"So much better since you guys are here. I know I'm about

to end my day with a bang!" she exclaimed excitedly.

"You got that right. Now just show us what you've got, boo!"

We left the store with about five bags each. We didn't have enough time to do any major damage, just a little something to make sure that I was the showstopper that night when I sashayed up in the club. I wouldn't have it any other way.

I called Carla and Dream to see if they wanted to roll with us. Dream declined because she had to work early in the morning. Charla, on the other hand, was all for going to the club and assured me that she'd be ready when I got there.

I hung up with them as we arrived at Michelle's house. Once inside, she turned on the light and I nodded my head in appreciation at how well she had put her house together. As silly as she was, her house was on point and I respected that to the fullest.

I noticed that she has redone her living room since the last time I was there; tastefully done in Queen Ann furniture with Cherry wood tables.

"You like?" she asked, watching me take it all in.

"Indeed, I do. This is really nice. I really like this. It fits the way this house was built, for real. This is very good, big sis. You did a great job."

"I know, right? Anyway, since we both have to shower and get dressed and you are slow as hell, why don't you go upstairs and use the bathroom in my room and I'll use the guest room."

"No, I ain't gonna put you out of your room. Everything you need is in your room. I'll just use the guest room."

I don't know why she called it a guest room. She never had any guests. There was not one stitch of furniture in that room. Oh, well, I wasn't there to sleep. I undressed and got in the shower. Once I got so fresh and so clean-clean, I dried off and put my panties and bra on. I bought a matching snow-white thong set with the push up bra. It looked really good against my skin tone. I didn't have any intention on fucking tonight, but hey, you never know when sexy panties will come in handy.

I bought two outfits to choose from, and I ended up going with the Christian Dior black, soft, leather pantsuit with the red bustier that goes underneath the jacket. That suit is hugged every curve to perfection, made just for me. I was gonna be killing em' with this leather. I re-checked myself in the mirror before I stepped into my black Manolo Blahniks with the five inch silver spike heels.

Oh, they are so not ready for this tonight, I thought to myself as I pulled out the black velvet bag that held my jewelry. My jewels were very classy but blinging just the same. I threw my hair over one shoulder so that I could fasten the diamond and onyx piece around my neck. It wouldn't be me if I didn't have the three and a half karat earrings to match.

I topped it all off with a three-inch cuff bracelet that sat beautifully around my thin wrist. I combed my hair up into a bun and let a little fall around my face. I flawlessly applied my makeup, pulled out my iPhone 6, and snapped a picture of myself. *Oh Yeah, I'm carrying it just like that.*

I grabbed my brand-new Fendi bag and put all the contents of the old bag in it before heading out to the living room to wait on my sister. To my surprise she was already there and waiting on me.

"What do you think?" she asked, standing up and turning a complete circle for me to check her clothes out. She tossed her hair from side to side and I had to admit; I was really impressed. She could compete with the best of them when she did her thing. She looked great.

She wore a navy blue Ralph Lauren strapless dress that stopped right above her knees and had a short cropped jacket that hung right under her breasts. She didn't wear stockings and her beautiful legs looked like they could go on forever. Her black Gucci open toed stilettos matched her Gucci purse.

Michelle never wore much jewelry, so she only had on a matching mother of pearl necklace and earring set. She was holding her own. I only had one question for her, "Whose hair is that you're wearing?"

"It's mine and it has been since I bought it last week. Why, are you jealous, Rock?" she asked me, looking indignant.

"Naw, I ain't jealous at all. It looks really nice. I was just wondering since I know that you didn't have any hair earlier." I snickered. "I might want to borrow that dress later too. That shit is the business."

"Don't worry; I knew you would be all over my dress, so I made sure that I got one for you too. Only yours is black."

"That's what's up!" I screamed as we left the house, prepared to party like only we can.

Chapter 11
Vip

To my surprise, Charla was ready when I arrived to pick her up. That is very unusual because we always had to wait for her. She came out rocking a badass one-piece Ralph Lauren blue jumpsuit that revealed the cleavage from her double D's. Her little pink toes stood out in her Jimmy Choo's. She had on the big ole school doorknocker earrings and a giant sized rope chain with a dollar sign medallion. She really knew how to throw her shit together when she wanted to.

"What's up, sistas!" she yelled jumping into the backseat. Of course, I let the valet park the Cadillac so that we could truly make a grand entrance. Jay-Baby caught my attention as soon as I stepped from the car.

****

He was swamped with the admiration of the gold-diggers and sac chasers. I shook my head and continued on my way into the club. Everyone stared as we strolled into the club. I felt like a celebrity. I smiled and took in all the admiration, knowing that I looked like a million bucks. I switched my way over to the bar and ordered some drinks before heading up to the VIP section.

When we arrived to the stairs that lead to the VIP section, I handed the bouncer three crispy one hundred dollar bills to ensure our immediate passage. He lifted the velvet rope and allowed us access. I could feel the heat on my back from the haters that tried to knock me off my square which wasn't going to happen that night. I laughed it off while me and my girls headed into the place where the big boys and girls play.

VIP was decked out and it matched our fly. It had been a minute since I was last there and I saw that Shy really stepped his game up. There were Italian leather sofas along the wall and a bar area just for "VIP Only," stocked with the finest liquors and wines.

For those who preferred to sit at tables, they were available as well, several of which were covered in white linen tablecloths. The tables were lit with colored candles that brought a sexy glow to the room. The phone located on the wall had a direct line to the DJ's booth in case we had a specific song we wanted to hear.

The ratio of men to women was about two to one, and everyone was representing. The atmosphere resembled a fashion show. The women had put away their street clothes and rocked designer wear by Gucci, Prada, Lauren, and Michael Kors.

The men were not wearing jeans and Jordans but instead were adorned in Giorgio Armani slacks and Kenneth Cole suits

Shy, the owner of the club, had taken it to another level. He was dressed to kill in a black Ralph Lauren Purple Label suit that fitted him to a tee. He looked like quite the dapper don.

As if I didn't see him, Michelle announced, "There go your man, Rocky. Damn, Shy is looking good as hell. Why did you guys break up anyway?"

"Stop minding grown folks business and go get us a table while I go over and holla at Shy real quick. And order me another Chivas Regal on the rocks, please," I demanded of Michelle as I straightened out my pant suit to get my sexy on.

"Okay. And Rock, ask him who that brother is he's sitting at the table with because I swear he looks like that man I want to marry and have kids with!"

"You are really silly as hell, girl, but I will gather that information for you. And Michelle, please try to be on your best behavior. Charla, keep an eye on her. You know how she gets from time to time."

"I got her covered, Rocky. She's going to have a good time. I don't anticipate us having any problems in here. If we do, then we will just have to handle them," Charla said, looking at me and giving me attitude.

Talk about the blind leading the blind; Charla keeping Michelle out of trouble is like me telling Diva to watch a T-bone steak and expecting it to be there when I return. That ain't gonna happen. I just hoped for the best when I walked away.

As I approached the table where Shy was sitting, he glanced over at me. The look on his face told me that he appreciated the extra effort I put forth in preparing myself for tonight.

He stood up and walked over to me after excusing himself from his table he shared with a woman, whose eyes were shooting daggers at me. I could only assume she was his girlfriend. The way that she mean-mugged me was actually kind of funny to me. I could tell that she wanted a confrontation with me and any other night I would have given her just that, but that night I was focused on more important things.

I had enough on my plate without having to worry about some chick who meant absolutely nothing to me. After all, Shy left her there to come sit with me, so I wasn't the one who should be mad anyways.

Shy turned to me as we sat on the couch and smiled. "Hey, baby."

"Hey, Shy, how are you doing? You look good tonight."

"You ain't doing so bad yourself, Ra'Quelle."

He leaned back to get a better look at me and then licked his lips. "How did you get all of that in them pants, girl? You are looking real hot tonight, for real. You making me catch flashbacks, and that might get you in trouble," he said flirtatiously.

"No, that might get *you* in trouble. Hell, you already might be in trouble. I see that girl staring at me like she's crazy. I hope that you have your pets trained well or else I might have to show my natural black pretty ass." I laughed even though I was dead ass serious.

"Naw, it's all good. That's Sasha. You might remember her from the hood. She found me about a month ago and presented me with a one-year-old boy she claimed to be my son. We have been trying to make a go of it ever since then."

From where Sasha was sitting, she had to stretch her neck and turn all the way around in her chair to see what Shy was doing, and trust me, she should have had a crook in her neck the way she was straining so hard to see.

"Damn, Shy, did y'all have a relationship? Are you sure, it's your son? Are you happy? Do you love her?" I tried to piece his story together, being nosey and asking one question right after the next.

"No all the way across the board, Rocky. But being the god that I am, I was forced to deal with a reality from my past. Whether I'm his father or not, I brought his mother into my cypher when I slept with her. So I'll continue to man up. The child needs some male guidance in his life and I'm willing to provide that. If the lineage of the child turns out to be negative for me, I'll still try to help her direct his path."

That's some real shit he just said. I wish more men would own up to the task of being a dad like that. Shy had always had a pure heart. That's why I always came to him for advice and what not.

"See, Rocky, if you hadn't left me high and dry, I wouldn't be in this quagmire. We would be happily married and making babies that I'd know are mine." His eyes pierced through me waiting for my reaction.

"Yeah, right, Shy!" I countered, thinking back to when we were together. "You were a totally different person when we were together. You weren't as righteous as you are now. You had a lot of shit with you back then. I'm very proud of the changes that you have made though."

"You are one hundred percent right, I have done a 180. I guess with age does come wisdom. At least in my case it did. I was pretty wild, huh?"

"You ain't even gotta ask."

"Anyway, it's always good to see you, but what brings you out to my neck of the woods? I thought that nigga had you under lock and key."

"Never that, boo-boo, never that. I have just been laying low and doing me. But seriously, I've got something to talk to you about."

"Is this about those agents being at your house?" he asked

curiously. "You never did call me back."

"Yeah. The feds were there for credit card fraud and identity theft. I have some moves I'm trying to make and then I promised Isaiah that I would go straight. My son is counting on that, but I'm tripping right now because the streets are all I know. I'm really stressing about this fed shit. On top of that, the thought of change really scares me." I stopped talking long enough to watch the waitress walk over in our direction. She was a pretty Latino girl with the body of a sister. I know she racked up on her tips.

"Excuse me, I hate to interrupt, but I have these drinks here for the lady that were sent over from that table," she said, pointing at the table where Michelle and Charla were sitting.

As I glanced in their direction, they both held their drinks up as if they were toasting me. Michelle lifted her eyebrow and tilted her head at Shy as if to ask, "What's up?"

I smirked at their gestures and shook my head. Charla pointed at the dance floor to let me know that they were about to dance. I just focused my attention back to Shy and the sexy mamacita who brought the drinks over. I reached for my purse to get ready to tip her, but Shy placed his hand over mine, pulled out his wallet, and handed her fifty dollars. She smiled, thanked him and reminded us that she'd be back around should we need anything.

I teased Shy about the large tip he gave the waitress. "You're still that nigga, huh?" I knew that it was for my benefit as well as hers. He was always going above and beyond to show love.

Amused at my comment, Shy leaned back in his chair and sighed deeply before speaking. "Ra'Quelle, I told you a long time ago to leave them credit cards alone, did I not?"

"I know, Shy, and you were right. I should have listened to you and everybody else who told me to stop." I knew he can hear the irritation in my voice, but my purpose of meeting him was not to be lectured.

"You can't keep doing the same thing and expecting different results. You should have known that eventually you would get hemmed up in it. The world just doesn't work that way. What you need me to do? How can I help you with this? You know that I am always here for you.

"I know, and I love you for that. I really just want to bend your ear about some things I want to do. I need your input on a couple of ideas, and I basically just want to talk to you whenever you have time."

"I always have time for you. I can get a couple of bottles of Cristal and we can talk right now."

"Umm, I don't think that's such a good idea. Sasha is already going to have whiplash from trying to see what we doing back here, and besides that, I have K.G. and Mel-G meeting me here. See how I solicit business for your club? When are you gonna put me on payroll?" I teased.

"Payroll? Hell, you've been in my pocket since I met you, Rocky. What's the difference?" he joked.

I slapped him on the shoulder and assured him that I would be getting in touch with him very soon. I got up and walked away with a little extra twist in my step because I knew that he and his girlfriend were watching me.

Before I take my seat at the table with the girls, I peeped Mel-G come into the VIP area looking around like he was looking for someone. I waved my hand so that he could see me.

He approached me, turning heads as he passed by. Mel-G was true to his own and he never switched up his swagger. There were no suits and ties for him, but he carried himself very well wearing a beige and brown Gucci argyle sweater, dark denim Gucci jeans, and brown Timberland boots. He looked like a thug with good taste because only he could pull off that outfit in the club. I had to give him his credit. He was definitely in a class all of his own.

I smiled to myself and thought, *This is my nigga for life.* I had mad love for him. I respected his gangster and I liked him as a person. He took a seat beside me and motioned for the waitress. When she came over, he ordered a Grey Goose straight up and asked if I wanted anything. I ordered a glass of white wine. I needed something to cleanse my palate because I was about to switch up my drinking.

"Damn, Rocky, where you get that suit from? Stand up again and let me look at that ass."

"Quit playing with me, boy, and sit down somewhere."

"When are you going to let me get with you and show you how a real man does it? Let me show you how good your life can be with you as my lady."

I looked at him and could see that he was dead ass serious. Now that would be something to see. He was sexy as hell, but I knew how Mel-G got down and I did not have the patience to train another man. It took me years to train the one that I had.

"Really, now? And what number would I be, Mel? Would I be number seven or number eight or what? Where would I fit in? You've got three wives, six baby mamas, five girlfriends, *and* you're doing your next-door neighbor's wife. What are you taking, Viagra, or something? How do you handle all those women?"

I glanced over and caught him blushing; he knew that I was telling the truth.

"You have more than you need on your plate right now. You can't handle me along with the rest of your tribe. Somebody would go lacking and trust me; it would not be pretty if the slackness fell on my day because I gotta get mines!" I held my drink up in my right hand to toast to him, then winked my eye, flirting outright with him.

He tried to convey a look of astonishment as he stretched his eyes. "Who me? I'm single, baby, and waiting for you to see things my way."

We both find that amusing because he's always been full of shit. We sipped our drinks and peered around the club.

"What's on ya mind, Rocky? What you trying to do?" he asked in reference to why I invited him to the club to meet with me.

I handed him a list from my purse. It contained a list of ten cars that I had been clocking and the details of each car such as paint color and model. I planned to have Da'quan steal these for me, and I need to know how much he would give me for all ten cars.

"How much will you be able to give me if I can deliver every car on that list within the next week?"

He read over the list very carefully. "You do know that

123

some of these cars like the 2015 Lexus 400 series have the kind of
alarm system that will shut the car engine off and lock the doors if
the correct code isn't entered within two minutes of driving,
right?"

"Yeah, my people know all of that. They have the means to
disable all of that. He's up on all the new shit. If it has four tires
and will go, he can steal it. No broken windows or any of that other
hot shit. These cars will not have one scratch on them when delivered."

Mel-G sat back and considered my proposition. He wanted
to know who and how, but he knew better than to ask.

"Okay, being that you're in a bind, I'm going to give you
top dollar and take some shorts myself. I'll give you ten thousand
cash for each car. That will be a total of a hundred thousand cash
money if you can deliver each car. Most of these cars are valued at
over fifty thousand, so I know that I will not have a problem selling them for at least ten or fifteen stacks each. Yeah, I can make
that happen for you Rocky."

"Say no more, consider it done." I relished in my business
skills and sipped my drink. "I'll be calling you in a couple days to
let you know when I am going to start bringing the cars into the
shop. I really appreciate you. You know I'm glad I can always
count on you. You always show me love." I tried not to get all
emotional on the man, but it made my heart swell when people
show me love.

"You just be careful out there, girl, and don't be adding fuel
to the fire," he schooled, talking about the investigation. "Oh,
yeah, what's up with that snow bunny that you have with you all
the time? I don't usually do white girls, but that broad is thick.
She's fine as hell and she got flava."

Mel-G and Charla? I wondered to myself. Yeah, I could see
that happening. She was just the one he needed to slow his ass
down. Charla didn't play no games when it came to affairs of the
heart, but she was a sweetheart as long as you didn't cross her the
wrong way. I always thought she really could be the one to settle
this nigga down.

"That's Charla, she's my homie. She's around here somewhere with Michelle."

"Yeah, I saw them when I came in. She was on the floor getting her groove on. Man, shawty is wearing the hell out of that jumpsuit. Damn, I need to get with her and see what's all that she's hiding in there," he said rubbing his chin with his hand like he was really trying to figure some shit out.

"Where did you see them?"

"They over there where I saw your girlfriend out there getting her freak on too." He watched to see how I would react to what he said.

"Oh, really?" I said and picked up my other drink and knocked it back. I reached over, took his drink out of his hand, and slammed that down too. "Well, come on and dance with me so I can get my freak on too!"

Chapter 12
Wildin' Out

I get up out of my seat and start to lead him to the dance floor, thinking of how pissed K.G. will be to see me dancing with Mel-G.

"Alright, Ra'Quelle, I don't want no shit out of your girlfriend because I don't discriminate. I will knock her the fuck out and think nothing more about it, and you know that I'm speaking the truth."

"It ain't even that serious. I just want to dance, boy. Come on, that's my song right there." I lead him out to the center of the dance floor and turn my back on him so he could wrap his arms around my waist.

We begin to groove to Plies, "Please Excuse My Hands." I can feel his dick pressed up against my ass and it won't be long before he's rock hard, so I turn around and face him while he grips my ass tightly and pulls me closer to him.

He stares into my eyes and squeezes my ass. "Damn, girl, you soft as hell. You about to make my dick get hard and if you do, girl, you gonna have to handle that," he whispers as I step into him closer and stare back at him seductively.

I'm just starting to groove with him when I hear Charla yelling. I look up and see her trying to catch K.G. by the arm.

K.G. approaches me and Mel-G. She looks at me furiously, and then turns to stare him up and down. It appears as if she's sizing him up. "Get your motherfucking hands off my girl."

She's standing there looking like she's about to have a fit. I wonder where the girl is she was with. She is really out of line, and

127

I do not feel like dealing with her tonight. Why is she looking at this man like she is about to swing on him? God help her if she does because this one ain't the one. He will really hurt her. He don't give a damn!

"Aye, yo, little man-bitch, you might want to take that shit somewhere else and get the fuck out of my face." Mel-G is acting calm as hell, which really scares me because I can tell that he is truly pissed. He's mad as hell for real, and I don't need for this shit to blow up in my face.

I didn't come here for this tonight. I just want to have a good time, but I knew that dancing with him would piss her off, so I guess I should have expected it.

Charla reaches for us just before Michelle does. She tells K.G. to go back over there to that girl she was all over a few minutes ago.

"Go back and dance with that fat ass girl you was just with. Why do you always have to make a damn scene?"

"Charla, if you don't get your Iggy Azalea looking, black girl wanna be ass the fuck out of my face, I will slap the shit out of you."

Okay, this is getting crazy. We are going to get put out of the club if Shy has to come over here to deal with this nonsense.

"Slap who? Me? Bitch, bring it!" Charla says, stepping up in K.G.'s face.

"K.G., you better not be fucking with Charla, and you damn sure better not put your hands on my sister or else, bitch, we're going to roll up in this club tonight," Michelle says, stepping in between Charla and K.G.

"Fuck both y'all bitches!" K.G. says as she grabbed me by the arm, pulling me from the dance floor.

I see Michelle taking off her earrings, and I snatch away from K.G. and tell her to chill out. I walk over to my sister and tell her it's cool and I'm okay. I also tell Charla to stop following K.G. up. I introduce Charla to Mel-G and ask him to keep her calm for me. Michelle asks me if I'm sure I'm okay and if I want her to go with me, but I tell her that I am good.

I walk over to K.G. and tell her that she really needs to

grow up and stop acting so damn childish and possessive all the time. "Where is your little friend that you were just with a few minutes ago? Why are you always trying to shine on me? You are not my girl anymore, and I can do whatever I damn well please. I hope you know that Mel-G was about to knock your crazy ass out!"

"And I would have shot the shit out that nigga too," she says, patting the waistband of her pants, where I assume she has her pistol cuffed.

"Where are you taking me?" I ask her while trying to keep up with her as she pulls me off the dance floor and through the club.

Before we get to the door, a little skinny dark haired chick with dreadlocks starts running in our direction, followed by some fat girl in spandex pants. Who the hell wears that shit to a club? Better yet, who the hell is still wearing spandex unless they are at the gym working out – which is obviously a foreign place to her since she is shaped like a perfectly round ball.

"K.G., I am telling you right now, I will shut the whole club down if one of your bitches tries to play me in here. If you can't handle your females, I will. I didn't come here for this shit tonight. Why don't you just let me go on about my business, and you do you."

"You ain't going no motherfuckin' where. Are you crazy, girl? Don't play with me, Rocky. Not tonight!"

I can see that she is serious, and it also appears that she has more going on with her than she is telling me. She looks really stressed, like she is going through it.

"I need you tonight, Ra'Quelle. I need to talk to you, need to be with you."

The eyes are the key to the soul and your eyes don't lie. I can tell that she is in a bind or something. I can't let her deal with it alone. I will always be a sucker for this girl.

"Okay, baby. Handle your business or whatever you have to do with that chick, and let me tell Charla and Michelle that I am about to leave. I'll give them the keys to my car so that they can get home."

I don't have to go all the way back into the club because they are right behind me with their shoes in their hands, looking like they're really ready to bring the drama.

"I tried to keep them inside the club, Rocky, but they wasn't even trying to hear me. It was either fight them or let them go. Since I don't hit women, here they are," Mel-G says.

I think he secretly wants to see a good fight. I doubt he even tried to keep them in the club. He probably told them to go kick her ass.

"I'm straight, y'all," I tell them as K.G. walks up behind me and puts her head on my shoulder.

"Bitch, you gonna make me kill you about my sister. You must be one pussy-eating bitch. That's just why I don't do women right there. You have a lot of shit with you, K.G., for real. Look how you got my sister out here dealing with your bullshit. I'm telling you that the head must be blazing!" she says more to the small crowd than to K.G.

"Yeah, you damn right, you already know what it's hitting for." K.G. laughs at how pissed Michelle is, pulls me closer to her, and bites me on my neck.

I ask Charla if she's straight to drive. I don't bother to ask my sister because she is feeling mighty good right now, and I do not want her driving my car. Charla assures me that she's straight to drive, so I hand her the keys to the car and tell her that I'll call her when I'm ready for her to pick me up.

"Take care of Mel-G. That's my homeboy, Charla, and he's good people."

"Oh, trust me, I will take damn good care of this fine ass man."

As soon as I turned around to walk towards K.G.'s motorcycle, which is parked at the front door, I see her going off on the little chubby girl who was trying to follow her from the club a few minutes ago.

"As long as they keep that bullshit amongst themselves, it's all to the good. My only concern is you!" Michelle says very loudly.

The chubby girl with the spandex pants attempts to turn

130

around and walk towards me. I put one foot out in front and lean back on my other leg with my hand on my hips. I watch this funny looking chick, and I know damn well she does not really want to run up in my face.

"I hope that little fat ass bitch knows that I will beat the breaks off her and not think twice about it," I say to no one in particular.

K.G. grabs her by the back of her hair and snatches her backwards. "What the fuck do you think you're doing? Why do you keep playing yourself? Why the hell are you following me? I told your ass I was 'bout to leave."

"Leave to go where and with who, her? Who the hell is she anyways, K.G.?" Chubby looks like she's about to cry.

"Why do you keep asking me who she is when you know who she is, Amber? You know good and damn well, who she is. That's Ra'Quelle, my wifey for life. You know that shit, so why you trying to front like you don't?"

"What?" the chubby one yells.

"We go through this all the time, you know what it is. You keep asking me where I'm going and I have told you repeatedly, I'm about to take my wife home with me!"

I think my eyes are deceiving me as I watched the spandex girl grow some big balls as she hauls off and slaps the shit out of K.G.

Oh, boy, it's about to go down. I don't even think about trying to stop K.G. because I know that my effort would be futile. When she is pissed, that's just that. I hope she don't do anything drastic. K.G. just stands there looking down at the ground and for a minute. I start to think that she might let the little girl have a pass. She has her hands on her hips and starts to smile.

Just when I really think she might let it go, she draws back and punches the girl in the face so hard that Mel-G yells, "Damn!"

She doesn't give big mama a chance to fight back before she's hitting her in the face repeatedly and cursing her out at the same time.

"Bitch, you knew what it was from day one. Now you wanna put your nasty filthy hands in my face like you run shit. The only reason I even fucked with your trifling ass in the first place was to get the connect from your brother. I'm done with your fat ass, I've got my own connect now. You know you was never really my girl. Look at you out here looking stupid as hell in spandex pants. You lucky I ever fucked with you in the first place!" She keeps talking and hitting her.

After she beats her for a minute or so, Mel-G intervenes. "Yo, dude, stop before you hurt shorty for real. You bout to catch a case."

I see that the chick can't fight back, and I begin to feel sorry for her. Nobody should get beat like that. "Baby, stop, please, that's enough. You're gonna kill that girl. Come on; let's go before somebody calls the police!"

I step over the girl, take K.G. by the arm, and pull her towards the bike. As we're getting on the bike, I look at Chubby and wink my eye. I wave at her as K.G. does a complete donut and burns rubber out of the parking lot.

Chapter 13
Can't Let Go

Riding on the back of the bike with K.G. was always an experience. She rode like a fool sometimes and scared me to death. When she pulled into Waffle House parking lot, I was happy to be get a break from the way she rides. I told her that I was still full from Ruby Tuesday earlier, so she just got her food to go.

I stayed outside and smoked a Newport. I heard loud music, but I didn't see a car or truck in the parking lot playing any. *Damn, who's knocking like that?* I wondered.

Low and behold, a silver 2014 Lexus truck with a chromed out kit, beating Tupac's "Shed So Many Tears" so hard that my chest vibrated. Who else but Da'quan? I smiled from ear to ear because he was just the man I needed to see. It felt like fate was on my side.

He exited his car thugged the fuck out. Black Dickie shirt and pants with a white wife beater under the Dickie shirt, black and white Dodgers cap and all black Jordans that didn't look as if they have ever touched the ground.

"S'up, Ra'Quelle? You smiling at me like you want me or something. Shit, you know that you can always get it. We can leave right now while ol' girl in there getting waffles!" He smiled, revealing diamond and gold fronts.

"Quan, I was looking for you. I have a business proposition for you. Come over here and let me holler at you."

He complied and I started talking as soon as he was close enough to hear me. "I need some cash real quick. I've got some problems I'm dealing with and I need to come up quick, you feel me?"

"Yeah, I heard them boys trying to do you something. What's good though? What do you need for me to do?"

I told him that I had a list of ten cars and I needed him to make that happen. I also informed him of the locations and the times the cars would be there, so it should be easy to find them.

"Day, if you can get me all ten cars in the next week, I'll pay you forty thousand dollars." That leaves $60,000 for myself, which is pretty damn good seeing as though all I had to do was put the list together and find a sale.

"No problem, Rocky. Give me the list, and I'll get on it ASAP. You know if it drives, I can get it. I've got a spot out in the country where I can park them until I have them all. I'll call you when the list is complete."

Day was my nigga, for real. He never asked any questions, no hesitation or nothing. He just agreed to help me out, and I loved him for that. When the business talk was over, he just stood there, staring at my cleavage, and licking his lips. I could tell that he was getting his nerve up to say something crazy.

"Shit, if you show a young nigga some love, I'll have those cars by tomorrow night! You know that I have been waiting to holla at you for a minute, Rock. I've been in love with you since I was just a jit," he said, trying hard to put his mack down.

"You still are a jit, nigga!" K.G. yelled, walking up behind Da'Quan. "How old are you?"

"I'm seventeen, K, but that don't matter. My dick still hangs long and goes deep. Too bad you can't say the same," he shot back, looking very confident.

"I don't need no dick, nigga. I ain't a man and I still keep my baby coming back. Ain't that right, ma?" she proclaimed and playfully slapped me on my ass before she smiled devilishly at him.

"Y'all nasty for real. I don't even want to know. Anyway, I've got you on that, Rocky, and I'll be in touch very soon."

"That's what it is," I said as I watched him take a seat at the counter. He was one cool ass little dude and I knew for a fact he was going to be hell when he reached full gown status.

"What's all that about?" K.G. didn't wait before asking what we were talking about.

"Don't be all in my business. I don't question you about how you handle yours, so please respect your boundaries." I turned my nose up at her and rolled my eyes as if she was getting on my nerves.

She playfully mushed me across the face. "What the hell ever, Rock. Let's go. You are going to make me kill you yet, just keep fucking with me, and see!"

I couldn't help but to laugh because I knew that she was playing. Well, at least I hoped that she is.

The whole ride to her house, I wondered how to tell her that I'd decided to marry Donnie. How would she react? Would she cry? Did I have to fight this girl or something? Would she try to shoot me? Should I give her some pussy before I tell her?

Maybe I'm just paranoid. She may not even flip out. One way or the other, I had to tell her the truth. I always kept it one hundred with her. I was so deep into my thoughts that I didn't even notice that we had arrived at her house.

K.G. turned around to look at me. I guess she had wondered why I hadn't moved off the bike since she couldn't get off before me without me falling. "Damn, ma, what you doing, back there sleeping?" she asked.

"Almost," I lied as I got off the bike.

We walked up to the door and she opened it and stood aside to let me enter before her, always a gentleman. She went over to the stereo to go through her CD collection until she found what she was looking for. "Always and Forever," by Heatwave was the song that she settled for.

After coming out of the kitchen, she handed me a drink and sipped on her own bottled water. I scanned her apartment and realized that she hadn't changed anything since the day I left.

The three-piece green and burgundy chairs with the oversized pillows and the glass and brass tables were still in the same spot we put them in. I bought all of that stuff when I first started getting big credit limits on the cards. We decorated her place together. At one point, I was just about living here. I was so in love

135

with her there wasn't anything that I wouldn't do for her.

She was really there for me when I was going through all of Donnie's bullshit. Damn, I really didn't want to hurt her, but I knew that there would never be a real future for us. That was just a fact that we both had to face and deal with.

"What do you want to talk to me about K.G.? What's going on with you?"

She never made eye contact with me. She just kept rubbing her bottle of water. I figured it couldn'tbe good.

"What are you doing, are you alright?" I questioned.

"I was out shopping for groceries today, and I saw Zay and your boyfriend at the store. Donnie looked mighty happy. He didn't see me, but I watched him and I must say he looked like he was on top of the world. I know that look and I know that it comes from being in love with someone so deeply and completely that it fills your whole being."

"I felt like that had everything to do with you, so I just wanted to know what was up and see where your head is at. I love you with all my heart, Rocky, but I also know that when I hurt you, I opened the door for him to come back into your life. I take full responsibility for that. I just want to know where I stand."

I didn't say anything immediately because I wasn't sure where to start. I knew that this day would come, but I just didn't think it would be this hard. I really didn't even want to have this conversation with her.

"Rocky, you have been avoiding me for a minute, not answering my calls and the whole nine. It's time to stop running and tell me what's really going on, so I will know what I need to do and how to conduct myself."

I took a deep breath and tried to keep the tears from falling. "K.G., when I'm with you, we always have a good time. I can talk to you about anything, and you have always been there for me. You spoil me rotten and even though you did your shit, I have always known that you love me. I love you too, but, baby, we were doomed from the start because I got with you for the wrong reasons. I was hurting and I used you to make it all better, then I fell in love with you."

"You will always, and I do mean always, have a place in my heart. I just need more than you can offer me. It's not just about me, you know. I have to do what's best for Zay as well. He deserves to be happy and to have a normal family. Donnie asked me to marry him, and I said yes. We both are getting out of the game and are gonna start living the right way. We've decided that we don't want the streets to take us away from our son. This street shit can only end three ways. You get out and live your life right, you go to jail or prison, or you end up dead. Those are the options. I'm choosing to quit while I'm ahead. If I can get past this fed shit, we are going to give it a chance and see if we can make it work."

I had no idea what type of reaction she would have; perhaps she would hit me. I knew I didn't want her to see my tears, so I held my head down, closed my eyes and waited for the aftermath.

Her reaction was not what I had expected. Gone is the angry, aggressive person I just saw thuggin' at the club and before me stood the compassionate, tender woman that I fell in love with the first time.

She lifted my head and gazed into my eyes. "I love you, and I'll be here for you no matter what. Whenever you need me, or whatever you need from me, it's done. I will wait for you, Rocky. I ain't gonna try and keep you from doing what you feel you must. Just know that I will be here waiting for you to come back home. I know that you will come back because with me is where you are destined to be."

I smiled at her response and expressed my love for her. I almost felt at peace because I wasn't gonna lose someone who was very dear to me. I slapped her on the butt and I told her that I was ready to go to sleep. I had a lot to do in the morning.

"Sleep? Sleep?" she asked me, cocking her head to the side. "Who said anything about sleep, where are you gonna get some sleep at? Just because you're about to leave me and break my heart by marrying ya' baby daddy, don't mean that you're not about to give me some pussy tonight. Don't make me beat ya' ass and take it girl!" She laughed and led me into the bedroom.

When I came out of the bathroom, K.G. was already undressed and sitting on the bed in her red and white Tommy Hilfiger boxers and a wife beater. The only light in the room came from two candles that she had burning on each nightstand. K.G. stared at me for about two minutes without saying anything. She just smiled and I was starting to think she wasn't going to talk to me.

"Take your clothes off for me," she finally said, giving me that smile that turned me on because I knew she was thinking dirty thoughts. At first I didn't move, I just stood there and thought to myself, *Donnie will kill me if he catches me here.*

"Take your clothes off for me baby and let me look at you please Ra'Quelle."

There was something about her that made all of my common sense go right out the window. In my heart, I knew that the only way I would ever really leave her alone is if she decided that she was going to stay away from me and she let me go, other than that, I didn't see it happening. My attraction for her was too strong, the love I had for her was too intense… like I was seriously in love with that girl. As if she were reading my mind, she got up, walked over to me, and ran her hands through my hair.

She kissed me softly, took my hand into hers, and said, "Ra'Quelle, what we have is real boo, but we will never be able to fit in this world like a normal couple. Society will never accept it for what it is. I can only marry you and give you my last name in a few states. You deserve to have the whole family thing and Zay does too, and as much as I hate to admit it, Donnie really loves you and he's a good dude. Trust me when I tell you that he is the only one I would ever consider giving you to. All I ask from you tonight, is to just let me love you one last time. I promise from here on out I'll keep my distance and I'll only come if you need me."

She kissed me again, except that time she kissed me with passion and a purpose.

"Do you love me Ra'Quelle?" she asked.

"Yes, I do."

I couldn't hold the tears back, so I didn't even try.

"Take your clothes off for me ma," she said and walked over to the bed to watch me undress. I pulled off my heels one by one, unzipped my pants and slid them down my thighs to step out of them. I took off my jacket and threw it on the chair; lastly, I unhooked my bustier one hook at a time. When I stood in front of her in my underwear, I was glad that I chose the sexy white lace thong set.

"Turn around for me baby."

I turn around slowly and once my back was toward her I glanced back over my shoulder at her.

"Come here baby," she commanded.

I went over to her and stopped in front of her; she grabbed handfuls of my ass and kissed my belly button.

"Ra'Quelle, you are so beautiful, I could look at you forever." I blushed and thanked her. She slid her fingers in my thong and gently pulled them down so I could step out of them. I breathed deeply and gazed into her eyes as she raised up off the bed; her eyes piercing my soul with desire. I wondered if that moment would really be the last time that I would be with her. I began to get emotional, so I turned away.

"Come here baby," she said, pulling me back into her embrace. She just held me for a long time, running her hands up and down my back. K.G. pulled the covers back on the bed and instructed me to lay down on my stomach. She straddled my back, poured warm lotion over my shoulders and back, and began to give me a deep massage. She continued to confess her love for me and that she was definitely going to miss me a lot. She reassured me that everything would be alright and that she'd always have my back. I closed my eyes and finally relaxed for the first time since all that crazy shit started. Once I became completely relaxed, she stopped and I rolled over onto my back. She leaned over me and kissed my neck, taking her soft wet tongue, and made a trail over to my ear. She slowly stuck her tongue into my ear and added just a little pressure. A moan escaped my mouth because my ears were a very sensitive spot for me and she knew that better than anyone. My breathing became more rapid as she massaged my breasts, flicking her fingers across my nipples making them harder instantly while she tongue fucked my ear. I felt my pussy getting wet and I tried to squeeze my thighs together to relieve some of the pressure. K.G. started to gently bite and suck on my neck and lick my shoulders. I just wanted to scream as I grabbed her by the back of her neck and whispered her name. She licked her way from my neck to my chest, down to my nipples making my body shiver in excitement. My eyes rolled back in my head when she took my nipple into her mouth and flicked her tongue across it. I could feel that sensation from my nipple through my stomach down to my pussy. She took turns licking and sucking my nipples one at a time, then both of them were in her hands, licking them at the same time. I could feel her bite my nipple and I responded by screaming out her name, "K.G., oh K.G.," I repeated while trying to maintain my composure. She released my nipple and came up to kiss me. I could have sworn I could taste fire and ice in her mouth as she wrapped her tongue around mine and sucked it for dear life. She sucked my tongue, my lips, and then my tongue again. She kissed my tears away and told me not to cry because she understood the way I was feeling.

"K.G., I love you so much, I love you," I confessed to her as she laid her head on my stomach and I could feel the wetness from her own tears. I ran my hands through her braids and tried to remember everything about that very moment because it may have been the last. She slide her knee in between my legs and put pressure on my clit, I felt my internal temperature rising and held my breath. She raised up on her hands and kissed my stomach, my sides, and my thighs. She used her tongue to create trails all the way down to my ankle and worked her way back up again. She slowly kissed the inside of my thighs. My pussy started thumping like some twelve-inch sub-woofers, my breathing increased as she sucked the inside of my thigh, circling her tongue around at the same time. She took her fingers, started at the crack of my ass, and ran it all the way up to the tip of my clit. That shit felt so damn good, she knew exactly how to touch my body. She looked up and gave me that mischievous smile that she was infamous for and slowly stuck two of her fingers inside my pussy. The way she felt inside of me was enough to make me yell. She removed her fingers and stuck them in my mouth and made me taste my own pussy juices off her fingers. She kissed me and sucked it all back out of my mouth. My body felt like it was on fire and I tried to be cool about what was happening, but I wanted her mouth on me and I needed it sooner than later or I was gonna explode. K.G. looks up at me, licks her lips, and says, "You know I love you right?"

I didn't answer her immediately because my mind was on something else.

"Kiss it for me baby please," I begged her.

"Tell me what you want me to do Rocky," she replied.

"I want you to kiss it for me baby," I said, anticipating what I knew was coming.

"You want me to kiss it like this?" she stated as she made her way down between my legs where she parted my lips with her tongue. I let out a breath I had been holding forever and my knees got weak. I stretched my legs straight out on the bed trying to control the situation.

"Un-un, no baby don't play with me girl. Let me get at my pussy like I want to," she said as she put her hands under my ass and lifted me up to meet her mouth. My legs wrapped around her neck and she devoured my pussy with an intensity that was unmatched. She tasted my pussy slowly from the bottom to the top and back down again where she placed her tongue into my opening that received her with gratitude. I wondered how she could get her tongue to be so hard; I would swear that it touched all my walls. She continued to tongue fuck me and I threw my soaking wet pussy in her face. She took her tongue out and inserted it back in again. She moved from my pussy and across my asshole in one swift movement. She locked her mouth around my ass and started to suck it until I screamed out her name, "Oh Kandace, yes baby yes!"

Just when I couldn't take anymore, she stopped, took her hands from under me and she blew on my pussy. I shuddered and my knees began to shake; I couldn't even think straight. She positioned herself on my side so that she could see what she was doing. She opened her mouth and closed it around my clit and nibbled on it very gently with her teeth before starting to suck on it. It felt like half the air had left the room, the only thing I could concentrate on was the small space between my legs. I needed to cum but I wanted the feeling to last forever so I tried to hold back. She locked her mouth over my clit and began to pull it back and forth between her teeth, she inserted her thumb in my pussy and her middle finger went inside my ass. She worked them both in a motion that was like opening and closing her hand. I felt my clit swell in her mouth, she pushed her thumb deeper into my pussy and the juices drizzled down her wrist, "Oh shit please" I whimpered out loud, no longer trying to hold anything back.

She pushed her thumb as far as it would go and she moved her middle finger forward in my ass and held it against her thumb which was deep inside my pussy. She released the lock she had on my clit and started to lick it faster than I thought was humanly possible. I screamed as my cum rained like never before. I came like a mad women, arching my back and bucking my ass so hard I almost fell off the bed. I had her head held in a death grip between my legs and I yelled, "Oh Kandace, oh my God, oh shit, I'm cumin."

I came for what seemed like an eternity and when it subsided, she removed her fingers from my pussy and kissed it. She went back to my love box and sucked the rest of my nut out. I shivered and moaned laying there unable to move. I pulled her up from between my legs because I couldn't take any more. I kissed her sweet lips and licked my love potion from around her mouth.

"I will ALWAYS love you!" I said to her lying beside her grinning like a Cheshire cat.

"I love you too ma, but did you call me Kandace, did you really call me by my government name? Damn, I'm doing it like that?" she teased me as I pulled the covers over my head and tried to hide from her.

"I'm sorry baby, I'm just teasing you. But for real though, you still got that blazing ass wet pussy, damn girl, I came twice myself!"

She pulled me into her arms and I lay my head on her chest and listened to her fast heartbeat. I gazed into her face and we talked for the rest of the night until I fell asleep and dreamed about what could never be.

"Stop calling my motherfuckin' house!"

I woke up to K.G. screaming into the phone. I assumed she was talking to her friend from the club last night. I opened my eyes and she was leaning against the dresser looking at me with her

142

arms folded against her chest. She tossed me the phone and motioned for me to speak into it.

"Hello," I said, trying to sound sexy and sleepy at the same time.

"When I catch you bitch, it's on!" Chubby cried into the phone.

"Catch me, what do you mean catch me? I ain't running boo-boo, you saw me last night didn't you? And I'll make damn sure you see me again," I laughed into the phone. I put the phone on speakerphone, threw the covers off me, spread my legs wide open, and used my right hand to open my pussy up so K.G. could see all of it.

"Damn baby, you have the prettiest pussy I have ever seen!"

"Do you want to taste this pussy baby?" I asked loud enough for old girl to hear me.

"Hell yeah, I want to taste it again," she said and walked over to the bed.

"I'm a kill you bitch, K.G. you better not touch her, I'm gonna fuck you up K.G. I promise you that," I could hear the tears in her voice.

"Touch her, shit you late bitch, I been in this pussy all night and I'm about to get back in it right now. BYE bitch."

K.G. laid on top of me and kissed me. I asked her if she wanted me to hang the phone up. She told me, "Good morning my love."

"Good morning K.G," and with that being said, I hung the phone up.

"That fat bitch gonna kill you when she catch you," I teased as the phone began to ring again. I kissed her and got up to go take my shower. On the way to the bathroom, I glanced over my shoulder at her and just shook my head.

"You are something serious, girl!"

Chapter 14
Plan B

After I got dressed and grabbed me a bowl of Frosted Flakes, I called Charla to come get me. She arrived shortly thereafter looking radiant.

"Damn, girl, Mel-G putting it down like that? You look like you had the time of your life!"

Charla gleamed, "I did, girl, and I'm going back for more. He is still at my house. He told me to tell you what's up, and he'll be hollering at you later."

"I know that's right!" I said and proceeded to drive her back to her house.

"Where is Michelle?" I asked.

"She hooked up with Shy's homeboy and they at the hotel. You know Michelle ain't about to take no nigga to the crib. She don't play that shit at all!"

"True, true," I agreed, thinking about how funny my sister was when it came to dealing with the opposite sex.

I could count on one hand the men that she had been with that she allowed into her home. She was quick to bring them to my house for inspection. She knew I could spot a lame ass man a mile away.

I told Charla about the crazy call this morning and we shared a laugh about it. I said that I would call her later when I dropped her off and then headed back to my house to change clothes.

I called Shy and asked if he could meet me at my house so that I could talk to him. He informed me that Sasha had the truck and for me to swing by and scoop him up. I agreed and let him know I'd be there in a few.

I showered again and changed into something real quick. Nothing special, just some Michael Kors jeans, and an Ed Hardy t-shirt.

I jumped into my car and cranked up the volume on the stereo. Listening to Mary J. Blige always put me in a good mood, singing about life being just fine. Since I had to pass the jewelry store on the way to get Shy, I decided to stop in and get my ring.

I walked into the store and was greeted by a very handsome Italian looking man, who was impeccably dressed in an all-white Armani suit that appeared to have been cut specifically for his body. He was a very good-looking man. I smiled and introduced myself.

"Ah, Ms. Summers, it's a pleasure to finally meet you. I have been waiting for you to come in to shop with me for some time now. I assume that your presence here is because you have accepted Mr. Benton's proposal of marriage. That's absolutely wonderful, dear!"

He waved his hands around the room as if he were testifying in church and that confirmed for me that that man was gay. Oh, well, to each his own had always been my motto.

I listened as he continued his performance. "I am called Jaque', and it will be my pleasure to serve you. Do you have any idea what kind of ring you are interested in?"

"No, I'm not sure. First of all, how much money did he leave for me to shop with?" I asked him, suddenly coming up with a plan to get some extra cash in my pocket and throw the feds off my trail.

"Well, price is not of importance here, Ms. Summers," he started before I cut him off.

"Look, Jaque' or Jack, whatever your name is."

"It is Jaque'," he corrected me, not at all intimidated by my attitude. So I switched the game up on him and approached him from another angle.

"Do you make commission off of each sale here or are you a salaried employee?" I inquired.

"It is salary with a commission bonus off of each sale," he advised me, and the look in his eyes let me know that I had piqued his interest.

"Okay, listen, I have another man that wants to marry me, and he wants to purchase an engagement ring for me as well," I said untruthfully.

"Oh, you're naughty little girl. Two men? Oh, that must simply be delightful!"

"Yeah, it is. Now, if you'll tell me how much money Mr. Benton left here with you, I'll tell you what I have in mind."

I watched him and gauged his reaction and saw a slight smile tug at the corners of his mouth. *Got him*, I thought to myself.

"Well, Ms. Summers, Mr. Benton left twenty-five thousand dollars in cash for your ring, and he left instructions for me to give him a call if you should see a ring that you want in a higher price range."

"How much money do you stand to make if I buy a ring for that amount?"

He broke into a huge smile, showing thousands of dollars of dental work. His teeth were almost perfect.

"My commission is twenty percent, so I will collect five thousand dollars," he said looking at me expectantly.

"Okay, girlfriend, so how much would you make if I bought a ring for seventy-five thousand today?" I added the today part to let him know that I was serious about doing business with him and not just running game.

Mr. or Ms. Cool – whichever he wanted to be known as – actually lost a little bit of that suave attitude and almost stuttered when he answered. "Why, Ms. Summers, I'd take home fifteen thousand dollars if you spent that much. That added to what we already have, my dear, would be enough to pay for Tomas to get pregnant and we could start the family that we always wanted. We have been saving up for this for a long time and that would be enough to have the procedure done. It costs a little over a hundred thousand dollars, you know." His eyes begged for me to make it happen.

What damn procedure, I wondered, and who the hell was

Tomas? That sounded like a man. I didn't give a damn how much money they had, or how many rings I bought. There was no way that a man would get pregnant and have a baby.

But that wasn't my concern. I was concerned with making that sale happen and using the American Express credit card that I had stashed in my wallet. The AMEX card was issued in the name of one of the men whose identity I've never used, but the card was mailed to my home address. I knew that Agent Garcia or Agent Wells would be able to get the receipt, and the signature would not match any of the ones that he had in his possession.

I was also one hundred percent sure that punk ass Jack or Jaque', or whatever the fuck his name was, would be more than willing to make sure they knew who used the card once they come to investigate.

Since my signature on that receipt wouldn't match the rest, they would have no way to prove that I used the rest of the cards. They would have to go with what they could prove, which would be that I used that one card. I'd give them that one card to charge me with in order to divert their attention from the hundreds of cards I'd been using. I was hopeful that that would be enough to stop them from digging in my business so much.

I smiled when I thought about how smart I was. It looked like I was going to be taking one for the team anyway; but just one, no more, no less.

"Okay, Jaque', why don't you show me what you have in the seventy-five thousand range, and instead of you calling Mr. Benton for the difference between what he gave you and what the ring costs, I'm going to charge the full amount to my other boyfriend's Amex card. You can just return the cash that you have for payment from Mr. Benton to me, and everyone will be happy. I'll have some extra cash in my pocket, and you and Tomasena can have a baby." I smiled at him because I knew that I said the name wrong.

"His name is *Tomas*, Ms. Summers, not Tomasena." He shook his head as if he'd wondered how I could be so stupid.

He led me over to the glass case where the rings were in the price range we had discussed. I chose a 7.5-carat D class diamond ring in a platinum setting. I patiently waited while Jaque' went to the back to retrieve the cash from the safe. I handed him the black Amex card, and we both waited for the card to be approved.

When the register printed out the receipt, that completed the $75,000 transaction. I was very excited when I heard the machine spit the receipt out. It was music to my ears.

I made sure that I used a distinct handwriting that was different from all the rest. I placed my new ring on my left hand and wished Jaque' luck on his mission to become a dad or a mom, whatever role he wanted to play. I told him that it was nice doing business with him and strolled out of the store feeling on top of the world.

INDICTED/*Keisha Monique*

Chapter 15
Mo' Drama

I arrived at Shy's house and blew the horn twice. He came out looking just as good as he did last night, only dressed down. Instead of a Ralph Lauren suit, he was wearing dark blue Polo jeans and a jacket with a collarless shirt. He had on all white high-top A-1's that I would bet were his very first time wearing them.

"What's up, Ra'Quelle?" he asked upon entering my car.

"You," I said while pulling out of his driveway.

"I heard about you having those women fighting over you out in my parking lot last night. You carrying it like that, Rock?"

I laughed at him because I thought he was trying to chastise me.

"Shy, you know how I do it. K.G. will always be my boo and her little fat friend just was caught up in her feelings, that's all. I didn't initiate the drama, but I did end it when I felt the shit was getting out of control. You can't just slap people in the face and not expect to get hit back. She better be glad she hit K.G. and not me because I probably would have shot that big bitch, for real!"

Shy laughed. "You are crazy, Rocky."

"You think I'm crazy? Crazy is running behind somebody that don't even want you, that's crazy."

When I turned onto my street, I instinctively looked for the police. I didn't see any, so I continued on to my house. Who did spot knocking on my door was Peanut with his crazy ass. I pulled around to the back and walked around to the front door.

"Peanut, why are you over here knocking on my door when you know I'm not home?"

INDICTED/*Keisha Monique*

Before he could answer, Michelle opens up the door.

"What the hell are you doing in my house, Michelle, and how did you get in?" I asked her wondering what her foolish ass was up to. She better not have had no damn man in my house.

"I didn't want Jamal to know where I lived at, so I got him to drop me off over here this morning. I can't let him know where I live at since I don't really know what kind of dude he really is," she said, looking all crazy like I had asked her a dumb ass question or something.

"You fucked him, but you don't know what kind of dude he is?" Shy questioned her.

"Yeah, duh!" she responded and turned around to go back into the house.

"Michelle, I'm a good dude. Can I get some pussy too?" Peanut yelled behind her.

"Yeah, right," was her response as she kept it moving.

I introduced Shy to Peanut, and he told me that he was looking for me to inform me that the feds were down the street earlier watching my house for about an hour.

"They didn't come all the way into the neighborhood. They just sat up there by the corner and watched your house for about an hour or so. I tried to call you, but you know you change your cell phone number so much that I can't keep up."

"Damn, that's what's up. Good looking out. I'll call your phone later on so that you'll have the new number on your caller ID." Shit, I was thankful that I wasn't home. I damn sure didn't feel like dealing with nor did I have the energy for the feds. "Rocky, look, if you have got all kinds of dead bodies buried in the backyard, you might want to go ahead and handle all that. I don't want to be on CNN trying to explain to the whole country how I could live next door to a serial killer and haven't noticed something was out of place. They might think that I helped you, and I ain't going to jail because you are the black widow reincarnated. I have an image to uphold and live up to. I don't even know why I'm over here talking to you now. They're probably up the street in a tree or something watching us right now with some high-powered long-range binoculars. I ain't with all of this shit. I'm a holla

152

at you whenever you parole out." With that said, he lit his blunt and blew the smoke in my direction, then walked to his house.

"Baby girl, you sure do surround yourself with some strange characters," Shy reminded me while he watched Peanut go into his house trailing a thick cloud of smoke behind him.

"I know, right? Peanut is good people though. He's just out to lunch a little more than most."

I opened the door and was surprised that Michelle didn't lock it when she closed it. I peeped into the guest bedroom, found it empty, and wondered where the hell she was.

"I don't know why you're looking for me in the guest bedroom. I ain't no guest. I'm in your room and I'm not moving. I am about to take a nap, so if y'all were planning on trying to get it on, take that shit somewhere else please." She slammed my room door and locked it. I didn't have time to deal with her crazy ass any more than the feds.

I took a seat beside Shy on the couch and bared my soul to him. I told him everything that was going on and shed a few tears while he held me in his arms. The peaceful moment was interrupted by the ringing of the phone and I just sat there looking at it.

"Rocky, do you want me to answer that?" Michelle yelled from the bedroom.

"No, let the machine pick it up!" I yelled back.

The phone stopped ringing after five rings, and the machine clicked on. I heard my voice filling the room. "Sorry I can't come to the phone right now, but if you leave your name and number, I will get to you at my earliest convenience. Have a blessed day." *Beep.*

"Ms. Summers, this is Agent Wells. Please give me a call as soon as you get this message. You can reach me at 803-777-8989. I have some new information that I wish to go over with you. Please don't try to avoid me, Ms. Summers. If you work with me, I'll try to work with you. We need to set up a time and place to meet, either at your home or my office. We need to discuss your impending indictment. Thank you very much."

I sat on the chair and more tears began to fall from my eyes. Michelle stood at the door looking at me and for the first time since I don't know when, she didn't have any silly shit to say. The only word that left her mouth was, "Damn."

She looked at me and asked if I was okay. I just nodded my head.

"Don't worry about her. I've got her. She's going to be alright." Shy held my hand in his and smiled at me. I was very grateful to have a friend like him. I always felt safe around him and I knew that he would always help me in any way that he could.

"Okay, ma, look, it is what it is. You ain't going to let this get the best of you. From what I can see, your cypher is tight. You don't have a whole bunch of useless people in your business. I don't really hear your name ringing in the streets like that, so any information that they have to use against you is gonna come from the banks that issued the credit cards and the stores where they were used."

"They're not gonna have any witnesses that are willing to testify against you in hopes of lowering their own offense level, you feel me? This is not going to be like a drug case where you have niggas that you dealt with five and six years ago trying to do paperwork on you 'cause they got caught up and are too scared to bid. Your whole case is going to be based solely on you and your home girls, but most likely you. They will use whatever they can to link directly to you and then try to get you to tell on yourself about the rest. I know you ain't falling for that dummy move, right?"

I nodded my head in agreeance and attempted to get myself together. I thought I just really needed to hear that to get it to become reality for me. I believed that I'd be able to deal with this a little better. I hoped the trap I laid for them would work.

"Ra'Quelle, you're going to be alright, queen. Your essence is pure, and your heart is full of love and not malice. You have a good spirit and you're always helping other people whenever they need you. I'm sure that your higher power will shine down on you with divine favor. You might have to go and lay down for a couple of months, but you're not going to do any real time. They're not that hard on white-collar crimes anyway. You might do a little Martha Stewart bid, so be easy, and stop crying. You're a trooper; you'll be okay."

"Trust me; the god knows what he is speaking upon. I wouldn't sell you no dreams if I thought that you were going to go to some serious jail time. If I felt like you needed to dip, I would make that happen for you. But this shit ain't even nothing to be trying to run from. You are straight. Matter of fact, I'm going to give you my lawyer's number, and I'm going to call him and give him a heads up about you and your situation. He's going to charge you a pretty penny, but I promise you that he is the one you need for this case. He'll walk you out of there with the least amount of time you can get, and if it's at all possible for you to bounce on this case, he is definitely the man to make it happen. I trust him with my freedom at all times, and you see I am still out and about."

I wiped my eyes. "Shy, are you sure they're not going to lock me up for ten or twenty years?"

"Hell no. Not unless you really are over here killing people and hiding them in the back yard like your crazy neighbor seems to think that you are," he teased me.

We sat around laughing and talking about a few more things. Shy would always be my dude. I wished he had been this calm and intelligent when we were together, maybe we could have made it happen. I guess what they say is true, with age comes wisdom.

Michelle came out of my room freshly showered and wearing some of my clothes. I started to trip out because she had chosen a Donna Karen sweat suit that I'd never worn before and she had on the brand new Air Maxes that I bought yesterday. I let it go though only because she was my sister, and I knew that she wouldn't trip if I ever needed to raid her closet.

I decided to change purses, so I took my pistol out and put it up in the closet. I didn't want to be strapped in case I ran into those people. That would be another charge that I didn't need.

I went back into the living room and sat on Shy's lap, facing him. I put my arms around his neck and thanked him for always having my back and being a true friend.

We all left the house together and got in my car. We laughed on the way taking Shy home about how crazy they were acting in the parking lot of the club. Of course, Michelle sparked a blunt.

I had to park in front of his house because his B.M. had the truck parked in the driveway crooked, so it took up all the space. We saw her unloading groceries from the truck. I told Shy that I would call him later about something I was trying to put into motion because I needed his input. By the time he opened the car door, Sasha was right there showing her ass and acting ignorant.

"Nigga, where the hell have you been? And I know damn well you don't have that same bitch from last night parked in front of my house!" she yelled, having a tantrum.

"Fall back, girl. First of all, this is not your house; this is my house. And don't worry about where I've been. I'm a grown ass man, and I don't have to answer to anyone."

I could tell that she was pissing him off because when he got out of the car, his whole body language changed.

"Rocky, call me later and let me know what's up. I'll be waiting on your call," he said and closed the car door.

"That bitch better not call your damn phone. I'll beat that bitch's ass!" she screamed.

Before I could get a chance to warn her that I wasn't gonna be too many more bitches, Michelle had already jumped out of the car. I watched as she came out of the sweat suit jacket in one fluid motion and stepped towards Sasha. "Who the fuck are you calling a bitch, you tramp ass hoe? I know damn well you ain't talking about kicking my lil' sister's ass!"

"Fuck you and your sister, bitch!" Sasha yelled, getting big balls because she was standing behind Shy.

I jumped out of the car to get Michelle because I had other shit to do, but while Sasha stood behind Shy popping her gums, Michelle just walked up to her and punched her in the face, knocking her off balance. She hit her one more time, and when Sasha didn't fight her back, she followed up with a flurry of blows that rained down on that girl with no mercy. Once Sasha hit the ground, that was all she wrote. Michelle stomped her ass for real.

I was about to kick her in her face when Shy picked me up and carried me back around to the driver's side of the car. He sat me down and looked in my eyes. "Rocky, stay here, stop it now.

156

Stay here and let me go get your sister before she kills that damn girl!"

"You better not put your hands on my damn sister, Shy!"

"Come on, Rocky, be for real. I'm a man. What I look like trying to fight your sister or any other women, for that matter? You have enough shit to deal with right now. Let this shit go, please!"

He looked back to make sure that I hadn't moved, and he went over to pull Michelle off Sasha. I noticed that he didn't seem in no big rush to get over there. He was probably tired of her mouth and glad that she was getting her ass kicked. He grabbed Michelle around the waist and lifted her up off Sasha, who was still laying on the ground threatening to fuck somebody up.

"When bitch, when?" I yelled as Shy put my sister in the car. She was surprisingly calm for someone who just beat the hell out of somebody.

I looked her over to make sure that she didn't have any mark or scratches on her that would make me try to kill that bitch for real. When I saw that she was good, I could hear Shy yelling to me to take her home and call him later. I blew the horn and pulled off, laughing.

"Girl, you are off the damn chain," I said to Michelle. "You know that I can fight my own battles, but I appreciate you looking out for me."

"Man, fuck that gutter bitch. Besides, that's what sisters are for."

I looked over at my sister and watched as she re-lit her blunt and blew the smoke out of her nose.

INDICTED/ *Keisha Monique*

Chapter 16
Nobody Move, Nobody Gets Hurt

With my focus on getting my money right, I called Jay-Baby and told him that I had some work that I wanted to get rid of. He asked me how much weight I had and how much I wanted for it. I explained to him that all of the pinching I had done off each package of Donnie's had come up to about 75 ounces, which was slightly more than two kilos.

"Damn, girl, how the hell did you do that without Dee noticing that shit and taking your head off?" he questioned, obviously surprised with the weight I was trying to sell to him.

"I just took a little bit at a time every time he got a new package, and I'd replace it with Isotol."

He laughed so hard, I had to pull the receiver away from my ear. "Girl, you are something serious, Rocky, but you are my girl so I fucks with you. How much do you want for all that shit?"

Being that I wasn't really a drug dealer, I wondered if he would try to beat my head in on the prices. It couldn't go down like that because although I didn't sell the actual drugs myself, I was around the sales every day. I knew that the price of coke had gone up because of the drought and things like that.

"I don't know, what do you think is fair?" I asked him, giving him the chance to either play fair or pull a bitch move.

"I'll give you sixty thousand for both if you want it today. If you can wait a few days, I'll be able to add about five thousand to that."

I was very pleased with his answer and glad that he didn't try to get over on me. It's always nice to know that the people you call your boys are willing to play fair with you and respect you enough to keep it one hundred.

"Naw, I need the money like yesterday, so I'll take what you've got. What time do you think you will have your money right?"

"Shit, what time you gonna have the work. My money stay right!" he reminded me with confidence.

"Okay, let me get back to you at around five or six. As soon as I get this shit together, I'll call you and tell you where to meet me, okay?"

"That's what it do, Rocky. Just be careful out there."

"For sure." I ended the call, looked over at Michelle and told her to shut up before she could even say anything about me creeping Donnie's dope. I didn't want to hear nothing she had to say.

Jay-Baby was my boy and all, but sometimes cocaine can make people do some strange things, so I called Shy to see if he would ride with me to meet Jay-Baby. I didn't get an answer so instead of leaving him a voice message, I sent him a text message. I explained to him what I talked to Jay-Baby about and asked him if he thought the price was straight.

I told him to call me ASAP to let me know if he could meet me at the carwash on Farrow Road around five. I hoped to hear from him soon. I called Jay-Baby back to tell him to meet at the carwash around 5:30. I needed to get there before him so that I could check everything out and make sure there were no police in the area.

"Ra'Quelle, so you're a drug dealer now. You think that Donnie ain't going to find out that you're out here selling damn two kilos of his fucking dope? Are you crazy, Rocky? What's wrong with you?"

Michelle's rants were really getting on my damn nerves, for real. I knew what I was doing.

"Chelle, listen to me, okay? I don't give a good goddamn if he finds out or not. What is he going to do to me? And, technically, I didn't steal the dope because he has always told me that what's his is mine," I recited, laughing like I thought the shit was a joke or something.

"I'm glad that you think this shit is funny. Well, I love you to death, but I ain't trying to get killed with your ass, and trust me, Donnie is going to kill you when he finds out. Sis, he is going to fuck you up, and there's nothing for me to say about it 'cause you are dead ass wrong. Anyway, I'm about to get started on those cards that you gave me and I've got some other business to handle, so drop me off at the house so I can get my car and go to work. I'll be calling to check on you so answer the damn phone, and please be careful. The federal guidelines on a drug case are way higher than they are on a credit card case, so please keep that shit in mind and don't end up getting a life sentence behind some shit that you ain't got no business doing."

Keep it in mind? How in the hell can it not be in my mind? The feds are trying to watch my every move and now I have to risk my life and freedom to handle this shit, I thought to myself. I let her have that moment to feel righteous and everything. The only reason I didn't curse her ass out was because I knew she was speaking out of love. She was really concerned for me and not just trying to be sarcastic.

"I promise I'll be careful. I've got this, and it's only a one-time deal. I'm not trying to make this a habit."

When I pulled up in front of her house, she turned around in the seat and looked at me. She asked if I wanted her to ride with me because she would if I needed her to.

"No, boo, I'm good. I'm going to run over to my storage unit real quick and grab this shit and head on over to the spot where I'm supposed to meet him."

"Okay, just be careful and call or text me when you're done to let me know that you're okay."

She got out of the car and waved as I pulled off bumping Tupac's "Me Against the World."

****

I parked the car in back of the rental storage building and went into my storage unit. I had so much stuff in there, and I needed to get rid of some of it. I have a complete living room set in there, and I had it arranged just like it would be at home. I went in there sometimes when I needed a real quiet place to think and not have to worry about being disturbed.

There were also piles of clothes and shoes in there. Some of it was mine, but most of it was Isaiah's. I thought to gather up some for that dumb ass girl that called my house about Donnie that time. Call me crazy, but my heart went out to people with kids that couldn't or wouldn't take good care of them. I couldn't in good faith throw these things away. I mean, there was thousands of dollars' worth of really nice clothes.

I sat down on the couch, reached under the cushion beside me, and pulled out my hard times stash. I had twenty names and social security numbers of people who had at least an 825 credit score or higher. I kept those in case I needed to get some American Express cards and have them sent to the house overnight mail. I could get over a hundred thousand in a couple days with those, but they were only for an emergency, like if I needed to go on the run.

I would have to use my real ID to go into a bank to be able to draw out that much cash, so I would set up an additional card to the account in my real name. I'd definitely be charged with using those cards, so that was only a last resort.

If the feds indicted me and wanted to give me 10 years or more, I would be out and they would have to do their jobs to catch me. I had never touched any of those socials, but I did check their credit report every so often to make sure that their rating was still up to par.

I glanced over at the picture on the end table and saw Isaiah in his football uniform after they won the Pee Wee League Super Bowl. Damn, I seriously was in need of a reality check. I had a son who counted on me to be there, to be his mom and to love and guide him on the right path. I really needed to keep my promise to him. That lifestyle was fabulous, but at what cost though?

I had to swallow that I was being investigated by the Secret Service and that I could very well go to jail. This was some very serious shit. Before I got too paranoid or emotional, I went over to the washer and dryer that I had before I did the upgrade. I kept it because it was only a couple months old when I replaced it, and there was nothing wrong with it.

I opened the dryer and pulled out some of the clothes that were in there. I found the coke just as I had left it. I grabbed one of Isaiah's shoeboxes and took the shoes out; some black high-top Forces that I didn't even think he had ever worn. I put the dope into the shoebox and placed that box into a Footlocker bag.

As I prepared to walk out of the storage unit, I heard a lot of noise and commotion outside. Aww, shit, all I need is for Agents Wells and Garcia to come running up in here. I would never see the light of day again.

This was that shit I be talking about. I was scared as hell which is why I didn't sell no damn drugs in the first place. I sat the bag down to go see if I could make out what all the fuss was about. All I could see were two white men having a tug of war over some yellow, silk ugly ass curtains.

Now, ain't that some shit? The way they were yelling and carrying on, I thought they were gay. Like they either went together or were in the middle of a break up or something.

"Let your new man buy you some window dressings, Tomas. These are mines, and I will not allow you to disgrace our memory like that. You will not have them hanging in your little sex den!"

"I have just as much of a right to those curtains as you do, girl. You're just mad because I have a new man. I have a real man, and we are going to have a baby soon and get married!"

The other guy said, "Well, he is butt ugly from what I can see. He kind of reminds me of Alf."

Wait a minute; did he say Tomas... and having a baby? Aww, shit, I wondered if that was Jaque's boyfriend Tomas? Ain't too many punks running around Columbia talking bout having no damn babies and shit. What are the chances of that?

Anyway, I'd heard enough. I grabbed my bag and a couple of more things that I had been meaning to run down there and get. I pulled the door down on the unit and locked it. I made sure the coast was clear before I got into my car and hauled ass.

I drove over to the car wash real early. It was only about 4:30 or so I figured I might as well clean the Caddy up and get it right since I'm there. Too bad that place was deserted because I

163

would have most definitely tried to get a nigga to wash it up for me.

My mind kinda of drifted off thinking about all kinds of shit as I washed the car and sang, "Hail Mary." I stood up to get the Armor-All out of the trunk and observed an old school box Chevy pull into the car wash with about three or four niggas in it. I didn't really pay it that much attention until they pulled up behind my car, blocking me in.

Shit didn't feel right. Something was about to go down and I didn't think it was going to be in my favor. Two men stepped out of the car and they were both dressed in all black. The first dude went around and stood between the driver's door and me. The second one approached me and looked around cautiously. He finally turned his attention to me and asked, "Aye, little momma, what's happening?"

I looked at him and I could tell that he was high off lean or coke because his eyes were all glassy and his pupils were dilated. I couldn't believe this was happening to me. Damn, shit was crazy.

"Not much, trying to get this car cleaned up some. I was just about to head out," I said, answering his question as best as I could without panicking and letting him see my fear.

"Okay, ma, check this out," the dude closest to me says, pulling out a chrome .45 caliber pistol with a pearl grip on it. He didn't point it at me directly, but he slid one in the chamber just to let me know what's up.

I looked behind me at the other man, and he was there holding two twin nine millimeters. I didn't know what the hell to do. *Lord, please don't let these niggas kill me out here.* I tried to figure out the best recourse for me to take or how to approach these men.

"I don't want to have to put you to sleep, but don't fuck with me 'cause I will if you push me. This ain't personal, sweetheart. This is strictly business, and I am dead ass serious. I will put a very sizeable hole in your fucking head if you try to play me. I'd hate to fuck up that pretty face of yours, but how you leave out of here is up to you, sweetness. We both know why I'm here. In case you're not sure, let me tell you. You've got two kilos of cocaine,

164

and I need to get that up off you. We can do it the easy way or the hard way, but either way, the dope is going with me. So, it's up to you to choose life or death. Either way, I am getting what I came for." He pointed the pistol slightly at my head.

All that talk about your life flashing before your eyes when in a near death situation was bullshit. I wasn't thinking bout nothing except making it out of that situation so I could raise my son, and how I would find that bitch ass nigga later.

I stood there, trying to commit to memory everything about that dude. I didn't want to miss nothing. I couldn't believe the shit was going down like that in broad daylight. I didn't want to give him the dope, but it wasn't like he wouldn't find it anyway, but I wasn't willing to die for it. I had way too much to live for. There was no way for me to make it out of this situation except to give him what he wanted.

I would make it my business to find out who they are, but at that moment, I had to swallow my pride and stand down. The man behind me was moving and I felt like he was getting a little anxious or something. I turned around and got a real good look at him as well; looking for distinguishing marks or tattoos.

I turned back the other way and pointed through my back window. "It's in the Footlocker bag, inside the Jordan box on the backseat."

That seemed like the hardest thing I ever had to say. Shit was crazy.

"Alright, that's what's up. Now, you reach back there and hand it to me, and please don't try no super hero type shit. I am sure that you have your cute little pistol in your Gucci bag, but don't even fuck with it. Just charge this shit to the game."

He opened the back door for me to get the bag, so I reached in, got it, and handed it to him. He took the bag and waited for his homeboy to get to the car. Then he backed away from me, keeping the gun pointed at me at all times.

"Stay right there, shorty, be easy. It was nice doing business with you." He jumped into the Chevy and they peeled out.

I didn't move for a minute or so. My body was shaking and tears rolled down my cheeks. Though I was thankful to be alive, the raging desire for revenge burned within.

Suddenly, I became consumed with rage. "Fuck, Fuck, Fuck!" I screamed. I jumped into my car and sped away, leaving my cleaning supplies scattered everywhere. I picked up the phone to call Jay-Baby, but I decided against that because I didn't know who set me up.

As I drove down Farrow Road, my mind raced in a hundred different directions. Somebody set me up, and I wouldn't have peace of mind until I found out who did that to me.

I didn't really have any enemies. I always tried to play fair with everyone that I dealt with, so that shit really threw me for a loop. I only told a few people what I was planning on doing and the place that I was going to meet Jay.

I figured I'd wait before I called anyone to see if who'd be the first to call me. Jay-Baby should've been calling me from the car wash soon to see why I was not there, and if he didn't then that would only confirm that he didn't expect me because he already knew what went down. I couldn't call Shy either. I'm not sure that he didn't set me up, although I hated to think that way. I had to cover all of my bases until I really knew what's what. That shit was unfucking believable!

I drove a little further and then called the one nigga that I trusted with my life with. Frank Nitty answered the phone on the first ring as if he already had the phone in his hand.

"Sup, Auntie?" he answered.

"Nitty, I just got robbed at the fucking car wash! I am so not in a good place right now. I'm really buggin' the fuck out trying to figure out how this shit transpired. You know somebody has to pay for this shit for real."

I was shocked that my voice was alarmingly calm. I felt as though most of the tension had left my body and was replaced with adrenaline for payback. At that point, I was more angry than scared. I guess just saying it out loud had made it more of a reality for me making it easier to deal with.

"Oh, hell no, are you serious? Are you okay? Where are you at? Who was it, do you know them, where are they at? Come get me. I'm ready to ride on a motherfucker as we speak!" I could hear him chambering a round through the phone.

"Let me make a few calls and see if I can find out who knows what, and you do the same. I'll call you back shortly."

"That's what it do, I'm on this shit Rocky; I'm on it!"

Nitty hung up before I did and then I threw my phone on the seat, contemplating my next move. I couldn't even call Donnie and tell him that I got robbed for some dope that I stole from him in the first place. If I called him, it would be a straight dummy move; on top of that, I really don't want too many people to know what happened. That way, if some shit went down, I wouldn't have a million people in my business. I didn't want to worry about anyone going to the police or no shit like that because trust and believe; I would be handling the shit my way!

I ended up on the other side of town and pulled into the projects, hoping that I'd be able to find Da'Quan. Sure enough, as soon as I made the last turn before heading back out, I spotted his Lexus parked and he was leaning up against it talking to two little chicken heads from around the way.

I pulled up and got out of the car. Da'Quan dismissed the girls and waved them off with the flick of the wrist. I guess it wasn't the first time because neither of them asked any questions. They just smiled at him and moved on.

"Damn, Rocky, you know I'm fast with the car thing, but I ain't done with that list yet. I ain't that damn quick. Hell, I only got three of them, but give a nigga some time." He smiled at me and blew smoke from his blunt through his nose.

"Day, it ain't even about that bullshit. This is bout some other shit. I need to holla at you about your other pastime hobby, you feel me?"

"What the hell are you talking about, girl? What hobby, jacking people?" he asked while squinting at me through the smoke as if he'd been trying to add something up.

Before I could start to tell him about the robbery, his eyes suddenly got big and started pacing back and forth. "Oh, shit, Rock, was that you that just got robbed? It never would have crossed my mind to think of you because you don't be dealing with no work and shit. Well, not that I ever knew of. I heard about the

167

whole thing, pearl white Caddy, female, two bricks, and car wash on Farrow Road."

"They asked me if I wanted in on it, but you know that I don't roll with niggas like that. I do my dirt by myself. Damn, Rocky, if I had known that it was you, I would have at least given you a heads up if I couldn't steer them niggas in another direction and tell them to fall back. They just came through here. Did they hurt you? Are you alright?" he asked, scanning me from head to toe to see if I was good.

"I'm straight, Day, but I feel violated. I can't just let this shit ride like that. It ain't even about the work. Hell, I'm about to marry the big man on the block. That was just some shit I had stashed for a rainy day. It's the principle behind this shit. I don't fuck with nobody and you know that. I treat everyone with respect. I laid down my flags a long time ago, but this shit here, this ain't gonna do. I gotta see them bitch niggas and introduce myself properly."

I wasn't really mad, but I had to deal with it and let the cards fall where they may.

"This shit here ain't cool at all. They rolled up on me, jumped out the car and next thing I know, I got pistols pointed in my face and shit. I didn't know if them niggas was gonna burn me or what. What part of the fucking game is that? You know I have no respect for niggas like that. These streets done changed, and there ain't no loyalty no more, no code of ethics or nothing. Motherfuckers just greedy and grimy as hell. They gotta be taught a fucking lesson and I'm just the one to teach it!"

"Damn, that was some grimy shit," Da'Quan said, passing me the blunt.

I smoked with him and we stood in silence for a few minutes, each of us in our own thoughts and both of us knowing what the very near future held.

"Rocky, you are like my big sister or some shit. You always keep a nigga in check, and you have taught me some real life lessons. You have put more food in my mouth than them niggas ever will. You ain't been nothing but good to me. I'm with you on this thing; however, you want to carry it. You cool with everybody, and

168

you always looking out for people. They done fucked up now. You really didn't deserve that at all." Da'Quan stared dead in my eyes. The love this kid had for me really touched my heart. It felt good to know that my efforts were appreciated this much.

"Da'Quan, I know that you would never do me any harm and that you will ride for me too, but I'm going to handle this another way. All I need from you is the names and locations. I give you my word that nothing you tell me goes any further."

"I don't give a fuck if it does, Rock, them niggas get what they get. They played the game dirty, so they gotta deal with that and anything that comes behind it." He said with irritation in his voice, like I had disrespected him with my words.

"It was them niggas from Hendley Homes – Xavier, Wrenice, and Geronimo, that's who you need to see. Yeah, my nigga Eric put me up on that shit a couple hours ago. Them niggas just flew through here on the way to Rose's house. They are always there and they always together, ma'fuckers act like they fucking each other or something. I heard them say that they were going to cut that shit and cook some of it back. Man, this shit is crazy. Are you sure that is all that you need from me? Them niggas ain't nothing to sleep on. They keep them pistols on them, and they will rock you to sleep if you don't come correct." I could hear genuine concern in his voice.

"Thanks for the info and the warning, but I'm most definitely gonna come more than correct. Of that please have no doubt, Day. I ain't playing with this shit, not in the least. They ain't even gonna see it. I'm trying to change my ways and whatnot, but ain't no way in hell I can let this shit ride. I gotta handle my business. I gotta see bout these niggas ASAP. I have never done no petty ass shit like this to anyone and never would. I hustle for everything I have, and I'll be damned if some fuck niggas just gonna come take my shit. Naw, hell no!"

I smoked a little more of his weed to get my mind right. I told Da'Quan again how much I appreciated his help before I lit a Newport and hopped back into my car.

"I hope that you know that I appreciate you, Da'quan, for real. Finish that car list and get at me. Let's get this money, baby."

"I got you, ma. Holla at me if you need me."

Pulling out of the projects, I could see him in my rearview mirror standing there shaking his head. I hoped those niggas enjoy their riches because I was about to bring it. On my life, they were about to see a side of me that I let hibernate for a long time. I only hoped that they were ready because I was going to get mines.

Chapter 17
When I Ride On My Enemies

I tossed my phone into my purse and pulled out the cheap little throwaway phone that I used when I needed to talk about shit I didn't want traced or monitored. I called Charla on the phone that she had identical to mine.

Charla answered the phone immediately. "What's wrong?" she asked. She knew that since I'd called her from the secret phone, something was not right.

"I got hit. Some niggas ran up on me at the carwash and robbed me. I just left the hood, and I already know who they are and where they at!"

"Fuck! Oh, them bitches must be crazy or something. What we need? How far are we going with this, and how long before you get here to get me?" I knew she had a lot more to say than that, but even though the phones were throwaways, there was still some shit that you just didn't say outright over the phone.

"I need some heat that we can toss, a couple of them. We are going all the way, and I'll be there in about 45 minutes."

"It's done" is all that she said before disconnecting the call.

I don't know where or how Charla came up with the shit that she did, but when it was time to put her game face on, one crazy ass white girl. I was glad to have her on my team. I hit Nitty up and informed him that I was on the way.

"I'm ready. I'm shootin' hoops; you know where to find me."

When I approached the basketball court, I didn't even have to pull in. I saw Nitty running top speed. He was already halfway up to the street where I turned in. He had always been thinking ahead. We didn't need a lot of people to see us together. We had a pretty extensive history.

I thought back to the night that I first met him and took him under my wing. I hadn't started making any major moves with the credit cards yet. I had a small two-bedroom apartment with Donnie and Isaiah. Zay was about six years old, and I used to let him stay with my neighbor, Ms. Pandora, sometimes.

She was an older woman who didn't have any kids or family, and she enjoyed his company. She was kind of like a play grandmother to him. One night, it was time for me to go get him, and I decided to walk through the cut instead of driving my car. It was only about 9:30, and the weather was nice, so I walked.

I saw a couple of people standing in the cut, which was nothing strange being that it was a known dope hole and people were always in and out of there for one reason or another.

"How are you gonna ask me for more dope and you haven't paid for the dope I already gave you?" I heard some young boy in a red hoody say to the older dude he was talking to.

"Man, fuck all that. I'll pay you when I'm good and damn ready. You ain't paid your dues around here yet, young buck. All I'm saying is if you want to sell dope in this here cut, you gotta go through me." The older cat stood there sounding all cocky and pounding his fist on his chest.

"Go through you, huh?" the young jit asked, as if he were considering the statement.

"That's what the fuck he said, and that's what the fuck he meant!" another cat said, who I could see clearly was nobody but crackhead Larry, an old head from around the way that was known for bullying the younger ones into supporting his crack habit.

Without looking behind him, in my direction or around him period, the young buck reached behind his back under his hoody and pulled out a black .40 caliber pistol and shot the first dude in the face, making the back of his head explode. He didn't miss a beat, turned, and hit smoker Larry twice in the chest without any hesitation.

"Well, that is what the fuck I mean!" the young boy said,

and he hawked as if to get ready to spit on smoker Larry's lifeless body.

"Don't you do it, don't do that!" I intervened. "Keep your DNA in your mouth. You are about to solve this shit for the police before they even get here and get a chance to investigate."

He spun around and pointed his pistol at my face. I continued to walk toward him. I held my hands out to my sides.

"I wish you no harm, lil' man. In fact, I'm trying to save you from spending the rest of your life in prison or worse, death row. If you value your freedom, you will do exactly what I say and don't ask me no questions right now. Do you understand me?" I asked.

"Yes," was all the response that I got from him.

"Are you driving?"

"Yeah."

"Who's car?"

"Stolen," he said, looking at me like he was trying to get a handle on me and what I represented. He wasn't sure if he should trust me or not, but he really didn't have much of a choice. Well, he did have a choice. I guess he could've shot me too.

"Go get in the car and pull it as far in this cut as you can and pop the trunk."

He did as he was told, and I helped him load the bodies into the trunk of the car, which happened to be an old Buick Deuce and a Quarter.

He appeared to be unmoved about the fact that he had just shot and killed two people. That little nigga was a gangster for real. The only thing he asked was if the footprints could be a problem, something the cops could trace back to him.

"Don't worry about footprints and shit. So many people come through this cut every day that they will be overlapping each other anyways," I replied.

I reached for the car keys. I called Ms. Pandora and asked her if she wanted to keep Zay a while longer because I wanted to go out with my friends.

"Mercy no, child, I don't mind at all. I was going to ask you if you would leave him with me until tomorrow anyways. He's already had his bath and is in my bed watching cartoons. You go on and have a good time. Maybe you can try to make another little one just like him. That way we both can have one." She was laughing, but somehow I felt that she truly meant what she said.

"You go on and shake a tail feather. He's alright, honey."

"Thank you, Ms. Pan. You take care."

After I made sure my son was squared away, I called Charla, who was my schoolmate at the time. "Charla, what's up? I need to go to your daddy's farm."

I hoped that she was somewhere close and be able to meet us.

"For real? You are in luck too. My folks are out of town, and I'm not too far away from there myself. I'll leave the gate open so that you can get in. I'm in the truck, and I'll head on over there right now!"

Charla didn't ask me why, what happened, or nothing. She already knew what it was if I needed to go to her folks' place. She was always mighty damn happy when shit like this turned up. There was something dark and evil about my friend, but hell, there must've been something even darker about me since I was always the one needing to go out there.

On the ride out to the country, I asked the young buck about himself. It didn't really faze me that we were riding with two dead bodies in the trunk. I had been dealing with that type of shit half of my life. My dad was a cleanup man for a couple of the old school drug dealers in the hood. I had rode with him on many occasions to get rid of dead bodies and evidence.

"What's your name, son?" I looked over to the passenger side and found him watching me curiously.

"My name is Frank, but they call me Nitty. Like Al Capone's hit man Frank Nitty," he proudly told me.

"Where are you from? I always see you around, but I don't know who your family is or where you live."

"That's because I don't have no family. I'm my own family. My mom is always tripping, and she be fucking up her money getting high, so I had to start hustling to feed myself since I ain't old enough to work. Then she started stealing my packages and smoking that too, and I didn't' want to disrespect her 'cause she my momma, so I left. I been on my own for a minute."

He sat beside me with the weight of the world on his shoulders, but he won my heart when he said that he would never disrespect his mom, even with the foul shit she was obviously doing. I knew right then that he was going to be alright. I was going to make it my business to make sure he was alright.

"But I can take care of myself. I just have to work on my temper. I don't let nobody play me."

I watched him as he stared out the window. He never did ask where we were going. He looked vaguely familiar to me for real though. I felt like I knew this kid from somewhere. It didn't feel like he was a total stranger to me.

"Is your mother's name Treese? Does she live on the west side of Gozales Gardens?" I asked him, wondering if he was who I was thinking he was.

"Yeah, that's my mother's name. How did you know that? Who are you?" He looked over at me, probably wondering how the hell I knew so much about his personal business. I had to admit the lil' dude was thorough, for real. He had the potential to be the shit when he grew up, with a little bit of help and encouragement.

"I'm Ra'Quelle. I used to live next door to you on Johnson Avenue. I used to baby-sit you. You were one little hollering ass baby!" I said, remembering the little curly headed baby named Frank.

Wow, he had really grown up, and it was a shame to see that his mother was still doing the same silly ass shit she was doing when I lived next door to her.

"Small world, huh? Well, I am not a crybaby anymore. I'm a grown man now," he said with pride.

"I wouldn't exactly say that you're a grown man, but you're growing up the hard way." I laughed at him because of his temperament. "Nitty, I must say that even though you handle yourself very well in the streets, I think that you should take another route for right now. I am going to put you all the way in the game, and I ain't talking about the drug game. I'm talking about the game of life. You are going to go back home tonight. From now on, I'll

175

cover all your school clothes and supplies, and I'll make sure you keep a little bread in your pocket."

"I'll make sure that you have food in the house. Treese is not going to mess with your shit or else she is going to have to answer to me. You will go to school every day, and you will graduate high school. There ain't shit out here in these streets except the same kind of shit you found yourself in tonight. Please promise me that you'll use this opportunity to get your shit together and stay out of them corners and cuts. When you get your diploma and you're of age to decide what you want to do, then I will respect that, but a child should not have to hustle to eat. I'd be less than a mother – less than a woman – to leave you out here in the cold like that. Do you think you can handle that? Does that sound like a plan to you?" I asked him hopefully.

I wanted him to do the right thing, but at the end of the day, the choice was his. Wiping the tears from his face, he asked me why I would do all of that for him.

"I'm going to do that for you because you're a trill ass little dude, and I like the fact that you remain respectful to your mom. Also, I have a son myself, and I never know if the day may come when he may need some guidance and help from someone. Besides, if I can help you get rid of two damn dead people, why the hell can't I help you go back to school?"

He laughed at my humor, but he did agree to go home and go back to school if I helped him. We rode the rest of the way in silence, leaving each of us to our own thoughts.

I pulled up behind Charla's truck and got the packages out of the trunk. Damn, those people seemed to weigh more now than they did when we put them in. I turned my head to try and keep from looking at the one who was missing half of his face. I swear it seemed to me that Charla loved that shit a bit too much.

I couldn't let them see that that shit was about to make me hurl, so I thought about pleasant thoughts, and I was all too happy when they were in the 150 gallon drums filled with a mixture of lye and diesel fuel. My dealings with Charla taught me that there were no remains from a human body when you burned it in that kind of fluid, not even bones.

I took in my surroundings and once again was amazed at my crazy ass friend. "Charla, I really wonder about you and your family with this place out here in these bushes."

"Don't ask me no questions and I won't ask you any. That has always been our mantra. Let's not use tonight to change it because I damn sure don't want to know why we are standing here with two dead ass niggas and a lil' boy who can't even be 15."

"True that. I feel you on that one, girl."

After we watched that shit burn for a couple of minutes, Charla took the keys to the Buick and drove it down to the water behind a building. I assumed it was a shed. She drove the car as close as she could, and then she got out and let it roll the rest of the way into the water.

I was wondering how many cars had been fed into that lake never to be seen again. Or how many people had found them drums to be their final resting place?

I tried not to get blood and shit on my clothes, but it didn't work. Charla took me in the house and gave me a sweat suit to put on. I laughed as I thought that I wouldn't be caught dead in her damn clothes.

We drove back to the city in Charla's truck, and she took me to take Nitty home. I walked him to the door and waited until he went inside before I told his mother what the deal was. I didn't tell her what had just transpired, but I did tell her about the arrangements I made with him. I told her that I was going to make sure he got everything that he needed, and all she had to do was leave his shit alone.

I told her that if she needed a hustle every now and again to support her habit, she could come holla at me or Donnie, but if I found out she was stealing his clothes and shit to sell for dope, I was gonna beat her ass real bad. Treese was so happy to have him home that I figured they would be alright.

****

Nitty opened the door to my car and jumped in. We continued up the street before he spoke. "How are we doing this, Auntie?" he asked, pulling his pistol out and checking the clip.

"Damn, Nitty, you haven't even asked who it is yet," I said, looking at the tall handsome young man he had grown into. "That's because I don't give a fuck who it is. If it's my daddy, oh well, too damn bad for him. Motherfucker's about to go to sleep tonight, and that's all there is to say about that. I don't hardly play no games when it comes to you. I don't fucking discriminate. Whoever they are, they are about to catch it. You are the reason I breathe free air right now. You taught me everything I know, and you have always been true to me. I'll die before I let a motherfucker lay hands on you, Rocky, and that's my word!"

Nitty lit a cigarette and I watched him exhale the smoke. Yeah, I raised him well. He was my soldier for life.

"That's what's up, and you know that I feel the same towards you. You're my lil' dude for life. I found out that it's them niggas from 48 that we're looking to see."

"Oh, you mean Geronimo and his goons? That's what it do; they can get it too. I always knew that one day they would run up on the wrong one and somebody would lay their asses to rest. It may as well be me. They done did more than enough dirt."

For some reason, I wasn't surprised at how callously he spoke about killing. I taught him to feel only when it was relevant to his family or his inner cypher. Other than that, show no mercy. People take mercy as a sign of weakness. Then they'll try you, and you end up having to prove yourself anyway, so you might as well come out the gate hard and solve all that shit at once.

We arrived at Charla's house, and she came outside dressed like a middle class hooker. She had on skinny jeans made by Baby Phat that showed off her ass, a tight t-shirt with red and white stripes, and a black hoody that zips up the front. Added to that, she had black high heel leather boots and appeared ready to roll.

"You look just right for the part you are about to play. You must have read my mind. I need you to go up in Rose's house and cop some powder and find out who all is in the house. Try to use the bathroom or something. Just be sure that you know every one that is in that house. You can't be guessing on this shit, baby, 'cause this ain't play time. Then you come back out and let us know what's what. We're going to go in your truck because your tint is darker than mine, and they won't be able to see into the truck," I said, already thinking ahead and trying to cover all the bases so that any mistakes would be unlikely.

"Okay, I got you. What's up, Nitty? I see that you're still lookin' good as hell," Charla flirted with Nitty openly and without shame.

"Girl, if you don't sit your old tired ass down somewhere and leave him alone. Why don't you worry about who we are going to see or what even happened? Do you care to know?"

I asked her because from the time I first called her, not once did she ask me any questions. I really didn't think she cared just as long as she would have the chance to do something dark.

"Rock, I know all I need to know. I ain't fucking retarded. If you called me on the throwaway and you come here with Nitty, somebody has violated someone I care about, and they about to get dealt with. That's enough. I don't need names and references; this ain't no job application. I do not care about their personal history. I say fuck 'em all and let the Lord sort 'em out."

Wow! She was really thrown for real, but shit, she was my girl. I expected no less from her. At least I knew that she wasn't gonna freeze up on me. I trusted her with my life.

We got out of my car and Charla set a black book bag on the trunk of the car and pulled out two nine millimeter pistols and two 380s, and a sawed off shotgun that had a handle so short I could probably put it in my purse.

She had duct tape and some rope, as well as a small bottle of gas and a damn digital camera. I wondered what the hell she was planning to take pictures of. She wouldn't be taking no pictures where we are going that night. I had always heard that serial killers like to take little keepsake mementos and shit, but that was the kind of foolishness that would get you life when the jury came back after a very short deliberation.

"Charla, why the hell do you have duct tape and a camera?" I questioned, really wanting to know.

"Shit, I didn't know what you were planning to do. I thought that you might want to get medieval on their ass or something. I thought we could try taking them to the farm while they are still breathing and put them in the barrels like that and see how long they can last."

I watched her as she smiled, thinking about that little scenario she just gave.

"Yo, Auntie, where the fuck you find Charla at for real, yo? I gotta keep it real. She scares the hell out of me sometimes. The sad part is she is dead ass serious, ain't she?" Nitty asked no one in particular.

"Serious as hell." Charla laughed.

"Naw, home girl, we can't do it like that this time. It's too much of a risk. Maybe next time you'll get to do a damn science project with somebody's life, but not tonight, sweetheart. We're just gonna be in and out real quick and real quiet. All we need is the pistols, the gloves, and the ski masks. We're going to leave them right there with the burners. Do you have any hair spray?" I asked her, wanting to spray all of our clothes and shoes so that we can minimize any transfer from us to the murder scene, which is exactly what that place will be when we leave it.

"I'm on that too, Rock," she responded by pulling out a can of VO5 hair spray.

We sprayed ourselves thoroughly, hopped into the truck, and rode out.

Chapter 18
Rock-A-Bye Baby

I parked across the street and up a little bit from where Rose lived and where the niggas we looking for were supposed to be. I went over the plan one more time with Charla and she went over to the house. Nitty and I sat in the truck in silence, watching the house very closely. Charla comes out of the house and sat in the driver's seat. She informed us that Wrenice, Geronimo, and Xavier were all in the house. Rose wasn't home and there was nobody else there. They were all high as hell and really feeling sure of themselves.

"What took you so damn long?" I asked while I began to put my ski mask on.

"Well, hell, Rock, you said to check the whole house out, so I had to give that nigga Wrenice some pussy just so I could have a reason to go into the back of the house. They don't have but one bedroom, so I knew he would have to take me there to get some. I knew he wouldn't be able to resist all this sexiness." Charla looked at me and batted her eyes playfully.

Yo, she was really demented. We were about to murk all these dudes, and she done fucked one of them and laughed about it.

"You've been wanting to fuck Wrenice for a long time, huh, haven't you?" I teased her.

"And you know this is the truth. At least he will die a very happy man, and it's such a waste of some prime dick too!"

"That's cold, Charla, that's real cold," Nitty said, exiting the truck. We walked briskly to the front door and stood off to the side while Charla knocked. If somebody looked out of the peep-

181

hole, they would only see her.

She knocked on the door until someone came to see who it was. I heard them walk to the door where they must've been looking through the peephole.

"Aye, Wrenice, it's that white freak that just left here. She must be looking for you again." someone yelled from the other side of the door.

"Yeah, let my new boo in. I told y'all she would be back," the one I assumed to be Wrenice replied.

As soon as the door opened, Charla walked in and Nitty ran in right behind her with his pistol stretched out in front of him. He pointed it at the one sitting on the chair playing a video game.

"Get it off your mind, nigga!" Nitty said, walking in closer to the guy on the couch. Charla was already in the bedroom, bringing Wrenice out with her at gunpoint.

I never gave the one they call Geronimo a chance to move beyond the door before I had my pistol pointed in his face, damn near in his mouth. I kicked the door closed and watched to see who would move first.

"You's one dead ass bitch, you know that right, white girl? You fuck me and then turn around and try to –" *POP-POP-POP!*

"Shut your bitch ass up!" Charla says calmly, after she shot him three times in the face.

The gunfire must have scared Xavier because he started trying to cop a plea. "We ain't got no work in here, but I have money in my car that I will go and get for you. Just don't shoot me, please," he begged for his life and I looked at him without any compassion.

"Shut the fuck up, man," Geronimo screamed at him. "This shit is personal, not business."

I could tell he had already figured out what was what.

I pulled my ski mask off and smiled. "I'm glad that you remember me, Gee. You're a very smart man. It's too bad that you didn't utilize any of that earlier when you took my shit and put that pistol in my face. Didn't anyone ever teach you that you don't point your gun at a motherfucker and then let them walk away? Nine times out of ten, they are coming back to see you later. So you already know that I cannot let you walk out of here alive. I always cover my bases. We know that payback is a bitch, and today, I am that bitch!" I schooled him, looking in his eyes.

"I know how the game goes. I knew that when I got into it years ago. It is what it is," he said, trying to be a man about it. He closed his eyes right before I shot him in the chest and stood over him, putting one in his head.

I guess because of the way that .40 caliber pistols sound when they release the bullets, I didn't even jump when Nitty shot Xavier, even though he was standing right in front of me. That particular gun made a sound more like a metallic pop than a sonic boom.

I didn't feel any sympathy or remorse for any of them as I watched the blood drain the last bit of the life out of them. It had been a minute since I had to body a nigga, but not much had changed. I did what I had to do.

I knew that some people may have been able to just walk away from the whole thing and charge it to the game. Well, we all can see that I wasn't one of those people. I felt that if we lived by the gun, then we died by the gun.

I made it my business to deal with others on a level of respect, and I damn sure expected it back. Although I lived a criminal lifestyle, I still honored the codes of the streets.

This was the path that they chose for themselves, so I felt that they were the only ones to blame for their week getting cut short, for real.

Nitty didn't even blink when he shot Xavier. When I looked up, all I saw was blood running down the big screen TV that was still playing a Grand Theft Auto PlayStation game.

We all wiped the guns off even though we are wearing gloves. Can't be too careful. I threw my gun on top of Geronimo and headed to the door when Nitty stopped me.

"You want this work back, Auntie? This is most of it right here."

"Naw, leave that shit there. They already paid for it. Anyway, it will throw the cops off. They'll think it was probably a botched robbery," I said, trying to think ahead and look at the bigger picture.

"Shit, one brick is enough to throw them off. I'm taking the other one with me." Nitty smiled as he loaded the dope into the footlocker bag. He left his pistol in its place. *I should've checked his stash*, I thought.

We all turned to leave, and Charla dropped her gun on the way out the door. I was the last one out of the house, pulling my mask back down over my face before I closed the door. We walked swiftly back to the truck and rode out.

After giving Charla her shit back and telling her that I loved her and would get with her later, Nitty and I got into my car, and prepared to return him to the basketball court.

"Don't forget your pistol in the glove compartment," I told him, not wanting him to be without his heat.

"Never that," he responded.

I handed him a blunt and some of the wood I got from K.G. and told him to roll us something to smoke on.

We sat in my car and smoked one right quick. The weed calmed my nerves down, and I started to relax a little more.

"Be careful with that work too, Nitty," I said while reaching for the blunt.

"I will. Do you want anything back off this package?"

"Naw, that's all you. Dope is not my thing and after this shit, I don't want nothing else to do with anything that looks like cocaine. It's too much shit that comes along with trying to hustle this shit. You go ahead and do you. I'm straight. I know I don't have to tell you how to carry yourself concerning this situation."

"I got this, Auntie. I ain't no fool to be broadcasting our business. You just be easy and stay out of the way of them feds."

I dropped him off where I had picked him up and watched as he carried the Footlocker bag and returned to his car before driving off.

I love that lil' nigga, I thought to myself on the way over to Michelle's house. While driving, I began to think about my life and everything that had happened. That shit bothered me a little more than I thought.

This shit wasn't for me anymore. I had way too much to

lose. I considered getting out of this shit in every aspect. I truly thought about honoring that promise I made to my son. This was only a one way street and nothing positive would ever come of it.

I'd collect all the money that I had coming to me and holla at that lawyer Shy was talking about. After that, I was done; it was a wrap.

I might as well get ready and face the feds because I knew that they were not going to go away. Just before I arrived to Michelle's house, I saw Charla's name come up on the caller ID right before the phone started to play Eve's "Who's that Girl?" That was the ring tone that Charla assigned to herself on my phone. I answered the phone wondering what she wanted since I had just left her.

"Rocky, I almost forgot to tell you with all that shit that just went down. When I was in the house with Wrenice, he was bragging about a lick his sister Sasha had put him up on that had paid off like a motherfucker. He was trying to convince me that he could take care of me and let me have all the coke I wanted. By the way, what should I do with this coke I got from him when I first went in? And ain't Sasha that girl that your boy Shy goes with, who Michelle swung on earlier?" Charla asked.

My heart dropped in my shoes. I didn't want to believe what she just said to me.

"I don't give a damn what you do with the coke. Just don't forget you have it and be riding around with it in the truck. You can flush it unless you know someone that uses it. But yeah, that's Shy's girl. Are you sure that's what the dude said?" I asked, not wanting to accept the fact that someone very close to me had something to do with me getting robbed.

"I texted Shy and told him what I was doing. I asked him to meet at the carwash right before them niggas showed up."

"What?" she screamed. "Hell no, Rocky, we gotta go see that nigga too. He ain't that damn special. He don't get no free passes when it comes to shit like this!"

"Man, Shy is my dude and I don't even want to think about him in that manner. I can't even wrap my mind around that concept for it to be true. Shy would never put me in harm's way like that."

I was defending my friend because I refused to think that he was responsible for how they knew where I was and what I had with me.

"Stop thinking with your pussy, Ra'Quelle, and see this shit for what it really is. He is the only one that knew where you were going to be. Damn, think about it."

"No, I told Jay-Baby too. He was the one that was supposed to buy the shit in the first place."

I could tell that she was getting irritated at me for taking up for him, but I would take up for her the same way if the tables were turned. If I trusted you, then I trusted you without a doubt, and I trusted Shy. There had to be something that missing from the puzzle.

"Rocky, I guess you didn't hear me say that Wrenice said his *sister* put him up on the lick. He ain't say shit about no damn Jay-Baby, he said Sasha. Now you sit here and act like you're fucking retarded all you want. I'll call Nitty myself, and we will go do that nigga since you act like you can't seem to get your damn mind right!"

I understood her anger but still, I had to do this my way. I'd have to accept whatever came with my decisions, but at that moment, I wanted to talk to him first. I always followed my first mind, and it usually led me the right way.

"Charla, let me get with Shy and see what the hell is really going on. If that is truly the case then it is what it is. I'll call you back shortly. Just chill and don't blow a fuse before then. Go get yourself a drink or something. I've got this."

I hung the phone up before she could try to change my mind. I saw that it was almost 10:00 and that Jay-Baby had been blowing my phone up all evening. I forgot that I turned the volume off. I called him back and he answered with a slight attitude.

"What's up, Rock? Why the hell you sell me that dream and have me riding around with all that cash on that hot ass side of town looking for you? You never showed up, nor did you call to tell me anything. I didn't know what the fuck to think. I thought all kinds of crazy shit waiting for you. I stayed there until I got paranoid and said fuck that shit, and left!" he said, talking damn near a hundred miles an hour.

I wondered how much to tell him, but it sounded as though he was telling the truth and I usually know bullshit when I hear it.

"Jay, I got robbed at the carwash before you made it there. Three niggas rolled up on me and drew down on me. There was nothing for me to do except give them what they wanted. I didn't call you because, to tell the truth, I didn't know if you had set me up or what. While you were having crazy thoughts about me, I was having even worse thoughts about you!"

"Damn, Rock, are you alright? Are you okay, did they hurt you? Do you know who those niggas are or where they be at? You know I will handle this shit for you. What kind of fuck ass nigga robs a woman with a gun? That's some bitch shit if I ever heard of any."

I could tell that he was pissed, but I'd already decided not to tell anyone what went down.

"Naw, I don't know who it was and I've never seen them before, but I would know them if I saw them again. I did get a good look at them. I guess I'll just have to charge that shit to the game." I said, hoping to convince him that I was going to leave the shit alone and chalk it up to a loss.

I really didn't want too many people to know what went down. If they found out I know who did it, they will automatically know it was me when the people turned up dead later on.

"Damn, ma, I'm sorry that you got caught up like that. Are you sure you don't need me for anything?"

I could tell that his sincerity was genuine and I assured him that I was straight.

"Well, holla at me if you need anything."

"I will," I said and hung up the phone.

Chapter 19
Street Justice

I called Shy and he answered the phone. "Where are you, Ra'Quelle? I've called you ten times and it went straight to your voicemail. I came up to that carwash and didn't see anyone there. I didn't know what was going on. What's up? Did you take care of that or what? I was really starting to get worried about you," he claimed.

Why would he get worried? Did he think that the people he sent to rob me had hurt me or something? Naw, that shit didn't even sound right. I couldn't believe that he would do that to me. He was probably worried because I wasn't where I said I was going to be and I wasn't answering the phone.

I had to trust my heart on this one, and my heart was telling me that Shy was still my friend and he hadn't ever sold me out like dat. I didn't feel that he was trying to play me because he had no reason to do some sheisty shit like that. I knew for a fact that he ain't broke and he had access to all the work that he could want. His brother was still doing it big even though Shy had retired. So I trusted him and decided to talk to him.

"Where are you at, Shy?" I asked.

"Just leaving the movies with ole' girl out here on Forest Drive by Walmart."

"Where is Sasha?"

"She's in the store getting something for Bre'shaun to drink. Why, what's up?" he asked. I guessed he wanted to know what was up with me asking all those questions.

"I called you and you didn't answer, so I sent you a text

message. Why didn't you answer or call me back?"

"I was in the shower when you called."

"You didn't have your phone with you? Where was your phone while you were in the shower?"

I tried to piece the shit together because every inch of my being told me that Shy didn't have anything to do with what happened.

"I didn't hear the phone, sweetheart. I left it in my room in my pants pocket. Why all these damn questions, Rocky?"

"Where was Sasha at that time, Shy?" I asked, ignoring the question he just asked me.

"She was in the house cleaning up. Once again, why all the questions, Rocky? What are you leading up to? What in the hell is wrong with you, what's up?" he asked sounding like he was getting irritated from my not answering him.

I figured that I may as well clue him in because I had to resolve that issue. I trusted him, and if I'm wrong, it ain't gonna kill me, but it damn sure might be the cause of his demise.

"Okay, Shy, check this out. I wasn't at the carwash because I got robbed. After you didn't answer the phone, I decided to go by myself. I went early so I could try and make sure no police were there and see if it was cool to make the deal. Some boys from 48 in a box Chevy rolled up on me and took my shit. They put pistols in my face and threatened to blow my fucking head off if I didn't give them the two kilos I had with me. They knew I was going to be there, and they knew exactly how much cocaine I was going to have with me."

I didn't say anything else after that. I waited for his response which would tell me all that I needed to know. If he was guilty, then it would definitely show. Damn, I hoped that I wasn't wrong about Shy. He meant a lot to me and if I was wrong about him, I would question how many others I had been wrong about? That would mean that I would have to reevaluate my whole team because if my judgment was off. That scared me.

His response immediately brought my attention back to the situation at hand. "What?" he yelled into the phone so loudly that I almost dropped it. "What? Man, what the fuck? Are you kidding

190

me? Goddamn, girl, what the hell happened? Who was it? Where the fuck they at? Where are you?" Finally, he paused and gave me a chance to answer.

"I'm okay. I was just shook up a little. That shit really caught me off guard. I wasn't expecting nothing like that to happen. I made a few rounds, and I found out who it was," I said, testing the waters.

"Who was it? Tell me who did that to you!"

"It was Wrenice, Xavier, and Geronimo," I informed him and waited to see how he would respond to that news.

"Whoa, whoa, whoa, baby girl! What did you say, come again?"

"You heard me right the first time, Shy. I didn't stutter." I got pissed because he acted like he didn't want to believe what I said. Hell, I was the one who couldn't believe it.

"Wrenice as in Sasha's brother, Wrenice?" I guess he tried to process what had transpired. He probably didn't want to believe that his baby mama almost cost me my damn life.

"I don't know of another one. Do you? That's the only fucking nigga I know named Wrenice. Now, you tell me, how the fuck did they know who I was and where I was going to be? Not to mention the exact time that I was going to be there and what I was gonna have in the car with me. Coincidence? I doubt it very seriously. It seems a little peculiar to me. What do you think?" I asked sarcastically.

"That bitch! That motherfucking bitch must have went through my phone while I was in the shower. That dumb bitch is always going through my phone. Usually I lock my shit whenever I set it down. Man, this shit is crazy. She must have been feeling some kind of way because I was with you, and then Michelle kicked her ass when y'all brought me home. Damn, Rock, I am so sorry about that shit. I can't begin to tell you how sorry I am. You know I'll replace or pay for what you lost, but later for all that. How do you want to deal with Sasha's sorry ass? What about them niggas? You want to go pay them pussy ass niggas a visit?"

I *knew* Shy was my boo. I knew I was right. He didn't do that to me! I was so thankful because I really valued his friendship.

It would have really hurt me to know that he could betray me like that, and it would've hurt me even worse to have to do something to him. That was the very reason why I didn't fly off on wild assumptions before getting my facts together.

"Naw, we don't need to deal with them. They're straight."

I didn't say any more about them, and he damn sure didn't ask. I'm pretty sure he knew exactly what I meant. I felt so much better knowing that he didn't betray me over no petty shit like coke. I knew I meant more to him that two lil' funky ass bricks.

"I'm glad to know that me and you are still me and you. I do need to see Sasha though." My mind was focused on dealing with that trick.

"Say no more. What do you want me to do? You want me to bring her to you? Where do you want me to bring her?" he asked, sounding just a bit too willing to bring her to me.

I really didn't think he liked her ass too much. He was happy to see her get beat up earlier and to be so willing to deliver her to me. He knew what time it was when he brought to me.

"Bring her to the gym at Hyatt Park, and wait for me to get there. I'm on the way. And don't tell her why she is going to the park. I want to be the one to tell her what the deal is."

"I'm about to be on the way as soon as she comes out of the store, but please remember that the baby is in the car, Rock," he reminded, showing love for the child that probably wasn't even his.

"I feel you, Shy. I got this. I would never put a kid in harm's way. I have a child of my own, you know me better than that."

I hung up the phone and started to think of a way I could handle this bitch and not have to take her life. Knowing her though, it's gonna end up with her and her brother being together after all. She didn't have any consideration for my life when she sent those goons after me, and for fucking what? Because she thought I was fuckin' Shy or 'cause Michelle got in that ass? That still wasn't no reason to do no grimy ass shit like that to anybody.

Those niggas could have killed me. That robbery could have went a whole lot of other ways. What if I didn't give up the dope, or what if I didn't have it with me? What if I had left it at the house or something? Those niggas wouldn't have believed that. They would have thought I was trying to play them and probably would have blown my damn brains out right there or kidnapped me or something. I reached over in the glove compartment to see if my brass knuckles were still there, and they sat just where I left them.

As I pulled into the park, I saw Shy and Sasha sitting on the same bleachers I sat with Zay yesterday when I talked to him about the shit that was going on. This was the confirmation that I needed to come out of the streets and get my shit together. I assumed the baby was in the car sleep since I didn't see him. I wondered why Shy hadn't drove the truck. He very rarely rolled around in his Benz because he liked to stay low key.

I could see Sasha's face frown up when she recognized my car pulling into the park. I put the car in park and pulled my hair back into a ponytail. She watched me most likely wondering what the hell she had gotten herself into. I slid my hand into the brass knuckles and got out of the car.

"Shy, I know damn well that you didn't bring me out this bitch at this time of night to play games with your lil' girlfriend!" Sasha said.

Her behavior didn't match her words. She tried to play that hard role, but I could tell that she was scared and attempted to put up a brave front. Good for her. Maybe she would go out like a trooper after all.

"You still coming out of your mouth sideways, huh, Sasha? It seems like you just like calling me out of my name, don't you?" I grilled as I walked toward her, still trying to figure out if she would live or die that night.

"Fuck you, bitch, I'm tired of your shit. Shy, let's go, take me home. I don't have time for this shit."

She still fronted like she was bout that life, but concern was scattered across her face. My mind was made up and she had just sealed her own fate. I had planned to give that bitch a pass on the strength of Shy and for her baby's sake, but her ass couldn't stop running her mouth and coming at me sideways, even after all that she has done. Fuck that. This bitch wasn't going to live to see the sunrise.

193

"Fuck me? Fuck me, Sasha? Really? You got the fucking nerve to stand there and say fuck me?" I laughed, deliriously but not because anything was funny, rather her bitch ass had a lot of nerves. "No, fuck *you*, Sasha. Fuck you, you stupid bitch, and guess what? Fuck your brother, Wrenice too. May he rest in peace!" I yelled.

"What? What did you say? What do you mean, rest in peace?" She started to cry. I guess she finally understood the point of my visit.

"Just what I said, hoe, though I doubt if his dirty ass will ever be able to rest in peace with all the dirt that he has done. Either way, his ass is done, boo. Did you think I was just gonna lay down and let them niggas get away with that shit? You had to have known that you were sending those niggas to die, bitch. Don't act like you don't know about me."

"I...I don't know what you're talking about," she stuttered.

She couldn't hide her fear anymore, and long gone was all that attitude she had been exhibiting earlier. I could see the fear in her eyes, through the tears and all.

"Sure you do, Sasha. You saw my text on Shy's phone, right?"

Her eyes grew wider as she realized that I knew everything, but she really started to panic when she noticed Shy walk away towards his car to leave.

"Where are you going, Shy?" she asked.

"Aye, look, you made that bed for yourself, so now you have to deal with it. You made this shit what it is, and now karma has come back to bite you in the ass. You played yourself and tried to bring harm to someone out of pure maliciousness and jealousy. I told you Rocky and me were just friends, and you refused to accept it for what it was, not knowing that if she wanted me, I damn sure wouldn't have been with you. Wisdom is knowledge, and God's cypher is divine. You must face the situation that you initiated. I'm about to take lil' man and put him to bed. If I don't see you in a couple days, I'll report you missing and tell the cops that you went to visit your brother and never returned. Peace."

Shy looked over at me and apologized again. When he

asked me if I was straight, I assured him that I would be just fine. Being through with the whole thing, Shy got in his car drove off and didn't even look back once.

Sasha looked up at me and tried to plead her case, but I was in a very forgiving mood. All I keep thinking about was how this bitch put my life in jeopardy over some bullshit. Those niggas could have very well blown my fucking head off, so it was whatever with me. I didn't want to hear shit she had to say, and she was really pissing me off acting like a punk about the shit.

She continued crying and begging for her life. "Rocky, please don't do this. I have a baby to take care of."

"And I don't, Sasha? Did you think about my son when you pulled that shit?"

"I knew that they –."

I never give her a chance to complete her sentence. I cocked my arm back and let brass meet flesh. I punched her so hard that her face instantly burst open. I didn't stop there. I began to hit her harder and faster. Every time I hit her, I thought about what would have happened to my baby if those niggas had killed me.

I thought about how much Isaiah would've cried if I had died and how I felt looking down the barrel of that pistol that was pointed directly in my face. I continued to beat that bitch to within an inch of her life. I didn't want her to die because people seem to weigh more when they are dead.

Maybe it's because all of their internal organs have shut down and the blood was no longer flowing. They would just become dead weight. Even someone that was half-dead weighed less than a dead ass person.

I had trash bags in my trunk and I spread them out, drag her ass to the trunk, and put her in. Thankfully, she was an itty-bitty bitch and I could lift her by myself. I got into my car and looked around to ensure that no one was watching me as I drove off.

I smiled to myself when rain began to pour down. At least I didn't have to worry about blood everywhere in the park. All I had to do was get rid of her trick ass.

I hope to hell I don't get pulled over, I thought to myself as

I drove away from the park and picked up my phone to call Charla. Charla answered the phone and I told her that I was right about Shy. He didn't know nothing about it, but his girl did.

"Charla, I have a present for you. I'm on the way to your parents' house, and it's still alive and kicking, so you might be able to conduct that science project you've been wanting to do. I don't know how long it will breathe in those barrels and I don't want to know, but you can have at it if you want."

"Hell, yeah! I'm on the fucking way, Rocky, right now!"

I swear I had to see about getting her some therapy or something. There was something wrong with my homie! But shit, she was my ride or die for life. I loved her just the way she was. And lately, I'd been making more trips out to the farm than her, so maybe we could go see the same therapist. Naw, later for all that, there was really nothing wrong with either of us. We just refused to take anyone's shit.

Chapter 20
Intervention

To say that I went through everything that I went through the other day, I sure as hell slept like a baby. I woke up and peeped that the clock read 1:15 pm. I must have been really tired. I never sleep that late. I had to get up and go see what I could find to get into.

"Get down, Diva, get off me. Stop it!" I yelled at the dog.

Wait a minute, what the hell is Diva doing here in the bed with me? Oh, Donnie and Isaiah must be downstairs in the living room. Let me go wash my face and brush my teeth so I could see my two favorite men in the world.

I grabbed my thick pink and white robe, slid my feet into my bunny rabbit slippers and handled my business in the bathroom. I ran downstairs super excited about seeing my boys.

"What the fuck?" I exclaimed. To my utter surprise, my damn living room was filled with people.

"What the hell are all y'all hoodlums doing in my damn house? Where did y'all come from, and what do you want?" I asked, trying to figure out why damn near everyone I knew and affiliated myself with was in my living room. I didn't think half of those people knew where I lived.

Donnie stood up off the couch and said, "Charla called us all and asked for us to come over here so we could all try to talk to you. Michelle had her key, and she let us in. Baby, will you please have a seat and listen to what we have to say?"

I may smoke a little weed every now and again, but I wasn't on any hard drugs. I didn't drink that much. So this couldn't possibly be for that crazy ass show, Intervention. I hoped they weren't trying to send me to a rehab or something. That shit bugged me out.

"Is this an intervention?" I asked, trying to make a joke to mask my anxiety. I wanted to figure out what the hell they wanted for real.

Isaiah came over, took me by the hand, and led me over to the love seat. I sat beside him and looked around to see what everyone was doing in my house. I saw Charla, Dream, Michelle, Da'Quan, Mel-G, Shy, Jay-Baby, and Frank Nitty. I didn't even think that all of them knew each other. What were they doing? "Man, what the hell do y'all want? Why are you here?" I started to feel some type of way.

Da'Quan and Mel-G were the first to speak.

"Rocky, we ain't got nothing but love for you. You always keep it one hundred, and we wanted to give something back to show that we really do respect you and admire you. We appreciate you for who you are," Da'Quan said. He looked at me, giving me a big ass Kool-Aid smile.

"Yeah, Rock, Day delivered all those cars to me and told me to tell you to keep all the money to help with your legal problems. I thought about it, and that was some trill shit, so I said to myself, 'Yeah, that's peace.' Since I know that I'll have no problems doing the math with those cars 'cause they are all top of the line, I decided to give you my cut too. I hope this helps enough and you think about all the shit that you have been through recently and get your shit in order. It's time to switch the game up. Do the right thing with yourself." Mel-G sounded ever so sincere. I could tell that he truly was concerned about my welfare. That wasn't an act; he was speaking from his heart.

How do I respond to that? Well, I knew that no matter what, I was *not* going to cry, especially in front of all those people. I took the money and gave my thanks. My voice betrayed me, and it was becoming apparent that I wasn't far from tears.

Shy stepped up next and looked at me like only Shy could. I laughed to myself. He had better be careful. Donnie was jealous as hell, and he didn't miss much.

198

INDICTED/ *Keisha Monique*

"Peace, Queen, you know I always try to pay my debts. I could never repay you for what you went through, but at least I could cover the monetary part. I treasure your friendship, Rock, and you need to get right. Allah is really shining on you right now, and you gotta take heed to the wisdom that is being presented to you in this room right now. Please try to find your true calling and leave the streets alone."

I didn't even care that Donnie was listening because I was quite sure the streets had already given a report about yesterday. Whether or not he knew what really happened or that I was involved, I couldn't be sure, but there damn sure wasn't anything I could do about it at that point.

Shy handed me several stacks of money and I didn't bother to count it. I still tried to keep my game face on because I didn't believe that this type of stuff happened to real people. This was some made for TV shit. But there were no cameras in my house, and we were all real people, so I guess that it really was happening.

"Give me a cigarette," I said to Charla.

She lit a Newport and handed it to me. I took a deep pull off it and exhaled looking up towards the ceiling.

Jay-Baby approached, me looking all serious and shit. Still sexy as hell, I caught myself staring at him and quickly averted my gaze before I started a riot in there.

"Baby girl, here is twenty stacks. Leave those people's fucking credit cards alone now. You are too smart to keep doing the same thing over and over. Them motherfuckers is hip to your hustle. It's time for you to switch the game up. You have been settin' an example in the streets for a minute. It's time to take that leadership and do something else with it. Do some legal shit."

"You'd be surprised at how many niggas look up to you and might follow if you show them that it can be done. You have that kind of influence over people whether you want to acknowledge it or not. Ain't shit in these streets. You can trust me on that," he preached.

Damn, he looked so good. Hell, I might change anything he asked me to. If I stared at him long enough and kept thinking nasty thoughts, I'd be changing my damn panties!

"Damn, y'all, I don't know what to say. I would have never expected this in a million years. This is not the type of shit that happens to people like me. I don't even know what to say or how I'm supposed to act." I sat in my seat and gazed down at my hands and played with my cigarette nervously.

"You wrong, Auntie, This is some real nigga shit. Real niggas always recognize real niggas. It don't get no realer than this. Ain't no punk ass people in this room. We are all soldiers in our own rights. You are the common thread that ties us all together. You're always helping people to the point where it's an everyday thing for you, you can't really see how much you affect other people's lives," Nitty said.

"You have absolutely no idea how much love you have in the streets. I'm telling you, Auntie, niggas will lay down their lives for you and not have to think twice about it. You found me when I was young and on the road to self-destruction. How many other motherfuckers saw me living out there as a child and left me out there to fend for myself? You made me go home, and you helped me through school. I have my diploma because of you. I'm about to enroll in college because of you. I used what I learned in the streets to get my money right, and now I'm about to be on some other shit."

"I'll still dabble in the pharmaceutical street business, but it won't be my only means to survive. I thank you from the bottom of my heart, Auntie. I mean that shit, you saved me. I got like fifteen stacks here for you. If you need more, let me know. I wish I could take this fed shit for you, God knows I would. You know that I'd change places with you in a heartbeat. Just be careful and look inside yourself for the truth like you always tell me." He handed me the book bag and kissed me on the forehead.

"I know that you would take this charge for me if you could, Nitty. I truly believe that."

I couldn't hold my tears back any longer. I loved my peoples. I didn't have any idea that they felt this way. Maybe this really was an intervention. I needed to really do what I had been promising to do.

Dream, Charla, and Michelle handed me a Victoria's Secret

bag with some money it in.

"You already know what it is with us, Rock. We need you to get right so you can stay on the streets. What would we do without you?" Charla said, looking like she was about to cry. I had never seen her show any kind of emotion. Hell, I didn't think she had any.

"We look up to you, Rocky, and I, personally, really need you. I love you a lot," Dream added, and broke down and cried.

I watched as Charla hugged her and took her in the kitchen.

"This is not what Momma had planned for us, Ra'Quelle. You're her pride and joy. If we stop all this foolishness, you know she'll welcome us with open arms."

Michelle's words were far more than I could bear. They just took away the last bit of my reserve. I missed my momma and I wanted to go home to see her and tell her that I would live the right way.

Just when I thought my guard was down enough, it was Isaiah's turn. "Ma, I have $64.00 that I saved out of my allowance. You can have it, and I don't want any new shoes or games if you have to do credit and go to jail. I need you to be home and take care of Diva and me. I know how to wear other kinds of stuff besides Polo. I can make anything look good," he boasted and he wasn't lying.

"I will get scared and cry if you go to jail because I think they are going to hurt you or not give you any food. I will cry all the time when you are in there. I don't know if the police are mean to you or if it's dark and scary in there. Somebody might try to beat you up or make you cry and who's gonna be in there to help you, Ma? Please try to change, Ma, I need you too bad! Please don't leave me, Mommy please!" When Zay broke down all the water in my body came streaming out of my eyes. The thought of my son being hurt tore my heart out. It felt like my heart stopped beating with each tear that he cried. There was nothing we had that was worth my baby's tears. Hell no, this shit had to stop.

I pulled him over to sit on my lap. "Don't cry, stank. I am so sorry. I'm done. I am done, baby. Please don't cry. It's okay, Mommy's got you, okay? Mommy's right here. Don't cry; please don't cry no more. I love you. You're my little man. It's okay, everything is going to be fine. I got you, I promise."

I glanced around at all of the people who loved me had surrounded me. I calmed my son down and wiped my baby's tears away when Donnie handed me some tissue. I told everyone how very thankful I was for the love that they showed me, and I believed I would retire and let the next person have that shit. I said my goodbyes, and then it was me, Zay, and Donnie left in the house.

"Are you okay, Ma?" Zay asked.

"Yeah, baby, I'm straight. Are you okay?"

After he promised that he was, I asked him, "Do you feel like taking Diva for a walk, or better yet, letting her take you for a walk since I know she is going to be dragging you down the street?"

"Yes, ma'am, I'll take her."

"Okay, be careful, and don't let her get away from you because you know that you will never catch her."

"I got her," he assured me and left the room to get the dog.

Donnie came over to me and kissed me. He put his hand under my chin, making me look at him.

"Baby, look, keep all of your money. I got the money for your lawyer and your bail if it comes to that. I been telling you this shit for a minute, but you won't accept it coming from me. Now, you have heard it from all your peoples. Let that shit go, Ra'Quelle. Deal with the trouble that you already have and leave them people's shit alone before you get caught up in some shit that you can't get out of."

"I'm going to wait and see what your situation looks like, and then I am going to make that run to Brooklyn. After that, I am done myself. Hold your head, ma. It's going to be okay. I'll always have your back. You should know that by now." He kissed me again, called me a crybaby, and ran as I chased him around the house.

Chapter 21
Facing the Music

I ran through the house the next morning trying to get myself, Donnie, and Zay ready. I was preparing to see the lawyer. None of us could seem to get it together. I had on my black two-piece Chanel power suit. My closed toe pumps said that I was ready to tackle the world. I grabbed my Chanel bag and checked on Zay. He was sitting at the table eating cereal and laughing at me. Donnie came out dressed in a long sleeved shirt and some slacks.

"Why didn't you wear the suit I laid on the bed for you, Dee?"

"Shit, I ain't wearing that monkey suit. I ain't going to trial. We are taking *you* to see *your* lawyer; I'm just here for support." He laughed.

"Fuck you, Donnie," I retorted.

"Calm down, Rocky. Damn, you running around here like you're on something. Are you ready or what?" he asked.

I looked around the house one more time. I had no idea why I kept thinking that would be the last time I'd see my house. I was really tripping. I pulled myself together and we got in his Escalade.

We dropped Isaiah off at school, and I began to get all emotional, but Dee stopped me. "Let the boy go, Ra'Quelle, before he is late to class. You'll see him when he gets out of school. I promise you that much."

I watched him out the window as Donnie pulled out into the oncoming traffic.

"Damn, you didn't see that car. What the hell is wrong with

you?"

"Shut up and let me drive," he said, speeding along like he had a damn license when he didn't.

We arrived at Mr. Shapiro's office in a really nice office building. It had about ten stories, made of all glass. He reigned king over the entire top floor. Well, at least I knew that he was making some loot. I also know that his shit up in there cost him a pretty penny.

His receptionist announced me and led me into his office. I shook his hand and checked him out. His whole presence screamed money, power, and respect.

"Hello, Ms. Summers, I've been expecting you. It is very nice to meet you. Our mutual friend let me know beforehand that you would be arriving today. It's my pleasure to help you, and this is?" he asked, waiting to be introduced to Donnie.

"This is my fiancé, Mr. Benton," I said, nodding toward Donnie.

"Great. It's a pleasure, Mr. Benton," he greeted, shaking Donnie's hand like he'd known him all his life.

"Ms. Summers, do you feel comfortable speaking in front of Mr. Benton or would you prefer to have him wait in the lounge?"

"I trust him with my life, sir," I responded.

"Very well. Let us get down to business. Time is very much of the essence. I will always be upfront and to the point. Now, the first thing to discuss is the money. I am normally paid by the hour in federal cases because they are so time consuming, but since you're a personal friend of a friend of mine, I will take this case for a flat fee of seventy-five thousand dollars. I will require fifty thousand now, and the rest at the closing of the case. If there is a need to appeal anything that will be an additional twenty-five thousand dollars."

"I understand that this is not cheap, but I assure you that you get what you pay for. I only deal with one case at a time in federal court. That way, it can have all of my attention. Federal court is about guidelines and loopholes. If you can't find loopholes, you are at the mercy of the court. Now, does this sound agreeable to you?" He sat looking at us and twirling his Mont Blanc pen. I wanted one of those, but I wasn't paying three hundred bucks for a pen.

I watched him as he leaned back in his chair as if he ruled the world. I decided that I liked him. Knowing that Shy's ass was still on the streets only confirmed that Mr. Shapiro was legit.

Donnie counted out $40,000.00 in cash and told him that we would bring in the other $10,000.00 before the close of business. Mr. Shapiro took the money and placed it in a hidden safe in the wall behind a beautiful oil painting of something that I couldn't really make out, but the colors were nice.

"Okay. I've been in touch with the agents who are investigating you, Garcia and Wells. I've also been in touch with the U.S. Attorney. You were formally indicted yesterday morning at 9:30 am."

My heart fell into my shoes. *Oh, shit, I'm going to jail after all.*

"What does that mean, indicted?"

"That means that the federal government has brought forth charges against you. They're charging you with multiple counts of credit card fraud and identity theft. However, their case is weak at best. They asked for a lot more indictments than were handed down. You seem to have been a busy little bee, Ms. Summers. Fortunately, for you, you have pretty much covered your ass. They won't be able to make most of it stick, and will drop the majority of them by the time you plead out."

"Going to trial in a federal case is not worth it. They'll hang you if you try it. They always win in their house. I'm concerned about your previous arrest record, though I'm sure that they will work with you. I believe the only one that will stick is a charge on an American Express card for seventy-five thousand dollars. They have the store salesperson, and he will be brought in to testify against you if you want to go to trial. Your offense level should not be higher than sixteen, and that is damn good."

He looked at me and went through some papers on his desk. I tried to hold myself together and be optimistic because I was confident that this dude was about his business.

"What happens now?" Donnie asked.

"If it's okay with Ms. Summers, I'd like to take her over to the federal courthouse so that they can serve her with the indictment. You'll either be allowed to go home on pretrial release, or you'll have a bond set today. I have my own personal bondsman that I use for all of my clients on standby, and he's ready to come bond you out today if it comes to that. You'll have to pay the amount the judge sets, however. We're going in front of Judge Gray, and he's a fair man. I think we can have you home by dinner if we leave now."

I looked at Donnie and he took my hand and advised Mr. Shapiro that we'd meet him at the courthouse on Richland Street in about 15 minutes.

"I got you, baby. Let's go. If they put any dollar amount on your freedom, then you are out of there today. Trust me on this, okay? You don't want to run away. This is nothing to run from. He said they'll probably drop all of the charges except one, and that's the one you told me that you wanted them to have, right? Well, it looks like your plan may work after all. Let's get this shit over with so we can move on with our lives. Do you trust me, big head?"

"Shut up, Donnie," I said, laughing. I was thankful to have a man like Donnie by my side.

We left the attorney's office, stopped and got something to eat real quick from Mickey D's, and then we headed over to the courthouse to deal with the demons I'd created.

Mr. Shapiro was waiting for us when we pulled up. We got out of the truck and all walked in together. After going through two separate metal detectors, we boarded the elevator and arrived on the third floor. I had to admit I was impressed with how the feds handled their business. It was a beautiful courthouse and I would like it more if I wasn't the one that had to be here.

The wood paneling and the oak furniture spoke volumes about the caliber of people that come through those doors. I felt like I had made it to the big leagues or some silly shit like that. I looked behind the judge's desk and saw the big seal that read, UNITED STATES OF AMERICA.

This is the last place that I ever thought I would find my-

206

self.

Mr. Shapiro showed us where to sit, and then he went over and talked to a gray-haired white lady who sat at the table across from me. I assumed that she was the U.S. Attorney.

Twenty minutes later, some people were brought in wearing shackles and orange jumpsuits. The bailiff entered the court and recited, "All rise. The Honorable Judge Malcolm Gray is attending."

We all rose to our feet and the judge entered the courtroom from a door hidden in the wall behind his desk.

"Please be seated. Are we ready to proceed, Ms. Sims?" he asked the gray-haired lady.

"Yes, sir, we are."

I felt my heart beating like a runaway slave. I had never been so scared in all my damn life. There were people that would come into this place and never see the streets again. The feds be giving out those football numbers, and it was damn near day for day. Man, shit, shit right here was not cool at all. I wished like hell I had listened to what my momma told me a long time ago. *All money ain't good money.* Now I was in there with the same kind of people who locked up John Gotti and Martha Stewart. If they sent Martha's ass to jail, why the hell would they care about locking my black ass up?

The gray-haired lady stood up. "Your Honor, the first case before you is the United States versus Ra'Quelle Monique Summers."

Damn, the whole United States against little ole' me? Not the State of South Carolina versus me, but the whole damn country. I felt like I would just fall out in there. I hoped this man was as good as Shy said he is, or else I can cancel Christmas because the party was about over for me.

"We are here to indict Ms. Summers on eight counts of mail fraud, nine counts of credit card fraud, and 20 counts of identity theft, as well as one count of lying to a government official," she said, reading off the paper in her hand.

I didn't know how Mr. Shapiro knew that I was about to fall out, but he put his hand on my shoulder and whispered in my ear for me to remember what he said about most of the charges not

207

sticking and being dropped at my plea hearing.

I was about to say, that sounded like 5,000 years' worth of shit right there, and what damn official did I lie to? I wanted out of there.

"Is Ms. Summers present here in the courtroom?" the judge asked as he looked around to see if he could see me.

"Yes, your Honor, she is right here with me," Mr. Shapiro spoke up and walked to the podium that was in the middle of the courtroom.

He motioned for me to join him. At first, I hesitated, and then I got up to go stand beside my attorney. Donnie attempted to walk up to the podium with me, but he was stopped by a U.S. Marshal. I stood beside Mr. Shapiro and I could swear that I could hear my knees knocking together. I was shaking like a leaf on a tree.

"Are you Ms. Summers?" the judge asked me.

"Yes, sir, I am."

"Very good then. Now, do you know why you are here, Ms. Summers?"

"Yes, sir. Mr. Shapiro explained it all to me earlier at his office. I am aware of the charges being brought against me."

I tried to maintain eye contact, keep a straight face and not look like I was about to have a nervous breakdown and start boo-hoo crying.

"Very good," he repeated.

He appeared to be pleasant enough as far as judges go. At least he wasn't yelling, screaming, and acting all crazy. I have seen judges have temper tantrums in the middle of a court hearing.

"Okay, Ms. Simon please read the indictment for this case."

She proceeded to read the indictment mentioning the various credit cards that I had been accused of using and the ones that were linked to me by my address. She also read about the receipts that they had and intended to present as evidence. She spoke about the mail fraud coming from me having the cards sent to me through the U.S. Postal Service, and identity theft in my usage of several devices that were issued in the names of others without their consent or knowledge.

"We have several accounts, your Honor, from Citibank,

Discover, Chase, and WaMu. These cards were issued fraudulently
and used several times by Ms. Summers and others that she gave to
use these cards. We will present the evidence we have as well as an
eyewitness to one or more transactions. We will present receipts
and photographs of items that were found inside the home of Ms.
Summers that were purchased with said credit cards." She sounded
like she wanted to go ahead and convict me right on the spot.

I wondered if Mr. Shapiro was gonna step in and object to
anything she was saying or are we just gonna go along for the ride?
I looked over at him and he held up his hand for me to be patient or
to be silent, one of the two. I listened as they continued.

"Ms. Sims, is the use of a credit card enough to warrant a
charge of identity theft?" Judge Gray asked her.

"Yes, your Honor, it is when that card was applied for by
someone presenting themselves as the person whom the card is
being issued to. As a matter of fact, the only way that a credit card
will be issued is if you present yourself as the person whose information you are using." She sat up and looked through some papers
on her table, but didn't say anything else.

"I see, I see," Judge Gray said as he wrote something and
looked back up at me.

"Okay, Ms. Summers, we accept this indictment. The Court
will enter a plea of not guilty today for you, and we'll set a date to
have you come back and either change your plea or make arrangements for a trial. Your attorney will help you to decide what the
best route for you to take would be in this matter."

He signed the indictment, and a marshal brought me a copy
of it. It was about ten pages long and contained all the information
that the U.S. Attorney had read.

Judge Gray continued, "Now that you have been issued
your indictment, there is the matter of your bond. Do you want to
stay home until your next court date or do we want to keep you in
the good custody of the U.S. Marshals?"

What the hell did he just say, keep me where? He had to be
tripping. I was not about to be staying there or any place for that
much. I wanted to go home the same way I walked in there, on my
own accord.

I was not about to cry, but I tell you what, I also was not that happy. This did not go at all the way that I thought it would, and what the hell is my lawyer for? He ain't said shit since I stepped in front of the judge, other than to tell the man that I was present.

"Ms. Sims, what is the court's recommendation for her bond?"

"The government doesn't have a recommendation for her bond, sir. We trust you and will go along with whatever you decide. We trust your judgment," she said smiling at the judge.

"Well, that is good to know. I'm glad that you trust me." He laughed and shook his head at her and directed his attention to my lawyer before looking back down at the papers he had in front of him. "Okay, Mr. Shapiro, I can see that you are ready to jump right in here at any moment. Tell me what we've got here."

Mr. Shapiro tapped my shoulder for me to accompany him to the other podium in the center of the courtroom. I walked over, stood by him, and wondered why we had to move from one to the other. I guess one was for standing and the other one was for talking. I attempted to occupy my mind off this hearing, but nothing was working. All I could think about was that I'd be going to damn jail.

"Thank you, your Honor. Ms. Summers is a 28-year-old single mother. She has an 11-year-old son that relies on her for his sole support. She is engaged to Mr. Benton, who is here in the court with her this morning showing his support for her. Ms. Summers didn't hesitate when I suggested we come down to this courthouse for her indictment. Actually, she beat me here. She is willing to turn over her passport, and I honestly don't feel that she is a flight risk. She has numerous ties to the community and this has been her home all of her life. I believe that she qualifies for the pretrial release, your Honor."

He stepped back and looked over at me like he felt he had just given an Oscar winning performance. He had damn sure better bring it better than that when it came to my trial or I could see myself going away for a very long period of time.

"Um-hum," Judge Gray uttered, and then he looked at me.

"Ms. Summers, what do you have to say about this matter?"

"Well, your Honor, I am ready to accept my responsibility in this matter, and I can assure you that I will appear at any court date you give me. I have no intentions on trying to avoid my due. I ask the court to please send me home so that I may continue to take care of my son and my fiancé."

I stood there feeling like the walls were closing in around me as I realized that what he said next was going to determine whether I went home or to jail. I couldn't believe the trouble that I found myself in. I had to make some major changes in my life because I didn't want to do that kind of shit anymore.

As much as I didn't want to cry, the tears began to fall from my eyes anyway. I tried to pull myself together, and Mr. Shapiro handed me a tissue.

"Very well, okay. Well, Ms. Summers, you have quite a little criminal history there, don't you? I see some previous convictions that are very similar to the ones that have been brought forth against you today. I'm not going to allow you to go home on a pretrial release."

My damn heart just stopped beating and I knew that I was about to die standing right there in that courtroom. How can that be? He said what? I must have heard him wrong.

"Oh, no, please!" I cried out without really meaning to. I just broke down and cried almost uncontrollably.

"Wait, wait, don't have a mental breakdown, Ms. Summers. I'm going to give you a bond, so it just won't be pretrial. You'll be able to post your bond. I am going to set your bond in the amount of fifty thousand dollars. It's a secured bond, but I'll allow you to post property or bond with a bondsman. I'm sure they'll take twenty-five percent if you don't want to post any property. If you can post that, then you will be allowed to leave today. They'll process you and release you after the bond has been posted. Is there anything else from the government?"

"No, your Honor, we're done for today."

"Anything from the defense?"

"Yes, your Honor. I want to go on record saying that I will be overseeing the posting of Ms. Summers' bond. A bondsman will be here in the next thirty minutes to sign her bond. Her fiancé is prepared to pay that amount now." He motioned towards Donnie.

"Very well. Next."

Someone else stood up I guess to get ready to call another person to be seen in front of the judge. Everything seemed to be happening in slow motion for me. I was very thankful because for a minute, I thought that they weren't going to let me go home.

"Relax, Ms. Summers. I'm calling the bondsman on my cell right now. He will be here in thirty minutes or less. Do you have twelve thousand, five hundred cash on you, Mr. Benton, or do you need time to go get it? You can also post property. Just keep in mind that if you post property, it has to be appraised, and all of that can take up to two weeks."

"That ain't gonna be a problem. I have her bond money right here."

I watched as Donnie pulled out a manila envelope with the money in it.

"Do you have proof of income just in case the feds want to know how you were able to post that much cash?" he asked him.

"Yes, I have the paperwork from where I collected a large amount of money from an insurance policy when my father passed away last year."

I looked at Donnie, but he wouldn't meet my gaze. Ain't that some shit? His damn daddy lived up the street from me. I laughed to myself as I wondered how he got those papers. Probably some chick he used to fuck with or might still be fucking with, for all I knew, and I really didn't give a damn as long as it worked in my favor.

"That's great. Sorry to hear about your loss. Okay, Ms. Summers, we'll handle this and you'll go with the marshal there so that they can do your fingerprints and whatever else they may need. I'll see you back in my office once I've had a chance to talk to the U.S. Attorney and see what they want to do and what kind of deals they want to offer you. You should hear from me within the month."

"Thank you, Mr. Shapiro. Dee, I'll call you later on when they are finished with me, and you can come back and pick me up out front."

"I'll be outside in the truck waiting for you, Ra'Quelle. I'm not leaving here without you. I told you I was gonna be there for you and make sure you get to see Zay when he gets out of school, and that is just what I meant." He smiled and patted me on my ass. He was just nasty and didn't give a damn who knew it, but I loved my man and I thanked God for him. He had never let me down when things were of the utmost importance. I knew that I could always count on him to have my back. That's my boo! I raised up on my tippy toes to kiss him on the lips, and then I followed the marshal through the door that led to wherever he had to take me.

Chapter 22
Back to Life

After a couple of weeks of sitting home and doing nothing but being a mother to my child and a wife to my man, I got tired of playing the Suzie homemaker role and decided that I needed to get out and about for a while. I called Michelle to see what the hell she was up to. I hoped she had some time to hang out with me. I planned to call the other girls as well.

"What's up, sis?" I asked her when she answered the phone.

"Damn, I thought that you fell off the face of the earth or that the feds had put you in the witness protection program, or maybe Dee had you on lock like that.

I laughed are her because she couldn't be anybody but herself, so I respected that.

"Never that, boo-boo. I've just been trying to lay low and get my mind right about all this shit that I'm going through with this indictment. But for right now, I'm ready to get the fuck up out of this house and get into something. What's up with you for the day? What are you smoking on over there?" I asked her, knowing that as sure as I was sitting there, my sister was getting high.

She informed me that her, Charla, and Mel-G were having a cookout and getting ready to throw some food on the grill.

"That's what's up. I'm on the way. Donnie and Zay are gonna do whatever it is that they do when they leave me here all by myself. You need anything from the store?"

I don't know why the hell I asked her that. That was mistake number one for me because she gave me a fucking grocery list.

"Hell yeah. Get some T-bones, some ribs, some chicken, some pork chops, some lighter fluid, and charcoals. We need some napkins and some plates. You can get some chips and soda and beer and liquor as well, if you don't mind." She said all of that like she had just given me a normal list.

That was everything that anyone would need for a damn cookout. I wondered if they had anything over there. I could just see them all over there now. Everyone was probably high as hell, and I'd bet my life that they'd try to get me to cook the food too. May as well though since I didn't have shit else to do.

"Chelle, how are you having a cookout and you need all of this shit? What the hell do you have over there?"

"I have a damn grill and some hungry niggas, that's what I have. Now, hurry up and get your ass over here. We were just talking about how much we all miss your stupid ass!"

With that being said, she hung the phone up in my face without saying goodbye. I didn't know why I even bothered with her, but she was my best friend as well as my sister, and I missed her dearly.

I went in my closet to find something to wear and chose a Michael Kors dress, but decided to keep it in the bag and get dressed when I got over there since I had so much running around to do, and would most likely be cooking and doing everything else.

The Christian Dior dress was really cute. It had four clear vinyl panels that made the dress appear to be skirt and top when it really wasn't. I had the cutest black ankle strap heels by Vince Cumato that set the dress off, and I wasn't going to mess my shoes up cooking on a damn grill.

I kept on the Donna Karen jeans that I had on with the matching t-shirt and my Air Max. I almost forgot to grab the clear cuff bracelets that I had to go with the dress. I believed the weather was just warm enough for me to pull it off.

I grabbed my pistol out of my closet and threw it into my bag and tried to find the long ass grocery list that my sister gave me. Once I found that, I put Diva on her chain and headed out to the car.

I was surprised not to see Peanut outside posted up somewhere or at least on his porch. I saw his son though and for some reason as soon as he saw me, he ran inside the house. I had no idea what the hell was wrong with that little boy, but he was tripping on something.

I went to check my mailbox and to my surprise, there was a Citibank Visa card in there addressed to Ella Lofton. Damn, I had completely forgotten that I had applied for that card earlier and hadn't gotten a response.

I opened the card and it had a $10,000.00 credit limit. It wasn't the best credit limit I'd had but hey, it was free money. I tossed that into my purse and closed the mailbox. I turned around to leave and walked straight into Agent Garcia. *Now* Diva wanted to start barking and growling after she let the man walk all the way up on me. That dog had more mood swings than me.

I tried to calm her down and put my game face on. I observed that he had come alone.

"Ms. Summers, how are you doing? I have been trying without any luck to get in touch with you for a couple of weeks now. Didn't you get the message that I left for you on your answering machine a couple of weeks ago?" He looked at me and it seemed to me that he was trying to read my expression or something. Maybe his ass was just crazy as hell. Well, at least there wasn't anything outside for him to break like he broke my damn table.

"No, I didn't get any messages from you, sir. My answering machine is broken and I haven't been able to replace it as of yet," I told him, hoping and praying that he didn't see me get the mail out of the mailbox. And to top all of that off, I chose today to want to carry my pistol around in my purse. Being a convicted felon, I wasn't even allowed to carry a weapon at all.

"Do you have a minute to talk to me? I have some other stuff that I would like to go over with you, if you don't mind."

This dude must have been out of his damn mind. They've already charged me with everything under the sun. Why in the hell would I want to talk to him about anything so that he could hand out more indictments? I think not. I tried to peer into his eyes, but he had on shades like Neo in the Matrix. "Uh, actually I was on my way out and my lawyer has expressed to me that I shouldn't answer any questions without at least checking with him first." I hoped that my voice didn't relay the fear that I was feeling at that moment.

"I was just about to check my mail, and then I was leaving to go handle some business."

"Well, go ahead and check it then," he snapped at me. All of a sudden, he had an attitude. Oh, well, he'd be alright. I was just glad he didn't see me get the mail out of the box. I turned back to the mailbox and open it once again, struggling with Diva's chain. I had trouble getting the rest of the mail out and then I felt her chain getting light and looked up to see K.G. taking Diva from me.

Where the hell did she come from? She had the biggest balls ever coming over here. I knew that she had warrants, and she shouldn't be in the face of this crazy federal agent.

"Hey, baby!" she said as she leaned forward and kissed me on the lips. *Oh, this hoe is crazy*, I thought to myself. If Donnie were here, he would kill her.

"Are you straight, ma? Who is your friend?" she asked me.

"He's not my friend. This is Agent Garcia. He's a federal agent who I've had some dealings with in the past. He wants to talk to me about something. Can you take Diva to the car for me while I deal with him for a minute, please?"

"Yeah, boo, let me hold your keys, and I'll put your purse and your clothes in the car as well. Try to hurry up or we are going to be late for the show. The dogs have to be there by two to get signed in."

I handed her everything I had in my hands. Damn, I loved that girl. She kind of fucked up when she said the show because what kind of show would we go to with a dog unless it's a dog show. I was glad that she was able to tighten that up.

I watched her walk off and Diva obediently followed behind her. I realized now more than ever that Diva really was a whore. Anything that was masculine, she would follow and just be straight trippin'.

I asked Garcia how I could help him he asked me to show

him the mail that I got out of the mailbox. I knew that he had no right to ask this because he didn't have anything that looked like a warrant. But I decided to let him see it anyway since there was nothing in there, nothing but my own bills. The shit that he really wanted to see was sitting in my purse safely in the car with K.G.

"Ms. Summers, you do know that it won't be long before I wipe that shit eating grin off of your face, right? You think you're so damn smart, don't you? Smarter than the U.S. government. But I'm here to remind you that you're not. I'm going to do my best to make sure that all of your indictments turn into sentences. And that, my friend, you can take to the bank," he said, acting all indignant.

I could not understand why they didn't require these damn people to undergo some kind of psychological testing to ensure that they were in their right state of mind.

"Sir, I have no idea once again what you are talking about. I don't think that I'm smarter than anyone, much less the whole U.S. government," I informed him, trying my best to be sincere.

"Lies!" he yelled and started with that foaming of the mouth again. Maybe he had post-traumatic stress disorder. He pushed the mail back into my arms.

"Everything out of your mouth is a lie. You're nothing more than an overdressed, dolled up convict. You may think that you're flying under the radar, but I can assure you that you are not. Honey, I have my eyes on you. You are going down, Ms. Summers. Your black ass is going down. You're going all the way down!"

He turned and walked back to wherever he had his car or truck parked because he didn't park anywhere that I could see it. I went back towards my house and saw the little dude from next door.

"Ms. Ra'Quelle, I told my daddy that I seen that white man watching your house. I seen him all the way up by the candy lady's house. Are you going to jail? If you go to jail, can I have Diva? If you go to jail, Isaiah can come to live with us and he can bring his PlayStation 4 over to my house. I only have PlayStation 3."

I could certainly tell that he was Peanut's son, just as bad as his damn silly ass daddy. Peanut came out of their house and ran the little man off.

"I was trying to warn you that the feds were out here some-where, but that nigga came out of the woods on your ass just now. Girl, you are on fire for real. What the hell are you doing? You must be fucking Bin Laden or something. I thought that I saw those Al-Qaeda people at your house the other day. I'm telling you, y'all should not have knocked down both of the twin towers at the World Trade Center. If y'all had only hit the south tower, the feds wouldn't be on your ass so hard, but no, y'all didn't ask my advice. You and your boy-toy Bin Laden just went and knocked down both of them, and that's why they're on your ass every time you turn around. I promise you, Rocky, that's where y'all fucked up at."

He took a pull off his blunt and looked at me as if he were awaiting a response, but how the hell do I respond to someone who had just accused me of going with the most wanted man in the free world even though he'd been dead for a couple years? He really had in his brain that I knocked down the twin towers. That must've been some good ass weed for real.

"Shut the hell up, boy. Let me smoke some of that shit that has got you all fucked up in the head like that."

He handed me the blunt, and I took it and walked off with it.

"Yeah, Rock, that's all right, you take that shit with you. You're going to need it with your hot ass. I don't want it back any-way. A nigga might just catch a bid if they're seen smoking with your hot ass. Take that blunt and get as high as you can. You need to try to get high enough so that they can't even see you." He fixed his lips to say something else, but changed his mind and walked into his house.

I walked around the back of my house and got into my car. K.G. and Diva were in there listening to the radio.

"K.G., your cousin is brain dead. I hope your family is aware of that," I informed her, still thinking about the encounter that I had just had with my lunatic next-door neighbor.

"Yeah, baby, Peanut is out there. He's been out to lunch for a long time, but he is good people though. Are you straight? I guess you must be. You're not in handcuffs or anything like that,

INDICTED/*Keisha Monique*

so that's always a good sign," she said, smiling at me.

"K.G., look, you know that you just saved my ass, right? You're my girl. I appreciate that shit, for real. I know that you have those warrants, and you don't really like to deal with the police like that. That's one of the reasons why I love you, papi."

I really had a solid appreciation for her. She had always been there for me, and this was not the first time that she has put her life on the line for me.

"I love you too, Rocky. I'll always love you; you're my wifey. I will do anything that I can to help you whenever I can. I was actually over here to give you the money that I have for you. I heard that they had took up money for you and brought it over to your house a few weeks ago for your lawyer and shit. I know that it would have been some shit if I had come over to the house to give it to you, and I don't want to kill your baby's daddy."

She smirked and continued. "Here is ten thousand for you. If you need any more, let me know and I'll get it to you." She handed me a book bag with money in it, and I almost started crying.

I had to work hard to keep the tears from falling. I knew that she had slowed down a whole lot with her hustling, she had her mom to take care of, and was helping to put her sister through school. So, I knew how much this money meant to her. I didn't even really feel right accepting it, but I knew that I would be insulting her manhood if I refused it.

"Thank you, boo-boo." I leaned over and kissed her. Diva started barking. I hoped that she knew that K.G. was mine, and she had to find her own.

"What are you about to get into? I'm getting ready to go to the grocery store and then pick up Dream. We're going over to Michelle's house for a cookout and have a few drinks and whatnot. I could use some help since I know that they want me to do it all. If I remember correctly, you're pretty nice with a fork on the grill, right?" I asked, hoping that she would come, spend the day with me, and help me with this cookout.

"I got you, ma, let's go. I have been missing your ass anyway, and I've been wanting to see you and spend some time with

221

you. By the way, who are these for? Me?" She looked at me hope-ful, holding up my black silk panty set that I had in my bag with my clothes for later.

"Gimme my damn drawers!" I yelled, snatching them out of her hand and hitting her with them.

"You are so damn country, Ra'Quelle. Who the hell says drawers?" I lived in South Carolina, what the hell did she expect? We are country as hell down and we loved it.

"Shut the hell up!" I told her as I pulled out of the yard.

Chapter 23
Cat Fight

Once we were quite a ways from the house, I had her hand me the credit card that I got in the mail dialed the 800 number and waited until someone answered the phone. I called off the 16 numbers on the front of the card and gave them the three digit V-code off the back of the card.

"How are you, Mrs. Alston?" the rep asked me, sounding ever so chipper.

"I'm fine, how about yourself?" I responded, giving it back to her the same that she gave it to me – fake.

"Mrs. Alston, may I please have the phone number that is associated with this account, your birthday, and the last four of your Social please?"

"Sure, the phone number is 803-777-9090, my birthday is February 3, 1965, and the last four of my Social is 4789."

I looked over at K.G. as she shook her head at my shenanigans. I winked at her, and she pointed her finger to the side of her head and motioned the "crazy" circles.

"Okay, Mrs. Alston, your card is activated and ready for use. Is there anything else I can help you with today? Can I interest you in a deferred payment plan in case you should ever need to have your payments deferred?"

"Not at this time, but I might be interested at a later date. You can send me some information in the mail so that I can read over it. For right now though, can you please allow me to set my own pin number? I don't want the one that the bank is going to send me in the mail. I'd like to choose numbers that are easy for me to remember, so that I don't have to write them down for security reasons." I held my breath and hoped that she'd buy the bullshit that I lain on her.

Citibank didn't like to allow you to choose a pin number because it gave you instant access to cash through the ATM machines. But they'd allow it sometimes if you asked the right representative to do it. I'd hoped that the cheerful creature on the other line was mine.

"I can certainly do that for you, Mrs. Alston. Just give me the numbers whenever you're ready."

Oh, yeah, I damn near broke out in a happy dance, except I I was driving. I tried to mask my excitement and gave her the numbers I wanted to use. We exchanged goodbyes and I hung up the phone.

"YES!" I shouted once I hung the phone up.

K.G. looked at me with her head still shaking. "I see that you still haven't learned your lesson. You still fucking with them people's credit cards, huh?"

"Who me?" I asked, playing crazy. "Look, I had forgotten all about this one, but there was no need to let it go to waste. This is ten thousand dollars' worth of shit that I need."

I didn't look at her right away because I wasn't sure if she'd start tripping or what. I understood that I was in trouble for credit cards already but, I also understood that no harm would come from one last shopping spree. I truly believed that it was meant for me to have that card. I knew which stores to shop at and which ones I needed to avoid because of the security cameras and such.

"Well, since you are determined to do this shit regardless of what anyone has to say, can I get a couple outfits and some J's?"

Now that's why I loved my boo because she let me do me. I knew that she really didn't want me to do it, but she knew that she couldn't stop me either.

"Hell yeah. I'll get you anything you want. Do you want to go to the mall or what?" I asked her, being more than happy to comply.

"Naw, I want to go to that new Ralph Lauren store on Two Notch Road," she said.

"Say no more." I made a quick and illegal U-turn in the middle of the street.

We got to the store in one piece and went into the store of K.G.'s choice. She chose three Polo outfits and the shoes and boots to match since the store didn't carry Jordans. I got Donnie four Polo sweaters that I wanted him to have for when it got cold again. I grabbed Isaiah some new Polo shoes and five sweater vests with the long sleeved shirts to go under them.

The only thing that I chose for myself was a navy blue two-piece pant suit. It was really nice and I loved linen. I also copped the purse and shoes to match.

The sales girl was smiling from ear to ear, obviously adding up her commission. She rung it all up and the total fell just under $4,000.00.

"Will this be cash, check, or credit card? Would you like to apply for an instant store credit card?" she asked me hopefully.

"Not right now, sweetheart, I don't have the time. I'll just put this on my visa account, and maybe I'll come in later and apply for a store credit card."

I slid my card through the machine and stood there once again anxiously awaiting the music I love to hear. The cash register started to spit out its receipt, and I smiled. I didn't know who was happier, me or Meagan, the sales clerk. I got some fly shit, and she just got a pretty decent bonus.

Since the food was on Citibank and it had been a minute since I'd been able to get out and about, I decided to turn this cookout into some kind of affair. I decided to go all out and have some fun with my peoples; I haven't seen them in a minute.

I swung by Michelle's house and dropped the dog off. I told her that I would bring Dream back after I got the food. K.G. pushed the buggy and I loaded it up. Of course, we got a bunch of stares and whispers from people in the store. It was easy to see that we were more than just friends. K.G. was a very affectionate person, and she'd always be touching me or running her hands through my hair or something.

I went to the meat department inside of Publix and asked the guy working the counter for two whole rib-eye tenderloins that I wanted cut into one-inch thick steaks. He informed me that it would cost about $140 each at which I responded, "In that case, make it three." Then I smiled and moved on.

I selected ten packs of ribs and all the fixings for the potato salad, and some chips and beer.

"Baby, will you make me some macaroni and cheese please? You know I love that shit and you be killing it for real, ma." K.G. said.

I agreed to make it added the things for that to the cart. I decided to make enough so that I could take some home to Donnie and Zay because they all loved my macaroni. When I told her that I intended on taking some home to my boys, she immediately copped an attitude.

"Who said that you were going home tonight?" she asked, getting all in her feelings.

"Girl, don't play with me, you know I can't stay out all night with you," I said, hoping that she wouldn't start a big ass argument about me going home.

"Yeah, okay, what the fuck ever."

Damn, why she always had to show out? She knew good and damn well, I couldn't stay out with her all night.

"Look, I ain't gonna promise you nothing, but I will see what I can do about spending the night with you," I said in a desperate attempt to calm her down, knowing damn well that I was lying.

Shit, I wasn't crazy by far, and I planned on taking my black ass home that night without a doubt. She better get in where she fit in and enjoy the little time that she had with me. I wasn't going to mess up my happy home for her or nobody else. I loved K.G., but still, I had to look at the bigger picture.

"Go and check on that meat for me while I get the charcoal and the lighter fluid, please." I grabbed her by the shoulders and turned her in the direction of the meat department.

I grabbed so much stuff that I was glad that I brought the buggy with me. I swung by and grabbed some pans, plates, and everything else I could think of. I'd have to send K.G. back to get more beer. I didn't feel like lifting all that shit. I had my Bud Light and that was all I really cared about anyways.

When I walked out at the end of the aisle, what I saw there almost made my heart stop beating. K.G. was standing there with some chick that appeared to be crying. K.G. looked at her very intensely. I won't even front; the bitch was bad. I couldn't take that away from her. She stood about 5'8" and maybe 140 pounds, big breasts and nice hips. She had legs to kill for. She wore the hell out of her Apple Bottom jeans, and definitely had the Apple in the back. Her heels were surely Jimmy Choo's; I'd know them anywhere.

I definitely wasn't mad at her at all because she was doing her thang. Of course, she wasn't me, but I believed that she could still be a triple threat – beautiful, black, and intelligent.

The question was, did I want to go over there and snatch her damn face off or could I be civil about it and just introduce myself? After all, I broke it off with K.G., and she was a good girl. She deserved to be happy too, right? It was obvious that she cared a lot about this chick, so maybe I should just let them be.

On the other hand, that wasn't even in my character. I had to put my game face on and see what was really going on over here. I straightened my clothes out and checked my hair, and walked over to where she and Apple Bottom were standing.

K.G. looked up at me as if she had seen a ghost. She looked like she just been caught with her hand in the cookie jar. Apple Bottom was giving me much attitude, so my guess was she knew who I was. I hoped she could keep it together because this wasn't what she really wanted.

I gave her a look that said 'I am not to be fucked with right now.'

"K.G., can you please put my steaks in the basket? I have to be on my way," I told her, daring her to say one thing out of her mouth that I didn't like, because if she did, I would go the fuck off. I didn't wish to hear about this, that and the third.

I really couldn't understand why it was bothering me so much to see her with someone. I had a man at home myself. But for some reason, I felt some kind of way about the shit.

"Excuse you!" Apple Bottom said with a little too much confidence in her voice.

"Bitch, what? Who the fuck are you talking to?" I questioned, ready to slap the bitch down. "K.G., you better get your little trick ass girlfriend and do something with her, put that bitch on a leash or something."

"Why don't you put me on a leash since you have so much fucking mouth?" Apple Bottom countered back.

"Say no motherfuckin' more," were the only words that left my mouth before I walked over to her and punched her in the face with a right hook like Roy Jones.

I grabbed her around her neck and squeezed as hard as I could while I hit her repeatedly with my other hand.

"Who the fuck you think you're talking to like that, you stupid bitch? You must really don't know 'bout me. Where is all that mouth now? You ain't got no more slick shit you want to say, huh?" I screamed as I tried to beat this bitch to sleep.

K.G. grabbed my arm tightly around the wrist and I was forced to let Apple Bottom's neck go. She used this opportunity to try and sneak in a punch on me, but K.G. saw it coming and blocked the blow before it had a chance to connect. She had better be glad because if that hoe had smacked me, I would have shot her ass, for real.

"Ra'Quelle, what the hell is wrong with you? What are you doing?"

"What does it look like I'm doing? I am teaching your little friend some damn manners 'cause she act like she doesn't have any. Better yet, what the fuck are you doing? This bitch got you over here crying and shit? You about one disrespectful ass broad for real though, but you know what? I don't give a fuck anymore. I told you that I was done with your ass anyways so you have at that bitch, okay. You go ahead and do you because I promise you that I will always go above and fucking beyond to do me, believe that shit!"

I looked at Apple Bottom, wishing that she would open her mouth and say something so I could get back in that ass. I turned around to leave, and K.G. grabbed my hand. I snatched it back from her and got ready to hit her in the face, but something in her eyes told me that it wasn't the day to be trying my luck with her. I was pretty sure that she could whoop my ass, but she had never hit me before, and I surely didn't want that day to be the first time that she did.

"Rocky, I was telling Nyia that I couldn't fuck with her anymore. I told you a while back that I had met someone that I was kind of kicking it with; remember? You was getting back with ole' boy, and I was trying to move on, but the simple fact is this, no matter what I try to do to get over you it doesn't work. I love you; Ra'Quelle, and nothing and no one can ever change or alter that. I love you when I don't want to. You are my wifey for life. Nyia is a good girl, but she ain't you, Rock."

"I'll never be able to love or care for anyone the way that I love you, so I was telling her that she deserved more than I can offer her. You have got me so gone, Rock, and that's some real shit. Even when I can't see you and I know that you are with him, I'm still loving you and waiting for you to come home because I feel that when it is all said and done, you will always come back to me. I love your crazy ass, girl."

She confessed all of this while the side chick was still trying to recuperate. It caused me to blush.

"She is only going to break your heart again, K.G. You need a woman who knows what she wants."

Oh, Apple Bottom was really trying me. She better be glad that there were a lot of people around right watching us, or I would have certainly beat her ass again.

"Girl, you got less than 30 seconds to get gone or else I am going to fuck you up, and K.G. or nobody else will be able to stop me this time."

I turned to K.G. and smiled. "Why didn't you just tell me that you were telling her that she could never be me, ever, ever? We know that I am one of a kind, and she can't fill my shoes."

I pushed K.G. toward the shopping cart and glanced back at Apple Bottom. As I walked off, I mouthed the words, "I'm a fuck you up." I shook my fist at her and turned around real quick before

INDICTED / *Keisha Monique*

K.G. could see me. We proceeded to pick up a cake and proceeded to the checkout.

The ghetto fabulous cashier was straight hating on me. I was sure that she hated my looks, my clothes, my girl, probably my damn groceries, just everything. She stared at me like she didn't have good goddamn sense. I slid the card to cover the $660.00 total.

"I need to see some identification," the cashier told me, looking at me sideways with an attitude.

"No, you don't. See it for what?"

"It's the store's policy that we have to check IDs on all credit card purchases. So, either show me yours or go put all this food back."

Oh, this heifer was really feeling herself. Luckily, for me, I shopped at this store all the time and I knew the store's policy for when you didn't have an ID or when you chose not to present it. I calmed myself down by taking a couple of deep breaths because I didn't want to make it worse by cursing the bitch out.

"Okay, Shaquanda, Sha-Nay-Nay, whatever your name is," I said trying to do my best to act civilized after I read her nametag.

"My name is Shaniqua."

"Whatever. I told you that I don't have any identification on me and I'm not going to put any of these groceries back. What you're going to do is hit the debit key instead of the credit key and I'll use my card as a debit card instead of a credit card. Since I have to enter my pin number, the credit card company considers that a form of identification. I believe that will settle the problem."

I stood back and folded my arms over my chest like, *Uh-huh, that's what's up.* She wanted to protest, but fortunately for her, the store manager was the one bagging the groceries and he advised her that I was correct; if I didn't have my ID, the policy stated that I could use my private pin number as proof of identity.

She was too pissed and hit that button so hard that it didn't register, and she has to do it again. "Enter your pin, please." The sarcasm was so thick in her voice that I could feel it.

"Sure," I said, so bright and cheery that K.G. started to laugh. I entered the pin that I chose over the phone earlier when I

230

activated the card, and the cash register printed out the receipt for me to sign.

K.G. got the basket, and I told the manager that "Shameisha" could use a crash course in customer service.

"My name is Shaniqua!" she yelled.

"Whatever!" I yelled back, and threw my purse over my shoulder, looked her up and down, and strolled out of the store.

Chapter 24
Good Times

"K.G., why the hell do you keep playing with my damn radio? Leave it alone," I slapped her hand away wondering why she loved to mess with my radio.

"Aye, bay, I wanted to tell you to stop at the liquor store so we can get something to drink and some blunts. You know that I'm not a big beer drinker. I need something stronger so that I can fuck your brains out later," she said.

The things that escaped out of her mouth never ceased to amaze me. The sad part was that she was dead ass serious. I stopped and got half-gallon bottles of Hennessy and Grey Goose. I could only find the liter sized bottles of Patron. I also grabbed three bottles of Cristal, so that I could pop bottles later on.

I arrived at Dream's house, and she came out the house looking just as cute as always. She had on a pair of oversized Polo overalls with a light blue long sleeved Polo t-shirt. She looked too cute as she got in the car.

"Hey, Rocky. Hey, K.G. Dag, I was starting to think that y'all weren't going to come get me. I thought that y'all forgot about me. I was wondering what in the world y'all were doing for so long?" She smiled, suggesting that we were doing something nasty.

"We are late because your home girl want be the light-weight champ of the world. She in the grocery store beating up on people and shit," K.G. squealed, looking at me, shaking her head, and laughing at my behavior.

"For somebody who don't give a fuck what I do or who I

233

date, you sure as hell are quick to jump on somebody that you see me talking to."

"Yeah, whatever, you're the one that let that girl make you cry. Hell, I was just trying to take up for you. Apple Bottom had you in there crying like a baby, and she is such a good girl, right? Please make sure you remember that shit later on, okay?" I mean-mugged her and pumped the volume on the radio, blasting my boy Maxwell.

"Don't start that shit, Ra'Quelle, okay? Ain't nobody trying to be arguing and shit with you all night."

"What-the-hell-ever. Just leave me alone, K.G., how about that?" I hit the gas petal too hard and Dream fell back into the seat.

Dream sat back and laughed. "You guys are crazy. That is why I don't date women right now."

"You don't date women or men do you, Dream? I thought that you were celibate."

"I am, and I'm going to stay that way. I can't be all in Bi-Lo fighting over no man or woman."

"It was Publix, not Bi-Lo. And K.G., why are you worried about what the hell she is doing anyway? Are you trying to get with her too? You gonna make me hurt you yet."

"Man, go 'head with that bullshit, Rocky. I ain't even coming at her like that. I was making a joke and you know that shit. Why do you always have to take it there with me all the time?"

"Because you ain't shit, that's why."

"There you go with that shit again. Is that why you wanted me to come with you, so you could fuck with me all night?"

She looked like I did or said something to hurt her feelings, so I decided to let it rest for the moment. I pulled a cigarette out and lit it, driving the rest of the way in silence.

Just before I got to Michelle's house, I had the urge to confront K.G. about that girl. I was really tripping, I guess. "K.G., you think that you are so damn smart, don't you?"

"Girl, leave me alone and just drive this car."

I wanted to know who she thought she was talking to. I stopped the car and prepared for a confrontation. I took my time putting the car in park; mind you, I had stopped almost in the middle of the street. I took off my seat belt and asked her what was really up. What did she wanna do 'cause I felt like there was some serious tension in the air.

"Ra'Quelle, please don't do this. I ain't in the mood for your antics right now."

"Fuck that. You should have thought about that when you tried to play me in the store with your bitch."

"Girl, you are crazy. Where is all of this coming from? Damn, we were cool just a few minutes ago."

"Well, we ain't cool now."

"Look, you know I have warrants. You got a pistol in your purse, I have weed on me. Let's just go."

I sat there and looked at her as if she wasn't even talking to me.

"I tell you what, you want to sit here and act like a damn kid, but if I go to jail behind this bullshit you pulling right now, I promise you that I'm going to fuck your ass up. Now get me the fuck from around here, and stop acting so damn retarded. I told you what was what with that girl right there in her face. What more do want, man?"

The look on her face told me that she wasn't playing and she'd been telling the truth. She was right, we really didn't need that drama at that moment. I couldn't explain why I totally lost all my composure when it came to her. I would get real elementary sometimes, and I didn't know how to control that. I put the car in drive and continued on my way.

"Keep on acting crazy. You look like you want to swing on me. Go ahead and do that so I can fuck you up real quick and show you why I wear the pants in this relationship. I'll beat your ass real quick and be on about the rest of our day. I don't want to do it, but you acting like you need that in your life right now."

I just kept driving like I didn't hear what she said.

"That's what I thought," she added.

When we pulled up in front of Michelle's house, I got my purse and told Dream to come on. Dream looked at K.G. and shrugged her shoulders as if to say it wasn't her fault. I got my clothes, slammed the car door, and left her there with all of the groceries to carry.

As I walked off, I could hear K.G. mumble, "Ain't this some shit?"

I chuckled and I told her that I would send Mel-G out to help her with the bags. I entered the house, took my Newports out of my purse, and put my clothes and purse in my sister's closet downstairs. I went out and greeted everybody, and asked Mel-G to help K.G. with the bags.

"What? She ain't man enough to get them by herself? Oh, I see, you need a real man to do the job," he boasted.

"Boy, get your silly ass out there and help that girl."

I went over and sat beside Charla. "I like them Red Monkey jeans, girl. Them things are hot."

"Yeah, I know, right? I got them in Charlotte last week when I went to meet Melvin's parents." Judging by her kool-aid grin, she was the happiest person alive.

"Oh, his name is Melvin now? *And* you met the family? Let me find out."

I gave her a high five and then asked her where my dog was.

"That bitch is upstairs in the bed watching TV," Michelle interjected.

"And Rocky, she got mad at me because I didn't know that she wanted to watch cartoons. I knew the damn dog watched TV, but I didn't know she had a special channel. Every time I got ready to leave out of the room, she'd growl at me. I finally sat on the bed, smoked me a blunt, and asked her what she wanted me to do. That's how I figured out that she wanted to watch the cartoon channel." Michelle's facial expression let me know that she was as serious as a heart attack.

I stared at my sister and the words just failed me. "Whatever you say, Michelle. Did she come out to use the bathroom yet?"

"Yeah, she just came out."

I went upstairs to see my baby and she was laying in the bed sleeping. When I walked in the room, she opened one eye and wagged her tail before going back to sleep. I scratched her behind her ear and went back downstairs.

I scanned through the CDs and found some old school shit, and cranked that up. I went into the kitchen, washed my hands, and started to prepare the sides while K.G. started the grill. Charla and Dream made the potato salad, and I fixed the macaroni and cheese.

Michelle came in cheesing and announced that she didn't have to do anything because this was her house. I knew she was smiling because she hit K.G. up for some weed. That's the only thing that made her smile like that.

I asked her how much weed K.G. gave her, and she responded, "None of your damn business. Don't worry about what goes on with K.G. and me. That's my brother-in-law. I like her better than Donnie. Why don't you go back to being gay all the time?"

"Girl, you like anybody that supports your damn smoke habit."

"This much is true."

We all laughed, and she rolled a blunt and passed that, and rolled five or six more. I went back outside and there were way more people than when I left to go in the house.

I got a bottle of Cristal and Michelle grabbed one, and we popped bottles. K.G. popped the other bottle and then we all drank up.

I leaned over to kiss her and apologized about earlier. I promised to be on my best behavior for the rest of the day.

"It's cool, lil' mamma. We all know that you are sprung, so just get used to it." She laughed and pulled my hair.

"Okay, sprung, you better spring your ass over there and check them ribs. Them niggas look like they eat food straight off the grill."

I went to check my food and heard my song and start singing, "Without you, girl, my life is incomplete." That was my jam. I loved me some Sisqo. That sounded like my ringtone. Wait a minute, where the hell was my phone? That *was* my damn ringtone. I had two missed calls from Donnie, so I called him back. When he answered, I tried to sound sober and stood up straight like he could see me.

"Sup, ma? Where are you at?"

"Hey, bay, I'm at Chelle's house, we cooking out. Where is Zay, and what are y'all doing?"

"He's in the chair getting his hair cut. Tell cray-cray I said, 'What's up?'" he said, referring to Michelle.

"K.G. is here." Now why the hell did I just blurt that out? I could do some stupid shit at times, and that was one of them.

I thought that he was about to go ham on me, but he didn't.

"Oh, that's nice. You better behave yourself. You sound like you are getting your buzz on. Are you straight, you gonna be able to drive?"

I assured him that I'd be fine and asked him if he and Zay were coming over.

"Naw, go ahead and do you. Enjoy yourself; just bring us some food. I'm about to bring you my truck though, and take your car since your windows are tinted and you might get pulled over. I'll take Diva home too. I'll be there in about twenty minutes, so be looking for us."

"Okay. I made y'all a pan of mac and cheese too." I looked over to see K.G. giving me the screw face.

"That's what's up. Go and get Diva out the bed and have her ready. Make her use the bathroom so she don't piss in the car."

"How'd you know she was in the bed?" I asked.

"Because that's your crazy ass dog." He started to laugh before he told me he'd see me in a few, then hung up.

I pulled my shit together and I got Dream to help me fix the food for them. I fixed them two plates of meats and two plates of everything else.

K.G. came in and questioned what I was doing. I told her that I was fixing plates for Donnie and Zay. She asked me if he was coming over here, and I told her yes.

"I know damn well you didn't invite me over here to sit and watch you entertain your man. I could have went home for this bullshit."

"K.G., please don't start no stupid shit. They're coming to get the food I fixed for them and that's it. I know today is our day to chill, so just be easy. Damn, I got you."

"As long as he don't say anything to me, I won't say nothing to him."

My nerves started to calm down a bit, and I went back out-side and saw Michelle dancing with two dudes that looked half her age. I lit a blunt and danced by myself when they played my song, "I Put on for My City."

Nitty came from somewhere and started to dance with me, and we repped our city to the fullest. I happened to look oversaw my little man bouncing to the beat. I curled my finger, telling him to come join his momma and trust me, shy and bashful he was not.

Isaiah walked out to where I was and showed his momma how it was really done. We jammed all through the song to the part where they say, "I put on all the niggas that I knew from the start . . ." I pointed at Dream, Charla, and Michelle, and held my glass up in the air toasting them.

When the song went off, I hugged my baby and walked over to my man. Of course, there was some little bobble head over there trying to holla. I informed her that he was mine and she kept it pushing. He laughed and gave me a kiss. He looked better than he did when I saw him this morning. He was wearing a throwback Magic Johnson jersey, some Aeropostale jeans and all white Forces. Zay was dressed like him, except he has an old-school Kobe jersey with the number 8 on it and purple Kobe Bryant Nikes, showing people that he was carrying it just like that. I was really proud of how handsome my men were.

Dee put his arm around my waist and rested his hand on my ass as we walked into the house. Not once did he even glance at K.G., but he was well aware of her presence. Isaiah came down the stairs with Diva. I asked them if they wanted to chill with me for a while, but they both declined, opting to go home and get on their PlayStation 4 instead.

I gave Donnie his food and a bottle of Yak that I bought for him. He gave me a long kiss that made my pussy thump, and I walked them out to my car. I got nervous when I got close to the car because I remembered that I left K.G.'s clothes in it. Oh, well, I damn sure ain't gonna try to get them out. I just hoped he didn't see them.

"Don't get too fucked up, and if you can't drive, call me or catch a cab. Don't wreck my fucking truck, girl," he said, acting like I was new to this.

"I got this, boo," I assured him and watched him get into the car. I waved as they pulled off. Before I could get back in the house, my cell phone rang and it was him.

"Don't make me fuck you up and kill that bitch, Rocky. Don't get it twisted. I trust you, but I will do that bitch this time."

"It ain't that serious, baby. I'll be home later. I know where home is and you know where my heart is." I hung up and went back into the house, where K.G. greeted me with nothing but attitude.

"You like playing with fire, don't you? I saw you kissing that nigga. I should slap the shit out of you," she was fuming.

"He's my fiancé, K.G. Don't start please."

I really didn't feel like going through this shit with her, she knew what it was with Donnie and me. I looked at her and got ready to spazz out, but she grabbed me and pulled me out in the yard to dance with her.

"I'm sorry, bay. You know I just get jealous when I see you with him. I love you, Rocky. I only think of you on two occasions, that's day and night," she sang in my ear.

"Girl, now you know that you are my boo, but you have to let BabyFace sing his own song." I laughed at her trying to sing and put my head on her shoulder and dance with my baby.

I went back into the house to get another pack of cigarettes out of my purse, and I run into Dream. She looked like she was feeling good. She was just smiling and swaying to the music.

"Rocky, let me ask you a question. Donnie is fine as well and you see that every time he's around, girls be all over him. Why do you treat him like you do? Why do you always go back to K.G. when you have a good man at home?"

Because she was my home girl and I knew that she really cared about me, that's the only reason she didn't get cursed out. I didn't feel up to answering any questions though.

"It's complicated, and I don't have the time to really explain it to you. Let me just say this. Donnie is my man, soon-to-be my husband, and I love him dearly. He ain't going nowhere. K.G.

is another story. What we have is different, and she will always be a part of my life. Now, stay out of grown folks' business and come on outside with me so I can keep my eyes on you!"

I observed as she double-stepped on the way to the backyard. A couple more drinks and her ass would be upstairs in bed knocked the hell out. She knew that she couldn't hang with the rest of us.

I went over to K.G., who was sitting with her head held down while the same bobble head that was trying to get with Donnie was all up in her grill. I walked over, sat on her lap, and put my arms around her neck and said, "This one is mines too. Bye, Felecia!" I waved my hand at her like she was a pesky fly or something.

"So, you going home with me tonight or what?" K.G. asked.

"Naw, I have to go home. I will get with you again sometime soon though, I promise." I hoped that she wouldn't start tripping.

"So, it's okay if I call Nyia and have her come here and get me and take her home with me?"

I know damn well this hoe didn't just try me like that. Did she really come out of her mouth like that? She must have lost her damn mind.

"You know what, why don't you do that? You don't have to worry about me showing my ass either because I am about to hop in that Escalade and go home and fuck my husband to sleep like I do every night."

I shouldn't have said that but she asked for it. I went over and fixed myself another drink; only I made this one straight and took it to the head. I walked over by Michelle and smoked a blunt with her. My sister was in the wind, and she was feeling no pain.

She asked if I was alright and I assured her that I was just fine. The song changed to Jodeci, "Cry for You" and K.G. came and took my hand. We glided to the next table, and she pulled me back down on her lap.

"I'm sorry, Rock. I swear this shit is driving me crazy. I can't stand the thought of not being able to be with you. I'm not

241

trying to see anyone else, not tonight or any other night. My heart is with you, and I will just have to wait on you to come back to me. Please just promise me that you won't ever forget about me and whenever you need me, you'll call, and that you will not stop loving me."

She looked like she was about to cry. This was why I didn't want to let her back into my life. Either way, someone always ended up hurt.

"What we have ain't going nowhere, and I will always love you. Dee is not a replacement for you. I'm just trying to live my life as normal as possible and give my son what he needs. What we have is not going to fade, but you don't have to put your life on hold for me. I will . . ."

Before I finished that comment, she wrapped her arms around my waist and stuck her tongue damn near down my throat. I kissed her back and enjoyed the moment knowing that it would soon end.

We chilled a little bit longer, and Nitty and Charla decided that they were going to the strip club. Everyone either would go home to change or changed upstairs. I decided that I would go home.

I asked K.G. what she was going to do, and she said that she was going back to Peanut's house, where she left her bike. I texted Donnie and told him that I was on the way home and let him know that I was dropping her off at Peanut's house so he didn't beat my ass and hers when he saw her get out of his truck.

I took the rest of the food, put it away, and grabbed the rest of the Bud Light. We said our goodbyes. I went upstairs to check on Dream who was lying across the bed under a thick comforter. Michelle locked the house up, and K.G. and I got into the truck and pulled off.

I parked in front of the house, and she got the clothes that I had bought her earlier and handed me the bags with my stuff in it. I guess she took it out my car when she took the groceries out earlier. I didn't even see her bring them to the truck. I told her goodbye and that I'd call her later.

She let me know that she'd be over there all night because

she wasn't in no shape to ride her bike. I hit the alarm and went into my house. I peeped into Zay's room. He was sleeping in his bed with Diva right beside him. I walked in, cut his TV off, and put the Wii game on the dresser by the PlayStation.

I came out of his room and saw Donnie standing by the window. "Hey, I didn't see you when I came in," I said.

"I know that you didn't, but I saw you when you and that bitch pulled up in my shit."

"I sent you a text telling you that I was gonna give her a ride," I said, hoping to avoid confrontation.

"Yeah, I got the text. That don't mean I like that bitch riding in my whip. Next time, let her manly ass walk wherever the fuck she needed to be. Better yet, don't let there be a next time. Stay the fuck away from her."

I walked over to him and put my arms around his neck. "I'm home with you, and this is where I want to be. I'm in love with you. You're the one that I am going to be with, so don't start no shit!" I smiled at him.

"I know, Ra, I'm just trippin'. Oh, yeah, you did the damn thing with that macaroni and cheese. We almost ate it all. That shit was blazing."

I thanked him and told him that I got him some clothes from the Ralph Lauren store.

"I hope that you didn't get me the same thing you got for your girl. Okay, okay, I'll stop. Come here, girl. Are you ready for daddy to put you to sleep real good?" he asked playfully pulling me into his arms.

I was relieved because I thought he might trip since he knew I had used another credit card, but he didn't say anything, thankfully. This was my life and I had to let her go. I had everything that I needed right in front of me. "I love you so much, Donnie."

I grabbed his hand and led him into the bedroom. After closing the door, I jumped into the shower. I slipped into bed butt naked as always, and let my baby make it do what it do. After I got me about three good ones, I laid in his arms.

He put his hand on my stomach and whispered, "This one

is a girl."

I smiled at him and drifted off to sleep, feeling safe and secure in his arms, knowing that I made the right changes.

Chapter 25

Judgment Day

Three months after I was indicted, my lawyer got the U.S. Attorney to drop the mail fraud and the other credit card charges that they really couldn't make stick. I pled to one count of credit card fraud and one count of identity theft. Someone from the U.S. Probation Office interviewed me and did my P.S.R.,(pre sentencing report).

After reviewing my P.S.R., Mr. Shapiro informed me that my offense level was 16, but would drop to 13 for accepting responsibility. My criminal points are seven, which puts me in a category 4. My sentencing guidelines were 21-27 months.

Mr. Shapiro filed three motions asking for a downward departure for family reasons as well as my traumatic past. He had argued a pretty good case, and I did qualify for the departure. The U.S. Attorney did not object to the motion.

I have really been blessed; the U.S. Attorney in this case was not out for blood, and she had pretty much gone along with everything that my lawyer had asked of her.

As I sat in my chair nervous beyond measure because I didn't know what to do with myself. I glanced behind me and saw all of my friends there to support me. I even saw K.G. standing on the other side of the courtroom.

The judge asked me to stand, "Ms. Summers how are you today?"

"Nervous," I responded.

He gave me a smile and nodded his head, "Ms. Summers, I hope that you know you have a great attorney, and he has fought really hard for you in this case. He has presented the court with some pretty good motions in his request for your downward departure.

Oh, Lord, I hope that he gives it to me. I really want to go home. I don't want to sit in jail for no damn year or so. I prayed that he would allow me to go home on probation or something. I vowed to myself to never touch any more credit cards. Well, not for a while anyway. Change takes time, right?

I saw Donnie smile at me and put his finger under his chin, telling me to keep my head up. I was shaking so bad, my earrings were sounded like little bells or something.

"Well, Ms. Summers, with all that Mr. Shapiro has presented me with, I don't see how I can't grant his motion for your departure in this case."

I let out a breath that I'd felt had been weighing me down for a year or more.

"With that being said, the only thing now is for me to decide how much I want to depart from your guidelines. Do I want to depart just a couple of levels and still send you to prison, or do I want to depart enough from it to allow you to go home on probation?"

Judge Gray sat there and glanced up at the ceiling with his hands folded across his chest.

Let me go home. Please, let me go home. I will be a model citizen from now on. I'll pay my taxes and vote. I stood there trying to speak the ideal sentence into existence.

"Okay, Ms. Summers," Judge Gray had made his decision He started to stack his papers together and then looked over at me. He picked up his pen and began to speak while pointing his pen at me.

"After much deliberation and thought, I have made my decision in this matter. In the case of *The United States of America v. Ra'Quelle Monique Summers*, Case Number 4:10-CR-00849-CME, Title and section 18:1341 and 18:1096(a), in the District Court of South Carolina, this court hereby imparts a sentence of..."

INDICTED/*Keisha Monique*

Find out Ra'Quelle's fate in "INDICTED II." Will she go to prison, or will she go home? Will Ra'Quelle really be able to leave the streets alone and do the right thing? Will she marry Donnie and cut off her relationship with K.G., or will the pull of the streets be too much for her to resist?

The *Best* of
BOTH WORLDS

A NOVEL BY
Cher Jones

VISIT LCB @LCBOOKS

WWW.LIFECHANGINGBOOKS.NET